PROGENY OF A KILLER

BY

J.M. SHORNEY

Prologue

Dublin, June 22nd 1982

It had been a long night. Now it was over.

Her baby was born and now lay in his plastic crib beside her bed. A little boy, and so dark. Darker than Dermot. He had not suspected a thing. Why should he? His mind had been too befuddled with drink to connect dates and times.

Exhausted, Marie barely listened to the blare of the television in her ward. She was so profoundly lost in her own retrospections the TV was merely a blur, a buzz. The two women in the adjacent beds were tutting and muttering something about the troubles in the Province, how they were getting worse.

But this little dark-haired child asleep in his bed and, wrapped in a blue blanket, was a far cry from those terrible atrocities. Besides, this was Dublin, miles away.

She wondered where Dermot was. He had also been a blur, fussing and faffing about her bedside sometime after midnight, before he had disappeared. No change there. Throughout the months of her pregnancy all Dermot seemed to do was to disappear. Clodagh had been her constant companion. Her sister and brother-in-law were unable to have children. Clodagh had been looking forward to the birth as much as Marie. Even more so because she was expecting another boy. She hadn't found a name yet. Marie thought perhaps 'James'. Both Marie and Dermot had agreed on Harry's name. Dermot was insistent that they call their little girl Bridget. That was his ma's name, and they called her Bridie. Marie hated her own daughter being called by that name.

"As further troubles escalate in the Province, last night saw a renewed occurrence of the violence. An incident occurred at midnight near a Crosmaglen checkpoint, when a unit of British troops opened fire on a company of four men. They had stopped the men to ask their identity, and to check the boot of their car. The men were suspected members of the Provisional IRA. Two of the men were armed, and attempted to make their escape, after opening fire on the soldiers. The boot of the car was searched, and assault rifles, including Uzis and Armalites, plus several handguns and detonators, were discovered.

"Three of the men were shot dead. Another, 31 year old Liam Doylen, was wounded and arrested. The dead men are named as William O'Bannion, 28; Damien Molloy, 23; and Connor McMartland, 27.

"McMartland's wife Catriona, and their 18 month old son Aidan, were shot dead on their doorstep by members of the Ulster Volunteer Force in South Armagh in February. Since then, it seems that McMartland had gone on a rampage of bombings, doorstep shootings and robberies in South Armagh and Belfast. Although rumours suggest that McMartland had already joined the Paramilitary in November, 1981.

"McMartland also leaves another son, five year old Daniel from his relationship with Mairead Corrigan. Miss Corrigan is believed to have sheltered IRA men on the run in her Ballymurphy home. She admitted to having an affair with McMartland, but she denied any involvement with the Provos. She suggested that when she knew McMartland he was not in the IRA."

"Och, there y'are. And is this the wee wain?" Clodagh Connolly returned Marie to the present as she bent over the baby's crib. "And how are you, Marie, darlin'? He's a beautiful child, so he is. And so dark, and so much hair," Clodagh remarked with her customary briskness, before turning her attention back to her sister-in-law with abject concern. "What is it, love? You've been crying."

"Sorry, Clodagh, I'm just a wee bit tired that's all. It's been such an emotional night." Marie attempted to swipe the tears from her eyes.

"Here..." Reaching for a tissue on the cabinet next to her bed, Clodagh pressed the tissue into Marie's hand, and tutted with a barely concealed annoyance. "Sure if there wasn't some terrible goings-on in the Province last night. Och, if it's not getting worse. At least it don't touch our lives." She paused to hurriedly cross herself.

"Sure." Raising herself up in the bed, Marie muttered feebly, but Clodagh's attention had already returned to the baby.

"They should turn that television off," she retorted. "Piping that into the room of ladies who have just given birth."

"So where's that husband of mine?" Marie quickly changed the subject, with the stark realisation that the man she loved had given another woman a child, besides his own wife and herself.

"Himself arrived at my house about 2 o'clock this morning. He and Sheamie have been wetting the baby's head ever since, so they have. I left them snoring their drunken heads off at my place. After I took Bridie to playgroup and Harry to school, I had to come and see you.

"Dermot wants to know what you've named his son. 'Typical woman,' he said, 'they can't make up their minds.' So you had him at midnight then? Sure, if it isn't the Summer Solstice."

"I guess it is. It all seems like a blur to me."

"And his weight?"

"8 pounds 2 ounces, I think."

"So?" Clodagh arched a speculative brow.

"Oh, his name..." Marie mused thoughtfully. "His name is Aidan James."

Chapter One

The Collector

London, 2012

The basement was more spacious and accommodating than I had imagined. It was reached by yet another staircase. This one remains uncarpeted. My boots echo noisily on the bare boards. Flicking on the shadeless bulb, I observe it's one of those low energy affairs. The light glows brighter, enough to illumine my surroundings. I kill my torchlight and slip it into my jacket. Pausing to light a cigarette, I scan the room in disbelief at the extensive amount of DVDs and VHS tapes occupying a couple of the large teak bookshelves. The only light in the twelve foot square room emanates from the bulb. A 42 inch TV, complete with DVD and video player, sits on a glass shelf.

To all intents and purposes, the basement appears innocent enough. A veritable haven for any movie buff. Except these aren't the kind of movies you can enjoy with a beer and popcorn.

There's a couple of hard backed wooden chairs facing the TV. I deposit my weight on one of them. I allow my gaze to traverse the room for anything that might be worthy of note. Nothing does, it seems, apart from that huge television now standing idly by, collecting dust on the glass top.

I rest a hand on the chair arm, thankful that I'm wearing gloves, because something that looks suspiciously like blood is caked into the arm.

The stench pervades my nostrils and I swiftly leap from the chair. I taste the sliver on the leather. It's definitely blood. I quickly rub the glove on a handkerchief.

Inspecting the shelves I read the titles. You certainly won't find 'Gone with the Wind' or 'Casablanca' here. Nevertheless the titles catch my eye. Titles. Dates. Martin Cartright worked for the gangster, Raymond Lamond. He's still working for someone, because Lamond's been dead since February. The dates on some of the DVDs are more recent. April. May. Up to August. Even two weeks ago.

My curiosity is aroused, and I remove the tape from the shelf. The smoke anchored an omnipresent fixture. A decidedly uneasy sensation now permeates my insides as I slip the DVD into the player. Sometimes, as now, I wonder what the hell I am doing here in a guy's basement, awaiting his return. Upstairs, Dennis Mitchell guards his woman, whom he's forced to the floor, before tying her up and gagging her. It was the reason why I volunteered to check out the basement. I couldn't bear to look into that woman's terrified features any longer.

Two masked men had burst into her Brixton home, pulling guns and forcing her upstairs. This is shit. I know it, but I can't help myself. It has to be my alter ego who flicks the remote of that DVD player. I wish to God that I hadn't. Our brief is to check out some of the stuff Cartright houses in his basement.

The static is momentary, swift to clear. And there it is. My heart pounds. A trembling hand traces my bearded jaw thoughtfully. The scene unfolds. A child. A little girl wearing a grubby dress. There's a suspicious saturation down the front, as if maybe she's peed herself. The film is black and white. Its only saving grace. She's wearing socks that were once white, but are now grubby. No shoes. Her feet and hands are securely bound to a chair. Who the girl is, or how old she is, I have no idea. She has a white hood, similar to the old fashioned flour sacks, pulled over her head, and tightened with a drawstring at the neck. I feel every tremble that she makes.

5

The two men with her are masked, balaclava hoods exposing only their eyes and mouths. One of the men is quite rotund, in possession of a stomach that is badly running to fat. In marked contrast, the other is positively skinny. Both are wearing camouflage. Because I cannot see their faces, they remind me idiotically of Laurel and Hardy. One thin. The other fat. 'That's another fine mess you've got me into.'

A laugh of sheer nervousness escapes me at the comparison, plus a physical sickness because I know that the fat one is Cartright. He's the one touching the child up, while she sits there helplessly bound to the chair. She emits small, animal-like whimpers behind the hood, which makes me believe that she is gagged as well. I freeze when I think of my five year old niece, Samantha. My wee baby girl barely six weeks old. I can't avoid the element of hysteria that rises. Only for it to subside, when breathing out. I'm conscious of the semi-automatic .9mm Browning that nestles behind my jacket, as if the gun were an old friend. Oh yeah, Cartright. It won't be much longer now, you bastard.

Cartright's laughter is ugly and forced as his big gloved hand slides up inside her, beneath her dress. I catch a glimpse of the young girl's almost hairless pubes. It's plainly obvious that she isn't wearing any knickers.

The skinny man. Treveleyan suggested his name is Louis Platt. It's Platt who rips at her dress. The material tears apart in his hands, as if the dress were rotten. The hand rises upward toward her almost non-existent breasts. I would put the child's age at around seven or eight. Aware that I should switch it off, I pull the tape from the machine, and crush the ungodly filth beneath my boot. But Treveleyan wishes for nothing to be destroyed. "Evidence, my boy, evidence."

So I stare as if hypnotised, when Cartright pours what appears to be an almost colourless liquid from a small red can over the child's head. I observe her entire body quiver inside her bonds. My stomach knots. My heart races so predominantly I can practically hear the rush of blood as it crashes through my skull.

Cartright and his companion evoke ugly, perverted belly-laughs. Their laughter is so sadistic and evil that I can barely believe that it emanates from a human being and not a demonic entity, summoned from the very bowels of Hell itself. Neither can I help but expel an involuntary gasp and feel the need to vomit simultaneously. Unable to watch any longer, I switch the abomination off and bury my head in my hands.

I have no idea how long I remain there, killing and lighting one cigarette from the glowing butt of the first. There's a sound of hurried footsteps on the stairs. Dennis Mitchell exclaims, "What the fuck, McRaney? I wondered what was taking you so long. Did you find anything?"

"Oh sure I found something." I attempt to clear my throat. Kill yet another cigarette. My stomach remains a bundle of knots. I swipe a palm across my eyes. There's no way I can possibly allow this guy to remotely detect that I have shed a tear. He'll think I'm not up to it. Maybe I'm not. But what else have I got left? Three eviction notices on my flat. My concern that my wife and baby will be homeless. It seems that no one wants to know an ex-con, especially someone who's been inside for manslaughter. "If you want to know what I've found, then take a look in that machine, man. See what that bastard's been doing."

Mitchell's eyes are of a strangely flecked hazel when they bore into mine. "I know what kind of shit he's into."

"Take a look," I urge, and pass the remote. "You take care of her then? The woman. How much do you think she's implicated in this?"

"I dunno. She lives with the bastard, don't she? The stuff's in the basement. What do you think?"

"Well, did you ask her? Were you able to get anything out of her?"

"I'm going to have to call the boss." His tone of voice borders on the sombre.

"What about? To send in the cleaners?"

"That won't be necessary. We'll take the bastards with us."

"The woman isn't the target," I point out. "We didn't know she was going to be here. We were led to believe he lived alone. That wasn't our brief, Mitchell."

"That's why I have to call the boss. See what he wants us to do."

"Let's concentrate on Cartright." I flick a glance at my watch. "How much longer? Maybe the wee bastard's got wise to us."

Mitchell purses his lips."We don't need to fuck up. I wanna get this over with as quickly as possible. Look, McRaney, why don't you see if you can get some answers from Cartright's bird?"

"Don't fuckin' tell me what to do, Mitchell."

I'm angry enough at what I have witnessed without him assuming an unwarranted authority. Nevertheless he is correct in his assumption. We need to get this over with. Had expected our target to be present. Disposed of. Then to contact Treveleyan to send someone in to seize the condemning evidence. That Cartright has been abusing young girls, most of them under 16. The girls are invariably masked, as are the abusers. The atrocities sold on forbidden Internet sites.

Apparently the late, lamented Lamond brothers were reputed to have had their depraved fingers in a lot of pies, that even I had been unable to guess at. I'd not remotely suspected paedophilia. But Raymond and Francis Lamond are now dead. Alternatively, as attested to by the recent entries on those incriminating DVDs, someone else is ultimately working the 'kiddie fiddling' racket. Martin Cartright, a known paedophile, is merely acting on their behalf.

Unable to forget what I've seen on that tape, I leave Mitchell to check out the DVD. I move into the room upstairs where the woman lies on the floor. Her hands are bound behind her, her feet secured. Duct tape seals her mouth. Rolling a balaclava over my face before she clocks me, I observe her move her head in my direction when I enter.

She offered her name as Rosie when Mitchell asked. I judge her to be somewhere into her mid forties. She's not bad looking I suppose, despite the addition of the peroxide blonde. Slenderly built, she wears pink pyjama bottoms with a tee shirt top. Rosie mutters incoherently behind the gag. I peel the tape from her mouth. She regards me without speaking from wide, terrified eyes. She obviously believes we are there to kill her. I cannot speak for my companion, but killing her is certainly not my intention. All I require is some answers. Hunkering down to her level, I warn, "Don't scream, Rosie. I don't want to hurt you, understand?" I talk to her gently. "Understand?"

"I… I understand." She starts to cry silently, allowing the tears to slide unchecked down her face. I wipe them away.

"That's good. Because I need to talk to you before Martin returns. It is Martin, isn't it?"

Her nod is perfunctory. I guess it's difficult for her to keep her head erect when she's practically eating the carpet. She lies half-in, half-out under the bed, flat on her stomach.

"Are you going to kill him?"

"Depends on what he tells us, sweetheart. You live here? I mean is this your house or Martin's?"

"It's his, M….Martin's."

"I need some answers. How much do you know about the stuff in the basement?" I maintain a carefully controlled voice, in spite of the perverse desire to grasp her by that peroxide hair so belligerently that it will make her eyes water.

"I don't know nothin'. It ain't nothin' to do with me."

"You're lying, Rosie. How can you not know when you're living with it in the house? I've just watched one of those DVDs. It was called The Burning. What do you suppose that means?"

"I… I don't know." Tears fill her vision, and she averts her head. "He keeps the basement locked and tells me not to go down there. Martin can be… be quite aggressive at times. I'm too scared to ask him questions."

"Well I'm asking questions, Rosie. We can do this nice and gently. I don't want to hurt you, but I can't promise that my belligerent pal downstairs will be quite so considerate. You know exactly what Martin's into, and yet you stay with him. Maybe he's a good shag, huh? Jesus, he's fat and ugly. Plus he's a fuckin' paedophile. Maybe more than that. Do you know what was on that tape, Rosie? There was a little girl. She was hooded and so were the guys with her. But I knew it was your fella. They were touching up this girl. She was just a child. I reckon seven or eight. Your fella and another guy were laughing as they poured petrol over her. Talk to me, Rosie."

Shaking her head she maintains that she knows nothing, except to suggest that we ask Martin.

"Oh don't worry, Rosie, we'll do that alright. The thin guy in the film. Is it Louis Platt?"

"I don't know."

"The other man?" I rasp.

"Yes, yes! Martin calls him Louis. That's all I know."

"If you've finished bellowing at that bird, mate, Cartright's here," Mitchell declares. A kind of bemused smile flirts around his lips, indiscernible in the narrow slits of the hood.

After replacing the tape, I ascertain that the ropes are secured. Counselling her not to move, I straighten to my full height. I enquire of Mitchell if he watched the tape.

He swallows hard. "Till the kid was fuckin' burning."

"I didn't get that far. I have kids."

"C'mon, let's intercept this fuckin' bastard." Mitchell pulls a Glock pistol and checks the clip. The smile, disappearing behind the mask, is swiftly replaced by a tightening set to his mouth.

Mitchell says, "By the way, I spoke to the boss," in a sort of conspiratorial whisper.

"And?"

For an answer, he positions a couple of gloved digits adjacent to his temple.

"Fuck man, I'm not going to be. party to that. She might be fuckin' innocent. I'm not touching her."

"Innocent? Jesus, listen to yourself. She lives with him. Screws him. It's fuckin' Fred and Rose West all over again. There's stuff in that basement that no mortal eyes should have to look upon. Any decent woman would have had it on her toes ages ago, but she stays. That's a fuckin' double bed. She probably lets him fuck her after what he's done."

"Fred and Rose didn't burn their victims. They just had more patios laid out. And maybe she puts up with it cos she's too scared to get away."

"And maybe we was fuckin' wrong about you."

"What's that supposed to mean?"

"You can be all fluffy-bunny and Daddy to your kids, but when we're on a job all that goes out of the window, understand?"

"I'm not fluffy-bunny. Jesus, man. I can prove it, okay? But I still say we don't kill the woman. She isn't our mark."

"It's okay if you don't have the stomach for it."

My mouth is tight, and I push him ahead of me. "Maybe it's not the stomach you gotta worry about. Maybe it's the conscience."

The woman isn't armed. She lies upstairs bound and gagged. Will I be able to live with myself again, with my baby, my wife and my ten year old son?

There's something Mitchell knows nothing about. At least I hope he doesn't. Since I've been doing this, a small hip flask has become my constant companion. I carry the flask inside my jacket adjacent to my pistol. Right now it's the former that I close my hand over.

"Look, man, you go ahead," I instruct him.

I hear the door bang downstairs. Cartright calls out. "I'm coming to get you, babe, ready or not," to Rosie. Which makes me positively cringe.

"I'll check on the woman again. Make sure she's trussed-up, okay? Don't waste him before I arrive, will you?" I attempt a modicum of humour. To which he merely shrugs.

I wait until he returns downstairs before I retreat back into the bedroom, casting a cursory eye over Rosie. She's trussed-up fine. All an excuse of course. I imbibe a much needed swallow before I return the flask to my jacket. The drink serves both to fuel my aggression and, more importantly, to lessen the guilt at what we are about to do.

Downstairs I discover Mitchell has Cartright pushed into a chair. The expression on Cartright's face is one of puzzlement rather than actual fear.

"Wh...what do you want? If it's money, I... I've got some stashed upstairs."

Cartright is a burly kind of guy, filling out the black tracksuit he's wearing. His hair is thick, but lank as if he hasn't bothered to wash it.

Fifty-five years old. He's been in and out of care homes since the age-of eight. Institutionalised for child abuse, which had actually begun while in the care homes. At 15 he'd sexually abused a nine year old girl. According to our brief, his predilection for children, particularly young girls, saw him moving from one home to another.

"Look, when you've finished beating me up, not that I haven't been beaten up before, call me an ambulance, will you?" he implores.

"When we've finished with you, you fuckin' perverted bastard, you'll need a fuckin' hearse," I rasp. Pulling the Browning from my holster, I fit the silencer.

Chapter Two

Cartright's Confession

"Who... who are you?" Cartright asks, now displaying an initial sense of fear. Particularly as Mitchell has yanked his arms so far behind him, the limbs are in danger of being snapped.

"Guns? I thought you were just going to beat me up. That's what usually happens. I thought you were them kids' dads or something."

"Shut the fuck up! You talk too much." The gloved fist I slam into Cartright's mouth takes him by surprise. He jerks his head back as blood drizzles from a lacerated lip. "The only talking we want you to do is to answer some questions." I return the Browning to my holster. I warn him that just because I've put my gun away it doesn't mean we aren't going to kill him.

"Is Rosie okay?" Perspiration beads his forehead, dripping from his hair into his eyes. He blinks it back swiftly.

"We ask the fuckin' questions." Mitchell binds rope around Cartright's hands, tightly interlacing the hemp to the back of the chair. While he does, Cartright emits an agonising 'ouch' of pain.

"Now, you fuckin' perverted bastard, you're going to tell us who that little girl is on the tape. The poor kid. You fuckin' set fire to her. She tried to scream, but you gagged her, you bastard." The blow Mitchell delivers resounds like a thundercrack as it connects against Cartright's jaw, causing the tears to spring into his eyes. His pleas for mercy go unheeded when another blow almost sends him reeling from his chair. Mitchell is a powerfully built guy. "I asked who was she?"

Our faces remain concealed. Cartright attempts to penetrate the masks, while his eyes are narrowed as if with recognition.

"You heard him, bastard!" My anger is a formidable, living, breathing force.

"Why should I tell you? You're going to kill me anyway, ain't you?" The words issue almost like a challenge, an open defiance. It's as if he's sure of himself, even when Mitchell, pulling the weapon from his jacket, unceremoniously whips him across the jaw. He wraps a muscular arm about Cartright's windpipe, practically shutting off his breath.

"That depends on you, you bastard. You want to live? Then talk. That little girl. You still haven't told us who she was. What did you do to her afterwards? And her family, how do you think they feel? I bet it didn't occur to you to think what they might be going through."

Cartright's nose is bleeding profusely. Blood continues to ooze from a split lip, seeping between a couple of shattered teeth. He spits out the blood, narrowly missing our boots. He regards Mitchell and I with an open defiance once more.

"She's fuckin' dead, ain't she? We fuckin' buried her. Go on, fuckin' shoot me, if that's what you've come for. He wanted us to do it. We didn't want to burn the kid. It was his idea…" He ceases his talk immediately, as if he's said too much.

"Who wanted you to do it? Who is behind all this? Because I don't think for a minute that you'd have the brains. Not that what you did needs brains." I listen to the impassioned anger present in my voice. It would be so effortless to simply plug the bastard where he sits, bound and helpless to the chair.

Cartright hesitates. I bring my face up close to his. Martin Cartright's bloodied lips remain firmly closed.

"I… I don't know his name. He ordered us to abduct the kids, film 'em."

"So was it his idea, whoever he is, to set fire to that wee girl

after you'd finished with her? She was hooded. Still alive..." I allow my words to trail. All this sickens me to the stomach. I never imagined how evil people can be even while I was in prison.

"You okay?" Mitchell enquires, concern in his voice.

I barely glance his way. My attention is centred on my attempt to discover more information from this monster. His bloodied lips negotiate a grotesque twisted line. He hisses, "If you kill me you'll know nothing."

"You only have to move your head, Cartright, and my pal will snap your neck. You said 'us'. Is Louis Platt the other guy in the film?"

Aware of his hesitation, I repeat my question angrily.

"What film?"

"The fuckin' home movie. Is that how you want to die, Cartright?" I mock contemptuously.

"What?" Perspiration breaks out along his brow again. There's an unmistakeable stench of urine pervading the room.

"You filthy bastard! Come on, we ain't got all night," Mitchell hisses impatiently. "Now tell us about Louis, where he lives, and about the bastard who's pulling your strings. We know it used to be Lamond, but he's brown bread. So who is it?" Mitchell wraps a gloved hand around a handful of Cartright's hair and yanks it hard.

"Okay, okay, I... I'll tell you. And if I do you'll let me go?"

Let him go? To inform the guy who's pulling his strings? Our orders are to obtain answers from Martin Cartright. It's the way Sir George Treveleyan works and this underground Agency of his. Discover as much information as we can from the mark, then terminate his life. Like I said it's shit. It's no wonder that I drink, as I find no other outlet from this heinous occupation.

"So, Mr Cartright, who are you working for?" I adopt a more conciliatory tone, conscious of Mitchell's eyes narrowed my way in the slits of his mask, warily. "Your pal Louis, you think he's going to care? Or the guy you're working for? They aren't going to shed any tears at your demise are they? You want to take this rap alone? We kill you, and your pal Louis and the boss man who's behind all this are probably laughing. They'll think you gave your life away to keep them in the clear. Ray Lamond's dead. We know you worked for him. So who's taken over?"

"He'll kill me if I talk."

"And we'll fuckin' kill you if you don't."

"He's like you. I mean he talks the way you do," Cartright stammers. I observe there's more urine leaking through his tracksuit pants.

"Filthy bastard, you fuckin' stink. You've fuckin' peed yourself again," hisses Mitchell.

I bring my face up close to Cartright's. "So, your pal Louis. His surname, is it Platt?"

"Yeah, his name's Platt. Louis Platt."

"Where does he live?" I insist.

"In Camden. He lives in Camden."

"And the boss man. Tell us about him."

Cartright is practically crying now, as evidenced by the drizzle of wetness that stains his cheeks. Tears intermingle with perspiration. As he's bound to the chair, he's compelled to allow both of them to fall unchecked. "I... I don't know his name, but he's a paddy. That's all I know. A voice on the end of the phone and a package in the mail when he wants a job."

"A paddy? You mean he's Irish, this boss?" I cup a forefinger beneath his chin. "He talks like me?"

"Yeah, but harder." His words are allowed to trail because Mitchell has wrapped both hands about Cartright's head, as if it's his intention to twist it right off. A singular twist in the correct place is capable of splintering the bones in the neck, enough to render him paralysed for the rest of his life, or to kill him.

"Jesus, man, let him up, he needs to talk," I tell him. "So this Irishman. He's taken over from Ray Lamond?" He nods but perfunctorily. "The tapes in your basement. Is this where you store the perverted stuff to sell on the Internet's forbidden sites?"

Cartright has trouble speaking, so that his words issue with a lisp. Blood continues to drizzle through what remains of his teeth. "He's from the North. Northern Ireland."

"So do we have a name? Where can he be found?" I remonstrate.

"I don't know, honest. I told you I don't get to see him. Neither does Louis."

"So, Martin, tell me how many children you and your pal Platt have tortured and burnt?" Although my tone remains in the selfsame congenial timbre, I cannot fail to avoid the rise of anger that gnaws and burns at my insides. The sensation is so predominant that it practically makes my head spin. The only thing helping me to sustain the pretence of a cool, calculating demeanour is the savouring of Martin Cartright's punishment.

"I ain't admitting to any of that."

"How fuckin' many?" This time the inherent anger is allowed to pervade and I rasp, "How many?"

"Ten, twelve." He offers the information so nonchalantly that Mitchell and I can't avoid a sickly exchange of disbelieving glances. "There's a lot of likeminded people out there that like to watch kiddies being touched. The boss knows that. I can't expect people like you to understand."

"Understand? Is he having a fuckin' laugh?" growls Mitchell. "Let's get him out of here before I throw up. Hood him so we can take ours off. My fuckin' face is beginning to itch."

"Where are you taking me?" Cartright sounds anxious again. "I thought you wanted to ask me more questions." He directs his attention to me, the guy that maybe he views as the good cop. The guy with the softly-spoken Irish accent. The proverbial iron fist in the velvet glove. One he fails to realise may yet come up with the metaphorical knife blade.

"Sure now, you're not going to tell us anything more, are you, man?" I say. I'm conscious that he's stalling for time, aware that we're going to kill him and it's obvious that his intention is to buy that time.

"I ain't lying when I said I don't know the boss's name, but Louis Platt, he lives alone in the house. He used to live with his old lady, his mother, but she died. Like I said, it's out Camden way. I ain't ever been there, so I don't know whereabouts. And the Paddy, the Irishman, all Irish accents sound pretty much the same to me. but you gotta softer way of speaking. He's a fuckin' abrupt bastard."

"Jesus, mate, he's either making a pass, or he's trying to get onto your good books," Mitchell quips.

"It's called gentle persuasion, my friend. It's surprising what you can get out of someone with a wee bit of that."

"So where you from then?" Cartright dares to enquire.

"Och me? Dublin. So if there's nothing more you can tell us..."

I've heard enough already. Besides, the place is beginning to give me the creeps. The small box-like lounge, the TV resting on a glass shelf in the corner, all so comparatively innocent. Nevertheless I have cause to wonder how many children have been lured to Cartright's Brixton home. The stench of freshly painted dark blue on the walls, in all likelihood, attests to its own depraved story.

Mitchell wraps tape around Cartright's mouth before slipping a black hood over his head. There is both an absence of either mouth or eye slits in the hood. Mitchell tightens the hood at Cartright's neck unceremoniously, enough to close off his breathing if he so desired.

I manage to suppress an involuntary shudder when Mitchell deigns to enquire about the woman. An unmistakeable sound of whimpering, reminiscent of a wounded animal, issues from behind the hood.

"What about her?" I ask.

Mitchell gestures upstairs. "I called the boss."

"And?"

He merely shrugs and purses his lips.

"I told you, she stays where she is. I won't be a party to that. And when this is over..."

"You'll what?"

It's my turn to shrug. "It doesn't matter."

"You always was a fuckin' moody paddy." Mitchell pulls the Glock from his jacket. Aware of his intention, I lay a restraining hand on his arm.

"You don't have to do this, man."

"It's okay, you won't be implicated, if that's what you're worried about."

"That's not what I meant. She's a...."

"A woman. Just get him into the fuckin' van." He gestures to the hooded figure.

I allow him to go upstairs reluctantly. The woman is probably innocent, plus I can hardly believe that Treveleyan would sanction such an action.

I grab Cartright unceremoniously by the arm, reminding him that if he makes any escape attempts that I won't hesitate to shoot him. I bundle him into the back of the van. One Mitchell had stolen earlier and consequently changed the number plates. I slam the door hard. I snatch off the hood and drop it into my jacket. Jumping into the driving seat, I swiftly imbibe a swallow from the hip flask before igniting a smoke.

"You'll fuckin' set fire to yourself one day, McRaney," Mitchell complains with his familiar growl.

"What the fuck's that supposed to mean?"

"The whisky. I know what it is cos I can smell it, and then lighting up a fag. So you going to let me have some?"

I reluctantly pass the flask.

"Fuck, McRaney, how long you been drinking?"

Clambering into the seat next to me he snatches off the hood. Cartright lies recumbently in the back of the Trafic. His hands are bound behind him. His feet strapped together. I had checked the tape and re-tied the hood.

"It's got nothing to do with you," I retort. "So I suppose you're going to grass on me to Treveleyan, 'that Aidan McRaney's an alcoholic.' Sure it's the only way I can get through this shit, man. So where we headed? I thought maybe out Epping Way. It's pretty isolated. So what about the woman?" I ask as I swing the van out into the street.

"You don't have to worry about her. If you ain't got the stomach for it."

"I didn't say that. It's just that I don't believe in killing innocent people, that's all. Nothing fazes you does it, Mitchell?"

"Oh it does, believe me. If you must know, I didn't kill the woman."

"You didn't?" I favour him with an unaccustomed smile. The first probably since we had taken on this business. "I'm glad to hear it."

"We didn't know the bird was going to be there, or how involved she is in this."

"Surely if the cops sanction this they'd draw the line at killing innocent people?"

"Innocent, law-abiding people yes, but that Rosie, she knew what he was doing. She must have."

"So what happens to her?"

"It's not our problem anymore. That is, however..." He gestures to the rear of the van. "So you think you'll be pissed by the time you do this? I knew you was drinking, mate. That's why I asked if you were okay. Look, there's gotta be better ways of handling this than getting fuckin' pissed, and maybe getting picked up on a drink driving charge. We're toting shooters, mate. That'll take some explaining, even if they are licensed."

My breath issues hard and ragged, while a cigarette remains an omnipresent fixture. I refrain from glancing at the other man as we head towards Epping Forest.

Chapter Three

Tarred And Feathered

Laurena Catherine McRaney
Born 17th August,1993
Died 21st November, 2011 aged 18 years
A sister and daughter brutally taken from this life

Early afternoon. The sun is out, yet the granite remains
conspicuously chill. Already thin fingers of mist trail the grassy
mound as if they belong to my sister's spirit.

My older sister, Bridget, rests a hand on my shoulder and I
rise to my feet. Her face is unaccustomedly ashen. She shivers and
tightens her coat about herself. With concern, I enquire if she's
okay.

"Not really. I had a bad shift last night. I came here because
you asked me to. I'm guessing this is the first time you've visited
Laurie's grave."

"You know it is. I couldn't bring myself to come before. It hurts,
y'know? I mean, she was so..." I am unable to finish my sentence.

Brid nods sympathetically. "That's why you asked me?"

I attempt a smile I'm far from feeling. After the episode
with Cartright it takes little to make me feel physically sick. Yet
somehow I am compelled to visit my sister's grave, brutally raped
and murdered by Stephen Fitzwalter a year ago.

"A right wuss, huh?"

"Not at all. Not everyone can bring themselves to visit a loved one's grave."

Changing the subject, I asked, "Are you working nights now?"

"It looks that way." she answered curtly. "As a ward sister I chose to."

"You look like shit, Sis."

She makes a face at my less than complimentary observation. "Sure. You too could look like shit if you had the night I have."

I am almost prompted to suggest that it couldn't have been any worse than mine. I refrained, however, content to allow my sister to moan. "I'm on the men's ward. Although I prefer that to neurotic women bitching all the time. Then I go home and listen to bloody roadworks after taking Sammy and Mark to school."

"The perils of being a nurse, I guess. You don't have to do nights all the time, do you?"

"I do. I put in for it."

"Why, if you look like that?"

"I don't want to discuss it, Aidan. Let's go, shall we?" She swipes a tissue across her eyes. I'm in time to witness tears in them. My sister Bridget. True to her faith. When she's not at work she spends a lot of her time at the Church of St Assumpta. Attending Mass while her brothers lapse by the wayside in all things Catholic. Graves and deaths appear to hold no apprehension for Bridget Collier. Today, however, she seems ostensibly contrary to her erstwhile beliefs. Doubtless the death, and the brutal capacity of Laurie's death, has upset us all.

"She's dead, Aidan. Nothing can bring her back." She shivers once more. I slip an arm about her shoulders, while I'm unable to avoid my consternation that something is radically amiss with my sister.

"I hear you're going to live in Esher." She changes the subject quickly.

"It seems so."

"Judy going off to California with Rafe and leaving Patrick with you. That's pretty generous of your ex isn't it?"

"Guess she and Rafe will be too busy with their plastics clinic to worry about a ten year old boy. Now, let's get out of here and you can tell me what's bothering you, cos I know something is."

With my arm remaining about her shoulder, we move in the direction of our waiting vehicles. Reaching my Cabriolet, I pause to lean against the car to roll a smoke. Brid requests a cigarette. I remind her that she's given up.

"I know that, but too much has happened. Oh Aidan..." My name is uttered in an oddly disconsolate tone. I can't help regard her with a frown.

"Oh come on, Sis, out with it. You've looked like shit since you've arrived. I know that cemeteries don't usually bother you. Not being the churchy woman that y'are."

"A young man was brought into the hospital last night. He was about your age. I've never actually seen anything like it. Although I had heard enough when...." Her hesitation is almost palpable. "When Dad..."

"What are you trying to say, Brid?"

"This young man," she expels a prolonged sigh, "had been tarred and feathered."

"What?" The cigarette almost slips from my fingers. "What happened? Is he dead?"

"He's barely clinging onto life. It's probably because he's young. Hot tar had been poured over him, even..." she pauses to swallow hard, "his genitals."

"Jesus Christ!"

"He looked as if he had been rolled in feathers. At first we thought he was one of those crazy people who covered themselves in feathers and believe they can fly. Only his face was left exposed. His head had been shaved. The tar had been poured onto the back of his head, and his scalp covered in feathers. Sure if it didn't remind me of the Troubles. What they did in the Province when I was growing up. What the 'Rah did to the women who slept with

23

the Brit soldiers. How these women had their heads shaved and covered in tar and feathers."

I attempt to placate her that it scarcely touched our lives when we lived in Dublin.

"It was on the news every night. Some wee bastard's been tarred and feathered in the Province, Dad used to greet me with that when I came home from school . I reckon Dad was on the side of the 'Rah, him being Catholic and all."

"So this guy. Who is he? Do you know?"

"Dr Welch said his name was Jason. I was at the Nurses' Station when he was brought in. He's on my ward. Of course he has a private room. He's assigned to me. Apparently he was found by this guy's dog sniffing him out in the bushes, not far from the hospital as it turned out. Jason was unconscious when he was brought in..." She falters again. I imagine she is about to burst into tears, and I hug her close.

It isn't often that my sister discusses her job at the Blackheath General. She loves nursing, while she invariably takes things, no matter how bad they are with accident victims and the like, in her stride. After all, that's what she claims she signed up for. Understandably, the tarred and feathered guy has hit her hard.

"I wandered into the ward to check on Jason. There was a woman by his bedside. I guessed she was his girlfriend or something. They didn't say that Jason was married. Anyway this woman took this laminated card from her wallet to show me, but she didn't leave the card long enough for me to read it properly. It was almost as if I had caught her out, that she was up to something. She looked quite official, and told me that she needed a few minutes with the man. So I left. The curtain was closed. I know I shouldn't have listened. And you probably think I watch too many movies, but I thought by the suspicious way she seemed to behave she might have something to do with it. Maybe not the actual tarring and feathering, but she might have known who did, and wanted to silence him if he regained consciousness. I know it sounds stupid, but she did seem rather cagey. If she'd been his girlfriend she would have been upset. The minute the woman left I burst into his room. Thankfully Jason was still alive."

"You mean you think this woman had come to kill him?"

"I know it sounds crazy. I guess I was just a wee bit scared because of how he came in. This woman spoke so authoritatively, almost cold and clinical, if you see what I mean. I don't think she was connected to the police. A couple of officers came later."

"Don't killers who want to silence someone usually wear white coats and masks, so they won't be recognised?"

She appears far too upset to appreciate my rather futile attempt at humour. "It's not funny, Aidan. I don't know what I thought. It's just so horrible. When you've lived under the shadow of these things as we have..." she shivers involuntarily once more, and pulls on her cigarette vehemently.

"So when are you on shift again?"

"Tonight. For the next two nights. I'm the Ward Sister. Those young nurses look up to me. If anyone wants a shoulder to cry on Sister Collier is always there to oblige. How will it look if I can't cope?"

A vibrating buzz emanates from my jacket. I carry two phones. One is for personal use. The other is the personal transmitter all Treveleyan's operatives are issued with.

"Sorry, Sis, I have to get this." I pull out my personal mobile by mistake before returning the former to my jacket.

"You have two phones, Aidan?"

I tell her that I keep one for Treveleyan's calls, but I don't elaborate further on who he is. I see that Treveleyan is calling. Moving out of earshot of my sister, I growl, "What do you want?" into the mouthpiece, purposefully neglecting to speak his name.

"Oh dear you sound a little aggrieved, my boy." I wish he wouldn't keep calling me that. "It's just to let you know that I have organised a special briefing for 9am tomorrow. Sorry it's such short notice, but something has come up, and I'd like you to be there."

I utter a barely audible confirmation.

"Good. In the conference room. I'm glad you saw fit to visit your sister's grave," he adds, before I realise that he has rung off. I catch myself shivering involuntarily, not altogether because of where I am. Or that those thinly filamentous trails of mist, reminiscent of gossamer wraiths, appear to have entwined themselves about my legs as if it is their intention to pull me beneath one of those granite monstrosities.

'I'm glad you saw fit to visit your sister's grave,' he had said. How the fuck did he know? As if he's capable of pinpointing my precise location with his accursed remote viewing.

"You okay, Aidan?" Brid's voice, ringing with concern, returns me to the present. I mutter absently that I'm fine.

"Let's go. It's cold here and you've gone quite pale. Was it bad news?"

"Not exactly." I manage a tentative smile.

I'm in the process of cracking open the Cabriolet's door when she asks, "What is it you really do?"

"You know what I do."

"A driver you said."

"That's right," I tell her non-commitally.

Grabbing my arm she confronts me squarely. "This Treveleyan guy, who is he really? Look, you can tell me. We've been through so much together. I'll tell you mine if you tell me yours," she adds, composing herself into the passenger seat.

"What's that supposed to mean? You make it sound as if we were kids again."

Her gaze is faraway, her tone wistful when she says, "I wish we were. Do you remember when I cut off your curls, because I thought curls were wasted on a boy? And Harry grassed on me to Mum."

"I don't remember that."

"Well, you were about three. Now that's enough of a trip down memory lane," she retorts briskly. "You've probably been wondering why I don't ask you over to my place anymore."

"It did occur to me. I thought you were pissed off with me about something. Or you had fallen out with Caitlan. I know she snapped at you one day when you offered to change Catie's nappy. You said she'd have a sore bum if she stayed in it too long."

"That wee girl sure has some issues. I know she's your wife, and I love her to bits, but I think she probably has post-natal depression. You guys reckon you suffer, but women's emotions are all over the place when we have a child. All she needs is love."

"Like The Beatles?" I smile.

"Like The Beatles," she nods, "maybe more than most women."

"You know I love her. "

"Then maybe you should show her more. Give her your 110 percent, and not just with sex. Buy her flowers. Treat her like a lady. Your lady. And you're avoiding the issue. I asked you what you really do for this Treveleyan character. Don't tell me it's just driving. What kind of driving? Taxi? Chauffeur? The next words that come from your lips has to be the truth, brother."

I can't help but heave a prolonged sigh. "Okay, since you ask. I'm not just a driver. Don't tell Caitlan. She believes that's all I am. She's a bit too delicate right now. When I tell you, you'll probably go off on one, and won't speak to me anymore."

"It would have to be pretty bad for me to behave that way toward you. So, I'm listening. There's only you and me in this car."

That's if Treveleyan isn't sitting in the back seat like a fucking ghost. I glance behind me. The seat remains empty. Still.

"You okay?"

"Sure." I swiftly pass off the sensation that Treveleyan might be observing me from some enigmatic, equally unknown location. "It's an Agency, like I said. We do other stuff."

"What other stuff?"

Notwithstanding, I have no intention of confiding in my sister what happened to Cartright at mine and Dennis Mitchell's hands. The discovery of the depravity filmed on the DVDs in his basement. "We go undercover sometimes. Like Special Branch."

"It sounds incredibly dangerous." She fastens a hand over mine. "Do you know what went through my mind when that Jason was brought in last night?"

Although I shake my head, I can practically sense what is to come.

"That it could have been you."

I slip an arm about her shoulders in an endeavour to placate her, that it won't happen to me. I hope I've managed to convince her. Truthfully that I also convince myself.

"Why do you do it? There must be other more normal jobs out there. Jesus, Aidan, you have two children and a delicate wife. Soon you'll be having your son full-time."

"You know I've had difficulty finding other work. Treveleyan was offering it on a plate. Once I get enough money I'll quit. Anyway you said if I tell you mine you'll tell me yours. Has it got something to do with you putting me off visiting you." She appears to take time over extensive throat clearing. "You're not pregnant, are you?"

"Good God, no! Jesus, Aidan, I don't want any more children."

"It's not Dad is it? He's not going into a home? You know how I feel about that."

"No, it's not Dad. It's Mark Collier. He's moved back in with me," she quickly adds. Closing her eyes, I sense she's waiting for the storm to break.

It does finally when I explode, "You've got to be fuckin' kidding!"

Mark Collier, my sister's husband, had walked out on her practically a year ago, in order to live with a friend of our late sister Laurena's. Penny Cronin, who was eighteen at the time, was allegedly expecting Collier's baby.

"You're not telling me you had the bastard back? I thought you were stronger than that. I'm guessing she's had the baby by now."

Brid appears suitably chastened by my outburst. "Only the baby wasn't Mark's. It was a fellow student's."

"Jesus, Sis! This smacks of rebound to me. I thought you said you'd never let him back into your life."

"He is the father of my children, Aidan. What else could I do? Apparently, Penny used him from the beginning. The student was penniless. Mark had a good job, so he could provide for her and the baby. She treated Mark more as a father than a boyfriend. The student got a job, and wanted to see his child. Seems she's been seeing him behind Mark's back."

"So he came crawling back to you? Have you told Ru?"

"Not yet. He'll be as angry as you. Anyway, Mark's sleeping in the spare room. I'm not ready for him to sleep in my bed just yet."

Chapter Four

The Girl With The Cobra Tattoo

I have little time to dwell on the revelation from my sister that her wayward husband has moved back in with her. I'm running late the following morning. It's almost 8:40, having to drive from Shooters Hill to South Lambeth.

Caitlan hovers around me while I adjust my tie in the mirror. A slice of toast in my mouth, a few hasty sips of black coffee, and I'm almost ready.

"You look nice, Aidan." Catie's in her arms and crying on her shoulder. We've called our baby Catriona Marie. She's two months old now. My wife paces the carpet in an endeavour to calm her down. At twenty, Caitlan is small and slight. She's already getting her figure back, simply because she eats like a bird.

"Thanks, sweetheart. Catie been fed, has she? Only she seems to be crying a lot." I address my wife's reflection in the mirror.

"Sure, I've fed her. She's just a wee bit grisly, that's all."

I finish my toast, checking I haven't dripped butter onto my suit, before I slip a hand around my wife. Catie instinctively stretches small fingers toward me imploringly for her Daddy to take her. For the umpteenth time I wonder why I'm pandering to that man yet again when all I want to do is to stay at home with my wife and child. "Sorry, I know she's been fed. In a couple of days we'll be moving into Judy's house in Esher while she's away. There'll be more room for the kids than in this old flat."

"I like this flat."

I scan the room with a critical eye. Caitlan appears to have precious little time for housewifery. I know she's young and Catie's quite demanding, but our daughter sleeps a great deal throughout the day, enabling my wife enough time to clean up. Before I married again, Brid used to clean for me. Then the flat was spotless. Now there's fluffy toys everywhere. The bathroom's filled with dirty laundry that Caitlan hasn't got round to sorting yet. I'm lucky to find a shirt that's clean. If I reprimand her about it, no matter how gently, she'll either start to cry, or succumb to a migraine. Her migraines seem to be a physical crutch for Caitlan. No, that isn't fair. I do love her, and we both have our own faults. I'm an untidy man. A fact Bridget has often criticised me for.

I regard my wife now, our daughter in her arms. My wife is wearing her fluffy white bathrobe. Caitlan's long dark hair cascades around her shoulders like a curtain. Eyes so trusting, innocent, and filled with such love for me, reflected in their depth. All conducive to allowing the terrible guilt to surface of what Mitchell and I had accomplished. My double life. One I hoped the sweet child I had married will never be aware of. She believes I'm merely a driver who ferries people to safe houses for The Treveleyan Agency.

Not that I carry a gun, and infiltrate the worst kind of criminal element and, if necessary, kill them. Ultimately, blood on the hands with which I caress the softness of her alabaster skin.

"Do we really have to move? Your ex-wife's house? There'll be photos everywhere. I'm sure she's still in love with you."

"Don't be silly." I smile and tilt her chin with a forefinger. "We'll put the photos away if they bother you. She divorced me, remember? Stop worrying. It'll be great, you'll see."

"You said I had to take Patrick to school. What if those women look down their noses at me? Your wife was so well-spoken."

"That isn't well-spoken. It's just snobbish the way she talks. You worry too much, my darling." I attempt to perfect a smile into those beautiful trusting eyes. "Now I really should go."

"Will you be long?"

"I don't know," I tell her with a shrug. "It's some kind of briefing, that's all I know. When I return, we'll get this place cleaned up. And you," I tap her nose affectionately, "start packing. You'll feel differently when we get out of..." I was about to add, 'this pig-sty' but I refrain. "You'll have a garden. You know how big that house is. I can hardly wait."

The kisses I crush to her lips are conducive to affording me an unwitting erection. Because I really am desirous of nothing better than to remain at home and make love to my wife.

With the slow crawl of the morning rush-hour, I arrive at the Agency a little after 9:15, with the realisation that I will have to enter the conference room beneath the disquieting regard of other more punctual operatives. Particularly Regis Bonner. Bonner is indisputably a guy to whom I've taken an instant dislike. From what I know of Bonner the dislike is mutual. In the main, my own disregard lies in the fact that he invariably refers to me as 'Paddy'. It transpires that I'm the only Irish person present. Bonner once intimated that if this was thirty years earlier I would be the last person whom Treveleyan would trust. This ultimately prompts me to suggest than I would like nothing better than to put a bomb up Bonner's pompous arse. Needless to add, Bonner seems to have developed suspicions of me ever since.

I am already late, so decide to polish off my smoke. Cracking open the Cabriolet's door, I step out. The cigarette signposts my lips when I see the woman. She's obviously in a hurry, as she quickly slides from a gleaming red Porsche. Her blonde hair is quite striking, upswept and highlighted with hints of red, although tendrils have managed to escape their pins, as if she has performed the task in a hurry.

The neat black skirt she wears with a matching figure-hugging jacket is cut at least three inches above the knee. Elegant ankles spill into high black stilettos. Her eyes are rendered impenetrable behind dark glasses. She reaches to the Porsche's back seat to locate a pile of books. A black leather bag is slung across her shoulder. The bag falling against the books is enough to send them flying. I hear her curse an impatiently muttered, "for Chrissake," beneath her breath.

I kill the cigarette, and quickly move to reach her across the forecourt. When I observe that one of the volumes happens to be entitled 'Tactical Weapons Training', I mention something about that particular book being heavy going. She murmurs her thanks when I place a couple of them into her arms, while I opt to carry the others.

"Oh not really. Thanks again. Are you here for the briefing too?" The semblance of a perfect white-toothed smile radiates dramatically high cheekbones, while the subtlest intimation of colour suffuses her face.

"Yeah, guess I am. And you?"

She accepts the proffered hand, and I introduce myself. The action is a fraction awkward because of the books. I offer to relieve her of the others.

"Thanks, Aidan. I'm LJ – Lorna Allardyce." It is odd how the colour swiftly abandons her face momentarily, as if I've told her some bad news. She removes the shades and piles them into her hair. I'm allowed an initial sight of the deepest pellucid green eyes. Heaving a prolonged sigh, she suggests that we should go in, adding, "I'm the one who is conducting the briefing, and I'm late already. I expect the old boy will look down his pompous nose with his usual disapproval, but I had to make sure that my son got to school safely. There's a lot of goddamned bastards around, huh?" To which I cannot fail to agree, although I wonder why she should have mentioned the fact.

What I've learned of Treveleyan's Agency in the few weeks that I've worked for them, is that we seldom encounter other operatives. As Sir George outlines, the fewer colleagues we meet when we go undercover, they won't be known to us. So I can hardly believe it when I see at least eight of Treveleyan's agents present, seated at the long polished table in the spacious conference room. Dark oak panelling adds an olde worlde and sombre quality to the decor. Paintings of eighteenth and nineteenth century art adorn the walls. I recognise a couple of Gainsboroughs, a Pre-Raphaelite, and even Hogarth. As a potential artist myself, I appreciate the collection.

The only two operatives known to me are Bonner, of course, and a guy of ample proportions I know only as Gregor. Gregor sports a black tuxedo jacket with a starched white shirt. The jacket is incongruously emblazoned with a red rose. Gregor appears more as if he were attending an evening function than a mere briefing.

Regis Bonner sports a familiar smug expression. I hear him whisper, "Paddy's late again," to the sallow-faced individual next to him, before he addresses me, "So what you been up to with sex on two legs, Paddy?" His gesture is impishly directed toward Lorna, who is in the process of erecting a blackboard and easel.

A TV monitor, plus DVD player, occupies the remainder of the space. There the Great Man sits on his throne, or rather in his wheelchair. As always, he sports the all-grey, nondescript attire. His beard is neatly trimmed. Those strange, perspicacious grey eyes scan his surroundings, before they finally descend to those grouped about the table.

I'm the last to take my place in one of the high-backed Regency style chairs. Composing myself, I afford Bonner a steely glance. If it is his intention to goad me into an argument, then he's succeeded. He knows if there is one thing that I resent it's being called either 'Paddy' or 'Mick'.

In his late thirties, Bonner sports that rather idiosyncratic fashion statement of the shaven head, which he believes is ostensibly attractive to women, though Mitchell once intimated that it's because Bonner is going bald. He is a quite thinly-featured man, with a narrow mouth that, with the bald head, affords him an almost skull-like, shrewish appearance. Or maybe I am naturally biased about the guy.

I'm incensed by that coldly surreptitious gaze. With the way I feel, if he's looking for a fight then I'll be happy to oblige. The man hasn't borne witness to my inherently hot Irish temper hitherto.

Nevertheless there appears to be more important matters at stake, hence the briefing. Dennis Mitchell for one. I realise that he is noticeably absent, when I could have done with the support. Practically a sleepless night and a crying baby have done precious little for my sense of alertness.

Lorna finally manages to erect her blackboard. While sorting out the books on her desk, Treveleyan says, "You were a little late, my dear," in reproving tones.

She explains about taking her son to school, before swiftly returning her attention to us as if with relief. Like me, I guess she probably finds those inscrutably grey eyes oddly disturbing, as if the man is capable of penetrating my very thoughts. That's why I figure that it's safer to blank them.

She is the only woman in the company of men. Predictably, Bonner crudely hisses how he'd like to give her one to his sallow-faced companion. I freeze when Bonner adds, "What was you doing with her, Paddy? You did arrive together?"

I really have had enough. Anger surfaces, and I can't help but retort, "And I'm not Paddy for a start. Regis? What fuckin' kind of name is that? Maybe you should be called Lyme. You should be buried in it, man."

"Fuck you, McRaney."

"Oh you remember my name then?"

"Mr Bonner and Mr McRaney!" For an individual who appears as frail as Treveleyan, he sure has a booming voice.

"Sir?" Both Bonner and I chorus.

"So Aidan," Treveleyan steeples his fingers, interlaces his palms and taps his mouth thoughtfully. "Did you have to take your son to school too to account for your lateness? I did say 9 am."

"No, Sir, just overslept."

"Still on the honeymoon period, hey, Pad..." Bonner starts.

The withering glance I flash his way halts him mid-sentence.

"Gentlemen, please!" Lorna rasps, angry colour spearing her cheeks. She raps with her pointer on the desk a couple of times. "I've seen better behaviour in my son's class of six and seven year olds. We haven't called this briefing for fun. Something happened last night. That's why I have called you here." Her tone conveys authority. Although her accent is a perfectly cultured English, other times I detect a hint of American.

"Jason Lang. Those who knew Jason…" There's a muted hush amongst the assembly.

"Knew? What do you mean? He isn't dead, is he?" Gregor asks uneasily, his face growing pale.

Jason.

Bridget had referred to someone called Jason who had been brought into the hospital. Surely it can't be the same guy, can it?

"Jason was taken to the Blackheath General last night. He had…" she pauses to clear her throat. "He had been tarred and feathered."

Exclamations of horror travel around the seemingly otherwise frozen silence of the room. This is definitely the guy Brid mentioned. So was LJ the woman she had seen at the hospital?

"Apparently his body was covered in tar. The kind they use on the roads. They must have rolled him in feathers, but left his face exposed. They also shaved his head. That too was covered in feathers. At the moment Jason clings onto life. We have yet to receive reports from the hospital. I went to see him last night. I managed to smuggle in a small camera to show you what we're up against. I don't think the Ward Sister was too pleased." She smiles wryly. "She seemed to be hanging around quite a lot. I couldn't divulge too much of course. I got out of there before the cops arrived."

There's a still of Jason on the TV screen. Jason as he was before they had tarred and feathered him. He is a good looking young man with short wavy dark hair, a warm pleasant smile.

"33 years old, guys. Now this is how he looks."

Once again shock and revulsion travels around the room. I've previously had no occasion to have seen anyone tarred and feathered. Lorna has taken a back and front photo, from his head to his lower back. Apart from the feathers of course, his torso is bare.

"Imagine having hot tar poured over your body as you scream in agony as your flesh is blistered."

It appears that everyone has lapsed into a kind of frozen silence. The feathers are of a grey and brownish colour. God knows from what. They are tightly packed so that it almost affords the belief that he was born that way. A veritable birdman. His face, still handsome, is left exposed, and his eyes are closed.

"The hospital staff had to pluck off all the feathers before they could remove the tar and bandage him up."

Someone laughs dryly. I think it's Gregor. The sound is harsh and guttural. I guess it's a laugh that's borne from sheer nerves. Although it isn't difficult to observe there are tears standing in the big man's eyes.

"I know you and Jason were friends, weren't you, Gregor?" Treveleyan sympathises.

"Indeed, Sir. He sort of looked up to me. So is he...?" he pauses to swallow uncomfortably, "all bandaged up now?"

"Apparently. I just needed to take these photos to show you what these bastards did. Although I think if I'd remained by Jason's bedside any longer, that Irish ward sister would have had me arrested."

Lorna flicks us a somewhat cursory smile. That certainly sounds like Bridget.

"As you know, Jason Lang was engaged in fieldwork." Further tendrils of thick strawberry-blonde hair have worked loose from their pins. She brushes the hair aside with irritation. I realise there is something on her hand; I glimpse it beneath the sleeve of her jacket. It's the head of a snake. A cobra. She has a tattoo. I find myself staring at the tattoo abstractedly.

Turning her back, she takes a chalk and draws what appears to be an octopus, or giant squid, on the blackboard.

Treveleyan sits motionlessly, content to allow her to talk. The lord on his throne. The only thing that is animated is the familiar steepling fingers that continue to flirt with those narrow lips, on which a smile of pure admiration for this woman lingers. The woman, whoever she is, who sports the tattoo of a cobra's head on her right hand.

Chapter Five

L J

Despite my love for my darling Caitlan, I can't help but find this woman both fascinating and attractive. She's slender and svelte in the figure-hugging jacket and skirt. A peach silk blouse complements the ensemble serving to accentuate every curve of a body I'd enjoy, if only once, to lie beside. Nevertheless, I bring myself up sharply for what I am thinking.

'You have a wife and children, McRaney.'

This woman is unobtainable. She is obviously married with a child. Although amidst the assortment of sparklers on her fingers none appears to be a wedding band.

Harland, Treveleyan's manservant, brings in coffee and tea, plus a plate of Blue Riband wafers on a silver tray, before excusing himself with a small bow of propriety.

"At the top," Lorna returns our attention to the giant octopus that she has chalked on the board, "is our man. His name…" She pauses, green eyes serving to encompass the eight operatives seated about the table. "His name is Daniel Corrigan. These are the tentacles. What we have to do is this…" She immediately rubs out one of the tentacles with the cloth. "So what have I just done?" she asks, as if we really are in a schoolroom. Someone speaks up that she's just rubbed it out.

"That's what we do, honey." Her voice is a purr. "With the accent on rubbing out." She duly erases a couple more of the tentacles. "The tentacles represent Corrigan's acolytes of course."

"What about Corrigan?" It is Bonner who asks the question.

"Mr Corrigan is another story."

A man's face appears on the screen, replacing poor Jason Lang's tarred and feathered body.

"Do you think this Corrigan guy is responsible then?" Gregor enquires.

"Although we are certain that he is, we obviously need to obtain proof."

Corrigan sports rumpled black hair to his collar, with long sideburns tapering to his jawline. It's a good looking, almost aristocratic face, albeit with a semblance of cruelty and salaciousness etching the mouth. The distinct possibility that the cruelty may extend to women. His eyes are darkly embedded, almost impenetrable. The faintest arc of a smile flirts with full-bodied lips, which attest to the vindictiveness this man is probably capable of. It's as if he's directing that darkly brooding stare toward me. I detect also an imperceptible familiarity about this guy, although I've never met him.

"Daniel Fergus Corrigan," she directs the pointer to the TV screen. "Born January, 21st, 1977 in Ballymurphy, Northern Ireland. This makes our man 35 years old."

"I fuckin' knew it, a fuckin' paddy."

I can feel the sensation of Bonner's eyes, as if they are capable of spitting lead, rivetted on me. I concentrate on the screen instead, refusing to look at him. I'm storing it all up though.

Lorna adds, "Yeah, he's an Irishman," quietly. "And there's good and bad in all of us. We also know that Corrigan's late father was a member of the Provisional IRA. He was on the run from the Ulster Volunteer Force in the early Eighties. We know that Mairead Corrigan, Daniel's mother, housed wanted Catholic men in her Ballymurphy home. Miss Corrigan, never married, died of cancer last year. She was the long-time mistress of a man who already had a wife and child in South Armagh. This man is reputed to have fathered other children in both the North and the Irish Republic.

That man is Connor McMartland.

"As we know, Corrigan had dealings with the gangster Raymond Lamond. So it's no surprise that Corrigan's moved in on Lamond's empire. This leads me to the paedophilia and missing children. Because we believe Corrigan is involved in something as equally, or even more despicable than terrorism. For those who don't know, I published a book recently."

A writer too. Jesus, what hasn't this woman done?

"The book is entitled 'Missing Past and Present'. It deals with the children who have inexplicably gone missing from their homes, probably since the fifties and sixties. Some of these children have never been found. So why children? Because there are always people such as the Lamond brothers, and now possibly Corrigan. Once they've had their evil way with these poor kids, they sometimes burn them, desecrate them, other terrible atrocities too inconceivable to relate.

"Jason Lang was sent in to infiltrate Corrigan's enterprises. The Ward Sister happened to mention something to one of the doctors, that the tarring and feathering reminded her of the Troubles. We know that tarring and feathering went on in Northern Ireland during the height of the conflict. Women who consorted with British Soldiers had their heads shaved. They would have hot tar poured over her scalp and feathers were stuck to her head. If it is Corrigan, and we're certain that it is, then he is bringing the Troubles to us."

"So why can't this Corrigan guy be arrested?" I ask.

"The most obvious question I know. The trouble is we don't have complete proof that Corrigan is our man. Unfortunately this business has to be handled with kid gloves. There are certain politics involved. If only his own personnel would come in and grass on him, but they're too scared. That's why we've had to send our agents in. All we know is Daniel Corrigan is in London, and has been since Raymond Lamond died in prison, maybe before."

We help ourselves to the coffee. Lorna deposits herself onto a stool and crosses her legs. The few muted wolf-whistles she receives she chooses to ignore. It's obvious she's used to commanding men's attention, not merely because of her briefings.

"Anyway, we'll wind up things for today," she declares, taking a sip from her coffee. "Has anyone got any questions?"

I enquire where Dennis Mitchell is.

"Dennis is on field-work, Aidan." Treveleyan volunteers the information.

Depositing her cup onto the desk, LJ leafs through one of the tomes she's brought with her. I observe the book is the one entitled 'Tactical Weapons Training'. Further surprised when I clock that the author is LJ Allardyce.

Reaching the Cabriolet, I roll and light a much-needed cigarette. I'm about to crack open the door when I hear the sound of heels on the pavement. Smoke anchored to my lips, I turn in time to confront Lorna Allardyce.

Because her hair is so thick and heavy, further tendrils have succeeded in working loose from their pins. "Oh this ridiculous hair of mine. It won't stay in control. I normally wear a scarf around it, but I couldn't find one to match the outfit. God, I must look a mess."

Now she sounds softly feminine, making me wonder that I have imagined she is the author of a book entitled 'Tactical Weapons Training'.

Undeniably she is a beautiful woman. Her complexion is clear and firm. Marginally highlighted with a little blusher. Her mouth forms a perfectly sculpted bow. And those eyes. I guess a guy could practically drown in those huge green-flecked eyes. Nevertheless I bring myself up sharply for the second time today. I'm a married man who is going to have his children with him soon. There are going to be attractive women entering my life all the time. The art is not to succumb to their allure. I ask her if I've forgotten something.

"No. But Sir George wondered where you had slipped off to. Only some of the guys wanted to have a fool around in the Armoury."

"Fool around? That doesn't sound quite the thing you should do in an Armoury. Anyway I have stuff to do at home. Clean up my flat for one thing. We're moving into my ex's house in Surrey tomorrow. And there's all the baby stuff to sort out."

I wish she would replace the shades, because those eyes are boring into mine. She carries a partially flirtatious smile – at least I imagine that it's flirtatious – playing about her lips, while she also appears to look remotely interested.

"Sir George said your wife has just had a baby. How lovely for you. I bet you have photographs."

"Sure I do. On my phone. So is that why you're here? To discuss my family? That Ward Sister you mentioned. Do you remember her name?"

"Sure I do. Sister Collier. Why?"

"Because Sister Collier is my sister. She told me about Jason. That a woman, I'm guessing it was you, was at the hospital."

"Then it's a good thing you are one of Sir George's agents. No one outside the Agency is supposed to have known I was there."

"If you don't mind me saying, you're not the kind of woman who can remain unnoticed." Now I sound as if I'm making a pass.

"Thanks. At least I think it's thanks. Though you do seem a little pissed off with me. Your sister does have an extremely suspicious nature, doesn't she? I had the feeling she thought I was there to pull out Jason's lines, or smother him with a pillow. Even though she tried to keep still, I could still hear her behind the curtain. She would make a good agent."

"Heaven forbid. My sister an agent? She'd try and run the place."

"But your sister isn't an agent and you are. And I'd appreciate you not discussing this particular case outside the Agency building."

"I know my sister is assigned to his ward."

"Well, just warn her not to speak of it outside. If word ever got back to Corrigan... You don't know him, Aidan. He's evil, a sadist. He'd give the Marquis de Sade a run for his money, I'm telling you."

"So you wanted me for something?" I remain on the defensive, although I have no idea why. Or is it because I really don't wish to be here, yet I am magnetically drawn.

I enquire, "Or is Sir George missing me?" with a sarcasm I can't help.

"He's going to be calling you in the next couple of days. He asked me to tell you."

"Why?" I pretend obtuseness.

"He has a job for you."

I kill the cigarette, slide into the Cabriolet. "Sure he does, but it has to be the last one. I have my family to think of."

"That's just it. You stop fighting. We all stop fighting, and your children will not be safe. Treveleyan said you saw the DVD, 'The Burning'. You know what those bastards are capable of."

"You threatening me?"

"Oh honey, stop being on the defensive. Just the opposite. We need you, and the other guys. Treveleyan said you could be difficult."

"Difficult. What the fuck does that mean?"

"That you don't want to do this. Your heart isn't in it. But do it for your children then. The DVD, surely it made you feel angry?"

"You know it did."

"And you and Dennis did a good job."

"Okay." I prolong a sigh. "I'll do whatever the old boy wants... for now." I fire the ignition. The motor purrs into instantaneous life.

LJ says, "And thanks for what you did, Aidan." Her tone of voice is strangely poignant. I'm astonished to witness there are tears in her eyes. I can only conjecture that she's referring to the hit on Cartright.

Chapter Six

The Contract On Platt

The post office isn't overly crowded at this time of the morning. It's a little after nine. I offer my name as John Marshall, the alias I invariably adopt in an endeavour to conceal my identity. The clerk behind the counter fetches the package.

Wearing a checked ball-cap and dark glasses, my jacket collars are pulled to my face. I manage an attempt at appearing incognito. Treveleyan's memo suggested I am to play a lone hand. If I am not happy with the situation, then he would send in either Regis Bonner or Gregor Johnson. I tell him that I'll probably end up putting a slug in Bonner. As much as I like the guy, Gregor might be a wee bit conspicuous because of his size. Once again, I enquire of Mitchell's whereabouts, only to be informed by Treveleyan the former is still engaged on fieldwork. He serves to irritate me sometimes when he prefers to growl rather than respond. I like the guy, however, and trust him implicitly. We have got each other out of scrapes often. I'm beginning to miss him.

A final instruction from Sir George: if you have to speak, lose the accent. With practice, I swiftly discover it's fairly easy to disguise my accent. I speak with a perfected English one now, like a native.

"Your package, Mr Marshall." The clerk passes a thin A4 size jiffy bag across the counter; I thank him in my well-rehearsed South London. This particular Post Office is located in South Lambeth, not too far from the Agency building.

Dropping behind the Cabriolet's steering, I roll then light a cigarette, scanning the car park. There's no one around, and I open the jiffy to reveal the photo lying on the top. Louis Platt's weasely countenance. Intense grey eyes regard me coldly from the black and white eight by ten. I realise how much he does resemble Stan Laurel. Except Stan Laurel would not have perpetrated the horrendous things this guy has done. I recollect the DVD. The little girl hooded and tied to a chair.

Platt's lips are thin enough to be practically non-existent. His cheekbones are high, prominent, affording him a somewhat gaunt appearance.

So is Platt merely another tentacle of Corrigan's empire? I've been far too preoccupied with the move to Esher to dwell a great deal on what LJ had outlined. Nonetheless, it had struck me that Daniel Corrigan was the son of IRA man, Connor McMartland.

I can't help but wonder if Corrigan is living in London, or why people are so afraid of him. He's just a man, isn't he? He's human. Flesh and blood. He can still be killed. I see Platt is 56, but looks younger. He resides in a basement flat in Camden, so easy access then. My orders are to observe him for a few days before moving in. Treveleyan has provided a map, plus the layout of the flat. Nighttime is best.

Although I have been reluctant to do this at the outset, I am now fuelled with an inherent sense of anticipation.

I hate having to lie to my wife. Mainly to spare her feelings. She's so delicate. I love her and wish for nothing untoward to occur that will hurt her. I explain I have a job that will take me away for the night. She remonstrates how she hates to be left alone in such a big house. Predictably, she enquires about the job, asking if it involved driving someone somewhere?

I hear her talking to her sister, Mollie, in Dublin. I know I shouldn't eavesdrop on her conversation, but I'm concerned that if Caitlan complains too much, Mollie will insist on coming over and whisking her back to Ireland, as she has frequently threatened to.

Caitlan assures me that she loves me, and has no desire to leave. She often refers to us living in Ireland. I know it is our home, but I'm not certain I wish to reside there anymore. I've lived in London for almost twenty one years now. It would mean that Patrick be uprooted from his school. In less than a year he will be attending secondary school, to which Judy's already assigned him. Plus I can't imagine leaving either Bridget or Ruairi.

Caitlan is curious of my destination. I painfully lie that I have to take a guy to Scotland. Scotland? Where did that come from? Naturally it will certainly account for my being away for a while. She suggests that he could go by train, that Scotland is such a long way to drive. Her questions are so persistent I have to request that she asks no more.

I drive Caitlin, Patrick and Catie to Brid's, but refuse to enter my sister's house, because – she informs me – Collier is there. Brid's concerned that I'll cause an argument. So, after kissing my wife and children, I am preparing to drive away when my sister, clutching my arm, begs me to be careful.

Somehow I'm not as apprehensive as I imagined that I would be. This bastard has to die, and Treveleyan has entrusted me to carry out the contract.

I refrain from using my own car of course. Treveleyan has his own garage and mechanics. Motors, which he's practically bought for a song, are stripped down, repainted and made ready to be used by operatives. I drive my own Cabriolet into the garage, where a mechanic hands me the keys to a dark green Toyota. After procuring a .9mm semi automatic Browning, I check the gun for the umpteenth time. I plunge the weapon into the holster behind my jacket, and slip the silencer into my pocket.

I've had Platt on ice for the past couple of days, with the realisation that the guy seldom vacates his residence. There's an occasional trip to the shops, but that's all.

Everything is in place. There's an easy access around the back. I scrutinise the layout briefly while I remain in the car, breathing raggedly before abandoning the sanctuary of the Toyota. Wearing gloves leaves no fingerprints. I make a final scan of my surroundings before rolling a ski mask onto my face, and hope that Platt is alone.

It's a little after one thirty. Street lamps are watchful sentinels and, I pray, my only witnesses. The Toyota is parked opposite Platt's residence, shrouded in darkness, away from the detecting street lamps. There's no CCTV, so Treveleyan assures me.

A final smoke. An equally final reach for my other travelling companion, the one I carry adjacent to the gun. The hip flask that contains my favourite Chivas. I am ultimately aware that I should not drink when I need my wits about me. As Treveleyan says, I am to play a lone hand. I need something, however. The whisky spearing my insides makes the business of what I am about to do more palatable.

I enter Platt's basement with a gingerly-delivered lift of an old paint-flaked window. I hold my breath expectantly when the window squeaks, in case Platt should wake and come at me. There is a chance he too might be armed. Treveleyan isn't certain of that. So it means it's wisest to assume that he is. The fact affords me the upper hand, and alerts me enough not to allow him a chance to reach for a weapon.

The night sounds are magnified. The distant hoot of an owl that, in reality, might not be an owl at all, but a warning signal.

I'm in and drop agilely into the room, one I deduce must be the lounge. God it stinks in here, with a foetid staleness. A mix of old newspapers and an unwashed body. Something else too. Something indefinable. Could the stench emanate from putrefaction. Maybe something's dead in here? It's not Platt is it? It will save me from killing the bastard.

Platt's lounge is badly cluttered, mostly with old newspapers. I discover a pile of them are indiscriminately thrown onto a battered settee.

Easing the Browning from my holster, I attach the silencer. Positioning the weapon adjacent to my face, I catch a glimpse of the stranger in the mirror. The hood concealing my features reveals the narrow slit of a mouth, while my eyes shine out blackly piercing in the semi darkness of the room.

Platt is in bed and snoring loudly. He has partially thrown over the covers, to reveal a suspiciously stained once-white sheet and a grey flannel blanket. Wispy grey feathers of what remains of his hair are raised up and awry about his head. Platt appears thinner, more emaciated than in the photo. In fact the latter is marginally flattering in comparison to this man.

Skinny and wizened, a bare torso undulates raggedly in the relief of moonlight. At least he's alone. No women are about to crawl out of the woodwork, if he's that way inclined of course. The small bottle of white pills on his nightstand testifies to the reason why he sleeps so soundly, and snores sonorously. Perhaps with the terrible atrocities he has committed it's the only way he can sleep at night.

Platt moans restlessly. I tense, but need not worry. He's well away. A sitting target, or rather, a sleeping one. I raise the pistol as my finger inches the trigger. Then... fuck. Caitlan's delicate white countenance and imploring green eyes rise to my mind's eye. She holds Catie in her arms. My daughter's arms are outstretched as if to say, "Daddy." Brid warning me to be careful.

Remember the little girl on the DVD, I counsel myself. Hooded. Sexually abused, and torched by this bastard.

"Wake up, you bastard, and fuckin' look down the barrel of this weapon before I blow you away."

I take a swift taste of the whisky before returning the hip flask. My body grows cold. I need to remain detached from this. Focus. 'It's just a job, McRaney.' Nevertheless, all I can visualise is my wife mouthing, "I love you, Aidan." My baby. My son.

Louis Platt twitches in his sleep. The movement seems unnatural as if he is about to have a seizure. A sharply discordant thud echoes close to my ear, simultaneously bright spots of crimson flower the torso of the man on the bed. He twitches again as another thud slams into his head, allowing the blood to drizzle from the circular hole that appears between his eyes.

Did I fire after all without realising? Although I fail to recollect remotely squeezing the trigger. I freeze. Realising I am not alone, I see the gun. It carries no silencer, in spite of the muted sound of the shots.

His arms drop limply across the bed. The harshness of his sleeping breath is ultimately silenced, composed in death.

I turn to confront the assassin. A black hoodie is pulled up over their head and close to the face. A bandanna mask is raked up over the nose, while the addition of dark shades render the features totally impenetrable. A black leather trenchcoat is open to reveal tight black jeans plunged into high leather boots.

"Come on, let's get the fuck out of here!"

I'm further astonished to hear a woman's voice issue from behind the mask.

Chapter seven

The Past Unfolds

I have no idea whose side the woman might be on, although I detect a familiarity about the voice. We move outside, heading to where I've parked the Toyota. Stashing the Browning, I observe she has tucked her own weapon away.

She shot Louis Platt dead while he slept. The bastard deserved to die of course. If it wasn't for Caitlan's anxious face, or my baby daughter's, surfacing in my mind, then I would in all likelihood have killed him myself.

Another car is parked adjacent to mine. A black Saab.

She's removed the shades, but the bandanna remains. Above the bandanna, green flecked eyes are rendered lynx-like and inscrutably feline when they flash my way.

"We'll go in this one," she instructs when I raise the remote to my own vehicle. "Trevelyan will have the Toyota picked up."

"Who are you?" I attempt to penetrate the mask. I'm still wearing the hood, and suggest that she probably doesn't know who I am.

"Oh, I know who you are. Besides, you can't drive, can you?"

"Why not?" I demand indignantly pulling off the mask. It is not merely the rising tide of anger that I'm beginning to entertain, but an intermarriage of both unease and foolishness because I had failed to kill Platt.

"Because you've been fuckin' drinking, mister. That's why not. You get picked up by the cops with what you're fuckin' toting, man, it'll only come back to us."

"I thought Treveleyan had people to handle that kind of stuff."

"Not if any of his operatives are stupid enough to get caught by the police. It's the same if someone breaks the law while you're working for him. He'll deny all knowledge of you. You're out on your own."

I climb into the passenger seat beside her. She fires the ignition and swings out the Saab. It's now a fraction after two in the morning. I reason how easy it would be to locate the flask once more, except those green eyes flash my way as if she's capable of interpreting my thoughts. I realise who she is now, while my assumption is correct for she lowers the mask to reveal herself as Lorna Allardyce.

"So what happened back there, McRaney?" Her tone is caustic and chill. "Was it the booze?"

I mutter, "I fuckin' froze, that's all."

"Why? Cos you lost your nerve?" Those eyes flash dangerously at me again. The hood remains up, and serves to maintain her features wreathed in shadow.

"Haven't you ever froze?"

"Not on these jobs I haven't. The day I freeze I may as well get out of it. I give my 120 percent. Treveleyan said you might lose your nerve. That's why he sent me in."

Her mouth is tight and set. The way she is dressed is a far cry from the woman who had tears in her eyes the day in the car park. When she had thanked me for something I'd done. Although I had never really been able to figure out exactly to what she had alluded.

"To spy on me?"

"In a way, I guess. Oh, we don't doubt your abilities, Aidan. It's that you seem so reluctant. You saw the DVD. That little girl was called Sally Carmichael, by the way, if you need to put a name to a face. She was violated. Her parents will never get over that what was left of her was found buried in a shallow grave. There's too much of this sort of thing going on. More children are going missing. The police are as angry about all this as we are. That's when Treveleyan's agents come in. Often the police are blamed for not finding the killers soon enough. The public tend to lose faith in them. Have you ever heard of the MRF?"

"I can't say I have. They sound like some kind of organisation."

"That's exactly what they are, Aidan. The Military Reaction Force. I'm not saying these guys weren't rather unorthodox in their methods, but Treveleyan knew some of the officers of the MRF who were deployed in Northern Ireland in the early Seventies, although he was still at police college.

"Their operatives were issued with photos of known IRA assassins. The MRF shot on sight, no questions asked. Sometimes innocents fell foul of their gunfire, but it got the job done."

Something akin to a reptilian anger surges through me at what she intimates. "You're saying that Trevelyan condoned it? It sounds like murder to me."

"There was a war on. I'm sorry that it was your countrymen. We need to know where your loyalties lie."

"What the fuck, LJ?" I regard her in complete disbelief. "What are you saying? That just because I froze tonight you think I might have an ulterior motive. I'm not the fuckin' IRA. Jesus. What is it with the British not trusting the Irish? I've been here for 20 years. This is my home."

"I'm sorry. I didn't mean anything by it. Boy, you are touchy."

"Do you blame me when you spout stuff about loyalties and shit. Anyway, what have this murder squad got to do with anything? Cos, it was a murder squad no matter how much you try to justify it."

"It's because we are no different from the MRF that Treveleyan admires so much. Except now we find out who's killing and debauching these poor children, and we take them out. We're not sanctioned by the Army, but by the police. It's dangerous times, and there's a guy out there who is acting as some kind of catalyst with his hatred of the British.

"So tell me why you really froze tonight. Your gun was levelled on him. Your finger was on the trigger. Then what stopped you?"

"I'd rather not discuss it."

"If that's what you want." She shrugs her insouciance.

"So I'm guessing you'll go straight to Treveleyan and tell him that I fucked up."

"I'm not a snitch. So does he know you drink?"

"Jesus, I'm not a fuckin' alcoholic y'know. I just needed a wee bit of..."

"Dutch courage," she interrupted.

I edge, "Sure," non-committally.

"In this game Dutch courage can cost you your life, Aidan. Not to mention spoil your aim. I knew you drank before a hit because Dennis Mitchell told me. I'm not going to tell Treveleyan. Just lose the bottle, that's all. And not your own."

"What's with the gun?" I opt to change the subject. "I didn't see a silencer. Where the fuck are you taking me? I need to get back to Esher." I remain in an ill temper, one that is fuelled by my own shortcomings in allowing a woman to do the job for me.

"I'm not driving down there at this time of the morning. I need my sleep. The gun..."

The sensuous mouth delivers a fluctuating kind of smile. It is conducive to sending my senses reeling. Until I think of my trusting, lovely wife and my children, aware I should not be negotiating these kind of thoughts for another woman. That was the old Aidan McRaney. The freshly released from prison guy compelled to make up for lost time. I'd turned my back on my family before, which resulted in almost losing my son. I have no plans to repeat the mistake.

"A particular invention of mine," LJ declares proudly, returning me to the present.

"You making your own weapons now? Is there anything you can't do?"

"Well, I don't do needlework. And I don't make those arty

crafty things. I don't knit. But I do cook. I love cooking. That is one of my hobbies. But yeah, the gun, honey," she drawls, "no, I don't actually manufacture my own weapons. Treveleyan has his own gunsmith."

"Course he does." I inject a modicum of sarcasm, but one to which she fails to react.

"I needed a pistol that could fit into a holster without having to maintain the silencer attached. Or having to screw the silencer on. So this baby," she pauses to pat her left side proudly, "suits me perfectly. The gun is based on a .9mm Sig automatic."

I remind her that she has made no actual reference to where we are heading. It is odd, but I don't relish returning alone to that big old house in Esher. Although it hits me all at once how much I'm beginning to miss Caitlan. That what has just happened back there has somehow assumed an almost unreal characteristic surrounding it.

"You're coming back to my house. Oh, don't worry," she arches a brow, "no strings, okay? Just to get you sobered up, that's all. Besides, I need to talk to you for a while."

"About the evils of drink no doubt. Anyway, I thought you said you needed your sleep."

"Oh I do, honey, afterward. You can tell me why Aidan McRaney has to have a drink before a hit. Because the more you feel the urgency to drink, the more it takes hold of you. It's like sex."

Judging by the flippancy of her tone it isn't difficult to assess that she is teasing me. Which prompts me to remind her that the booze is nothing like sex. Unlike sex, I don't exactly enjoy the whiskey. Its only incentive is that it makes what I'm doing a whole lot more palatable.

Luckily for me she neglects to tender a response. I see also that we have arrived at our destination, wherever that is. She slides the Saab smoothly into the drive of what I can only describe as a small manor house. Its numerous lead-paned windows are screened in darkness, save for one small upstairs light.

The house stands alone. I can make out a white painted facade illumined in the orange florescence of the street lighting. The drive is spacious enough to accommodate three vehicles. She parks adjacent to an outmoded Sixties style orange mini. Next to the mini, a small black Fiat.

"It's big isn't it? The house?"

I can't fail to agree as we alight from her motor, and LJ flicks the remote, while leaving me to gaze up at the magnificent abode. There's even a couple of Palladian-style pillars at the front. "You live here?"

"Yeah, I live here." Again, with every response it isn't difficult to interpret the element of derision in her tone, as if she finds everything amusing. Or maybe it's me she secretly finds amusing. "With my brother, my mom and my son. Guess it's big enough for all of us. To think I was doubtful when Mom married again. But she married a rich guy, and he left her this place, as well as the bookshop where she works."

Fitting her key into the door, LJ ushers me inside, before she precedes me into the hallway. This too is spacious and carpeted with several multi-coloured Indian rugs. Interconnecting doors lead off from the hallway. She moves ahead, entering a room I discover to be the kitchen. I thought Judy's house was spacious. The units are a soft cream colour, and topped off by black granite worktops. There are so many cupboards I wonder how easy it might be to locate the coffee.

"Coffee?" she asks, as if interpreting my thoughts. "Black I'm guessing"

I say sure, and wonder how she can possibly know that.

I observe she has removed her coat and hood, to reveal a black shirt, one that's noticeably figure-hugging. The pistol nestles in a holster adjacent to her right breast. She shakes free all that copious strawberry-blonde hair, so that it spills to her waist in a shimmering pennant of waves. Although something unwittingly stirs into arousal behind my jeans, it scarcely matches the fact I am missing my wife so much. No matter how beautiful and alluring LJ Allardyce is – and she is, undoubtedly – I really am longing to be with Caitlan and my children.

"You do take it black don't you? Aidan?" She echoes from somewhere in the distant realm of my subconscious.

I make an attempt to clear my head. To focus.

"It's this kitchen isn't it?"

"The kitchen?" I frown, uncertain of her meaning. "Sure I'd love a coffee. And yeah, I take it black."

"People who come here reckon all that white is too dazzling, like you have to wear shades, you know." She laughs. "He was a great guy was Mike. What little I knew of him. I mean he wasn't as exciting as Pop. But he was steady and he was rich. Mom did well there, I guess. The trouble with Mike, he had no taste in decor. When he died, Mom and I re-decorated. Look, I'm sorry about what happened tonight. Guess it's bound to sometime. Maybe you need a spot of counselling. I do that too."

"Now why doesn't that surprise me? Though I guess if you were doing the counselling, I could live with that."

"Thanks." She manages to locate a jar of Nescafe from the bowels of her numerous cupboards. "Sir George reckons I'm a pretty good listener. So is instant okay?"

"Instant?"

"Coffee, hon," she laughs. "You seem in a daze, Aidan. I told you the drink won't do you any favours. Jesus, I should know. Has anyone ever told you that you have such warm brown eyes? I saw the way you looked at me tonight when I first turned up at Platt's place. Do you know you can tell a lot about a person from their eyes?"

"So I believe."

"I guess it's time I laid my cards on the table as it were." She pours coffee into two black china mugs as she talks.

"Have you ever spent time in the States? Only your accent sort of gives it away."

"Yeah I was in the States. Five years to be exact. Before that, until I was about 20, I studied business management." Her voice seems oddly distracted, as if she were speaking to herself. I detect a note of regret in her tone too. As if maybe she wishes that things were different. "I worked hard at book-keeping and stuff," she pauses to swallow hard, "until my sister was murdered."

"Jesus! I'm sorry, LJ. Lorna."

"I prefer LJ. All my family have the same initials. I'm Lorna Jane. My brother is Luke Jeffrey. And my sister..." She allows her words to trail, as if she discovers it far too painful to continue.

"If you don't want to talk about it I'll understand. Maybe more than most. My sister died a year ago. She was only eighteen. She was murdered too. So I guess we have something in common."

"Then I'm sorry too. My sister was shot and killed in 2003. Then my father was found shot dead in his car a year later." Her mouth tightens fractiously.

It is then that a peculiar kind of danse macabre rhapsodies my spinal column. One that prompts me to enquire who her sister was. Sipping from the coffee, I pause to regard her speculatively above the cup.

"Look, maybe I shouldn't have brought you here. I don't know." Now she appears the indecisive, lip-biting woman, who had had tears in her eyes that day in the car park. The woman with the recalcitrant hair, forever despairing of her tresses.

"Who was your sister, LJ? Because I think I know."

"When she came home weekends she never stopped talking about this guy she'd met. She hated having that awful gangster pawing her, when all she wanted was this young Irishman."

"What Irishman?" I ask, my senses reeling. Although she refrains from tendering a response momentarily. While the interim silence allows me to dive right in. "You're talking about me aren't you?" All I receive is a perfunctory nod.

"Was Leanne Harlow your sister? You look so much like her. I thought so the first time I saw you."

"Yeah, I'm Leanne's sister. Maybe if she and Dad hadn't been killed, I might have been managing my own company by now. I have always wanted to work in a proper job, like a normal person. Not become a woman who carries so much hate and revenge inside her."

"Why was your father murdered?"

"Because he knew too much about the Lamond brothers' activities. He accused Frankie Lamond of Leanne's death. That he was as responsible for that as if he had actually pulled the trigger himself. And the cops didn't care. They didn't even bother to investigate Pop's death, not really. They just reckoned that those who run with the bad guys end up that way eventually."

I opt to change the subject, in the main to spare her feelings. I would have to be totally insensitive not to see that what has happened in the past is upsetting her.

"So tell me about you. You have a son, you said."

"Gabe. Gabriel. He's six. I was married once. Ross, my ex, filed for one of those quickie divorces."

"Jesus! Why?" I dare to wonder how any man can possibly allow this woman to go.

"Because he could, Aidan. Ross Allardyce is a top lawyer in Washington. I hated living there. I think that's when the rot set in between me and Ross. I love the West. So maybe I'm a crazy chick." She laughs once more.

"Not at all." I smile with her. "I think the West is fascinating too. Though I've never been any further than England and Ireland. Oh, and Spain."

"I wanted to see all those places. Arizona, Texas and the like. Before I met Ross, there was this guy, Todd Howell, a couple of years older than me." Her voice conveys a sense of wistfulness once more. "Todd was a bad boy. I mean, real bad. He had a criminal record. What is it about the bad boys that women like? Mom married Johnny Harlow. He was small time, but my dad never really wanted to go straight. Anyway, I used to hang around this roadhouse with Todd and his mates. We drank, smoked, did drugs. We did other stuff too. That's why I ended up in a Correctional Facility in New Mex."

"For doing drugs?"

"Not exactly." Her smile is oddly coy. "For armed robbery."

"I have to admit that surprises me, and yet..."

"Pop and Leanne's deaths changed me. Guess I'm not so pretty on the inside anymore. Anyway, Todd shot a guy when we robbed a liquor store near Roswell. A real Bonnie and Clyde we were. Fuck, man, I must have watched that movie countless times.

"I met Ross when I was at the Facility. As a lawyer he got me let off with a shorter sentence. I grew fond of Ross. I knew he was madly in love with me. He reckoned that it was a pity a woman like me should be incarcerated with so many hard-faced bitches, that I would only end up looking like them. So he got me out. I hadn't killed anyone. Two years later I became Mrs Ross Allardyce."

"So this Todd guy, what happened to him?"

"Death Row, hon. They flooded his body with lethal injection. He was only twenty five. Even after I'd married Ross I cried alone in my bedroom when I heard about Todd."

"So why did Ross divorce you?"

"Because I cheated on him... twice.He forgave me the first time. The second time he reckoned he'd had enough. The reason why I have sole custody of Gabe is because after I'd cheated, Ross refused to believe that Gabe was his."

"So why do you work for Treveleyan? I'm sure there's a better way of life for you."

First Verdi. Now LJ. What is it with these women who believe they have some vengeful kind of axe to grind?

"I could ask you the same thing. You have a wife and two children. Why do you work for Trevelyan? My reason is that I believe in what he is doing."

"The way he believes in that murder squad you told me about?"

"The MRF?" She shrugs nonchalantly. "If you like."

"I reckon I was coerced into it."

"Coerced? In what way?"

"For a start, I had two eviction notices on my flat. Whenever I tried to get work they wouldn't hire an ex-con. Even working as a cleaner or porter at the Blackheath General where my sister works, was out of the question."

"Why?"

"Because of that Criminal Records Bureau thing. They find out I've been to jail and why I think Trevelyan exploited this."

"I still don't understand why Trevelyan should have anything to do with that."

"He seems to thwart me at every turn.I have a young family. I can't rely on handouts from my sister all the time." I run a hand across my eyes, with the realisation of how tired I am feeling. "Trevelyan seems to have made it his life's work for me to come and work for him."

"You're tired. Do you want me to show you where you can crash?"

"Maybe the coffee's sobered me up now. I'll drive home."

"Oh sure. In a car that's figured in a hit. I'll have the Saab and Toyota picked up in the morning. Booze stays in your system for thirty hours. Like I said, Trevelyan won't bail you out if you get caught for drink driving."

"So how long you been working for the Great Man?"

"Almost three years now."

"How come we haven't met before?"

"Maybe because, as you know, Trevelyan doesn't like too many of his oppos encountering one another. He enjoyed my book on Tactical Weaponry, and he called me in to discuss it and some other blogs I'd posted. Trevelyan reckoned he'd never met a woman who knew as much about weapons as I did. Course I had to give him a demo. Guess that sort of clinched it. I really don't like to boast, but I have become quite proficient with weaponry. It's a hobby of sorts. I know it's probably not the safest of hobbies. You should see what I have to fill out on my insurance policies." Her laughter is infectious. I discover myself being drawn along with it. Yet, beneath the humour I sense a sadness. That losing both her father and her sister practically simultaneously has taken its toll on this incredible woman.

"It's not all gun proficiency. I can use a crossbow, a normal bow, and even a sword."

"Impressive. But there isn't much call for swords these days."

"Now you're mocking me."

"I'm sorry. But why do you feel the need to use those kind of weapons?"

"For sport. I fence, and I teach fencing and archery. I write and I ride. You should try it sometime."

"One, or all of the above?"

Her laughter is silvery. "That wicked Irish sense of humour will get you into trouble one day. I meant the riding. My friend owns a stable near here. I've talked about myself. What about you, your little baby? You're a lucky man, Aidan." She passes a slender braceleted arm over her eyes. "I'm feeling bushed too. I'll show you to your room."

"Why do you care what happens to me? We hardly know each other."

"Because my sister loved you so much. You made her happy for those few months before her death. She was so beautiful, wasn't she?"

"Sure. There's no denying that."

As much as I loved her, and maybe I still do to a degree, Caitlan is my life now. LJ is assuredly a beautiful woman. She so resembles Leanne, they could have been twins, but I feel nothing other than sympathy for what she has gone through. The past is simply that. In the past. It's taken me a while, but with Caitlan's help I believe I've finally made it. I can face the future, and turn my back on what has gone before.

Chapter Eight

Luke Harlow

The room I've been allocated is on the third floor. LJ informs me this particular floor alone houses three more rooms, plus two en suite bathrooms. The second floor is used by her son and her mother. That her brother's room is on the third floor, reached by a black wrought iron staircase.

After bidding me goodnight, LJ returns downstairs. I manage to locate the bathroom. All marble tiling, cream matching units, even a bidet.

I can barely believe that LJ is Leanne's sister, although she resembles her so much. When I had first met her, with the realisation as to who she was, I wonder if I should have allowed her to talk me into coming here. Although she is undoubtedly a beautiful woman, as Leanne was, I entertain no feelings for her other than admiration. While she fails to indicate any other interest in me except as a colleague, nothing more. She is simply allowing me a bed for the night. The chance of Trevelyan washing his hands off me.

The hangings surrounding the four poster bed are fashioned from soft white satin. A delicate rose motif traces a pattern on the quilt. On the dressing table there is a photograph of Leanne. My heart quickens when I see it, noting the resemblance between the two sisters.

Leanne, the way I remember her. Her lovely face framed by all that glorious strawberry blonde hair, huge laughing eyes. I fancy I hear her breathe my name in the stillness of the room. The sound accompanied by the subtlest intimation of laughter. Now I know why I am here. For the exorcism to free me of the ghost which has continued to haunt me.

I run a hand through my hair, over my beard, and realise how much I need to shower. I should be going, resolved to take the shower at home. The roughness that is omnipresent on my tongue reminds me that I could at least use a coffee. Pulling on my jeans and shirt, I wonder if I'll ever manage to locate any in those cavernous cupboards. No one had deigned to give me a call, not even LJ.

Recollecting where the kitchen is, I head in that direction, when I hear a man's voice. Entering the room I discover a small boy, an unruly mop of hair hanging in his face, with his head bent over his cereal bowl. Instinctively the boy raises his eyes and I am looking into LJ's eyes. The child's are of a similar green-fleck and wide. His lips full. He twists the lower one with both indecision and an ill-concealed curiosity.

A young man with dark wavy hair that sweeps to the collar of a red check shirt, a wispy beard contouring his jawline, is intent on searching the contents of the refrigerator. With his hand on the door, he mutters something about not having any peanut butter, before exclaiming a surprised, "hello," when he sees me.

"Hi. I just wondered if I could get a coffee."

"Course." The smile reaches his eyes. In marked contrast, although his hair is dark, the eyes are definitely Harlow eyes.

He extends a hand, which I accept briefly, and introduces himself as Luke Harlow as if to confirm the fact. "You must be a friend of my sister's." Enlarged green eyes search my face indefatigably, as if in an attempt to satisfy himself whether or not I slept with her. I maintain a guarded expression. I simply explain that I am a work colleague.

"This is my nephew, Gabriel." Steering his gaze away, he finally introduces the boy, who swiftly pops up with the question, "Are you one of my mother's boyfriends?" as if LJ invariably brings men home on a par with stray cats. Maybe she does. The boy's accent is American, and contains the subtle trace of a Southern drawl.

"I'm so not," I hasten to point out, offering an indecisive smile. "Just a colleague, that's all."

"You wanted a coffee?" Luke reminds me. "Help yourself, Aidan. Sis is out riding at the moment. She always gets up early on a Saturday to go to the stables."

After helping myself to a black coffee, I join Luke and Gabriel at the table, enquiring where LJ goes riding. The question is merely an endeavour to make conversation, more than wishing to know.

I really am missing Caitlan. Last night was exactly that. Now I've sobered up.

"Her friend's mother owns the stables about a mile away. Lorna has her own horse."

"It's called Midnight because it's all black," Gabriel informs me before returning to his cereal

"So you work for the Agency too?" Luke asks.

"Sure. That's how I met your sister."

"So I guess you stayed the night then?"

The question sounds a trifle accusatory. Although I'm not certain that is his intention.

"In the spare room," I hasten to add. "I should be going."

"Aren't you going to wait for LJ?"

"She'll probably be gone a while. Like I said, we're just colleagues. She brought me back here because I was a wee bit worse for wear," I add with an awkward smile.

There is the subtlest intimation of a smile flirting about his own lips. "So you got a bit hammered hey? Actually I had a few jars myself last night. I should be getting to work. I promised the old dear I'd help in the shop later."

"I suppose it gets busy on a Saturday, does it?"

"Not really. The place never really gets busy. The books are mostly for purists. It's not a normal paperback, chit-lit store," he laughs. "Now it's almost Hallowe'en. And ma has lots of books on the occult, even the Malleus Maleficarum."

I regard him blankly. The boy obviously knows his way around books.

"The Hammer of Witches. Jesus, you'd never believe some of the stuff Ma got in her shop."

Making a face, Gabriel gestures at his Uncle. "He likes all that horror stuff, especially about vampires and werewolves. Mom tells him not to tell me scary stories. That I'll have nightmares."

"Little does she know, hey?" Luke ruffles his nephew's hair. "Why is it that birds think kids are scared of that stuff? I wasn't at Gabe's age."

Gabriel finishes his cereal before pushing his bowl aside. Luke suggests he go upstairs, brush his teeth and wash his face before mummy returns. "So you're not going to wait for her then?" he asks again.

"I don't think so. I need to get back."

Luke waits for Gabriel to vacate the table. He does so with a polite, "thanks, Uncle Luke," plus a cursory smile at me.

As the boy leaves, Luke lowers his voice conspiratorially. "So you and my sister were on a job last night?"

I stiffen involuntarily at the question, and tell him "sure," sotto voce.

"I'm her brother. I know exactly what she does. So does Mum. I agree with her of course. But it won't bring either Pop or our sister back. I knew who you were the minute I saw you."

"You did?"

"Yeah. Leanne kept a photo of you in an album. I was still at school when she was killed. But I don't feel the way Lorna does. Neither does Ma. Although she hated that gangster. Then Pop was murdered. Ma reckoned that it was inevitable. After Leanne was killed, Dad warned the Lamonds he would grass on them.

"I know you're the guy who shot the man who killed Leanne, and went to prison for it. And so does Sir George Treveleyan. I reckon when it comes to it, Treveleyan's the most manipulative bastard of them all."

I can't fail to agree with that statement. It appears that Treveleyan has been manipulating me ever since our initial encounter.

"So why do you do it?"

"What do you mean?"

"Kill for a living. Oh, I'm not some wet-behind-the-ears kid."

"Jesus, man, it's not something I want broadcast. Anyway, there's nothing else out there, and I have a family to support."

"So what do your family say about it?"

I entertain the notion of rising colour to my face. "My wife thinks I'm just a driver who ferries people to safe houses."

"Maybe that's for the best. What do you think she'd do if she ever found out?"

"Leave me probably. But once I get enough money I'll get out. I don't like what I do. That no one should have the power of life and death no matter how bad people are."

"Then you admit you're just in it for the money?"

What is it about this young man? The way he talks, the scrutiny of dark green eyes. Is all conducive to making me entertain nothing but discomfort. "Now you make me sound like a mercenary."

"Lorna believes in what she does. There's a lot of evil people out there, she says. I reckon she'd do it even if it was voluntary."

"What I meant was I have a young family, and I can't find any other work. If it were just me then I definitely wouldn't do it."

"I'm sorry, I didn't mean anything by it. It's your life. Don't worry, I'm not likely to tell anyone what you or Lorna does. But Ma and me worry about her putting her life on the line the way she does. You have a young family. What would happen to them if you were killed? Lorna has Gabe."

"I guess I hadn't thought that far. Anyway I was assured that Treveleyan will see the families are okay."

At this juncture Luke Harlow arches a disbelieving brow. "You sure about that? I wouldn't trust that man to give me the time of day, mate. If he said the sky was blue I'd have to go outside to check."

Chapter Nine

Gardening Leave

The following morning I receive the inevitable call from Treveleyan, urging me to collect the familiar package. Garbed in my habitual disguise, the collars of my jacket piled to my ears, I head out to the post office in South Lambeth.

With the package tucked beneath my arm, I'm immersed in my own preoccupation, when I fail to see the woman until I practically collide with her. When I clock who it is, my senses reel because of what I carry. The fact that the name on the package is John Marshall. The alias that I invariably use.

"Aidan? It is Aidan isn't it?"

"Sis? Yeah, it's me. Wh… what brings you out this way?"

"You look as if you're hiding from someone. So what's that?" She gestures to the package.

I furnish the lie that I had to collect a parcel for Treveleyan.

"Treveleyan? It says John Marshall on the front."

Trust my sister to be so infuriatingly observant. "He's one of our operatives. What are you doing out this way?"

She's wearing a black wool coat, high leather boots. Her red gold curls are upswept in their familiar style. "I had to see a patient." There is an obvious hesitation in her voice.

"So you making house calls now?"

"No." She laughs awkwardly, her face crimsoning. It isn't difficult to deduce that we're both lying to each other. "I thought I'd see how he was. He… he broke his leg," she adds quickly. "I promised I'd see how he was doing now he's been discharged."

"Him?" I arch a speculative brow.

"It's nothing like that. Look, you busy?" She asks, linking her arm through mine.

"I should be going."

There's nothing I would like better than to spend some time with my sister. If only I wasn't carrying something that could, in all likelihood, freak her out.

"Surely you've got time for a coffee."

I really should make my excuses. Albeit I sense that she wants to talk, so I agree to join her.

She directs my attention to a cafe called 'Marina's' across the street. "It's early. It should be quiet in there."

"What about your patient? Is he expecting you?"

Did I imagine her brows knit a frown at the question, as if she has no idea to what I'm referring? I remind her about the guy with the broken leg.

"I didn't actually say a time. You're more important. You don't mind?"

I manage to suppress a reluctant sigh. In reality, my one desire is to get this business over with. In spite of that, however, I'm aware that I should allow some time for my sister.

We locate a table nearest the window. The only other patrons are a group of workmen enjoying their habitual full English.

Brid removes her coat to reveal a flattering green cord pinafore dress with a white polo sweater. The masculine attention she receives she ultimately chooses to ignore. The pinafore complements her auburn hair.

Removing the shades, I lay the package onto the table. Predictably her gaze returns to it. A world-weary waitress arrives to take our orders and we opt for coffees.

"So, Aidan," Brid lowers her tone conspiratorially when the waitress departs, "who is John Marshall when he's at home?"

"I told you..."

Her hand descends to my leather gloved own. "You said he was an operative, but I think that you're John Marshall. It's me you're talking to. You couldn't pull the wool over my eyes when you was a kid. Now you're a grown man, I still deserve the truth. If you're worried, Caitlan won't hear it from me, but you really shouldn't lie to that poor girl. She's devoted to you."

"And I feel the same, you know that. So what makes you think I'm John Marshall?"

"Sure, if I haven't told you the truth either. It's time, as they say, to lay our cards on the table."

The waitress moves away after depositing the coffees. I ask what my sister is referring to.

"I'm not really visiting a patient."

I can't avoid a grin. "I didn't think for a minute that you were." Stirring my coffee absently, I regard my sister with speculation.

"You haven't answered my question. Are you John Marshall?"

"Okay," I raise a hand in mock submission. "I am he."

"Oh Aidan, I was worried about you. That's why I followed you."

"Why would you do that? To spy on me?"

"I suppose it was. I told you I was concerned."

"I thought you would have been in bed at this time of the morning. Weren't you on the night shift?"

"No, no I wasn't. They..." Her hesitation is almost painful. Descending her gaze to her coffee, she spoons in a sugar absently. "They've let me have some time off. I broke down at work in the middle of my shift, would you believe?" She raises her eyes finally. I'm astonished to observe the pain reflected there.

"Broke down? I'm sorry, Sis. Whatever happened. That's not like you," I ask with concern, and reach for her hand.

"A man was brought into the hospital. He had black curly hair like yours. He was also about your age. This young man had been beaten half to death until he was unconscious. They think he'll have brain damage. I… I thought it was you at first. I rushed to his bedside. And do you know what I did?"

"What?"

"I screamed. I actually screamed your name. One of the male nurses had to pull me off this man. Maybe this job is getting to me. After that poor Jason Lang was brought in tarred and feathered. So it was suggested that I take gardening leave."

"Gardening leave? What the hell's that? There isn't much you can do in the garden at this time of year is there?"

Brid allows a small smile to crease her lips. "I don't have to actually do any gardening. It's just time out. When I can't cope. I'm on full pay."

"I'm sorry, Sis. Have I done this to you?" I take her hand, press it to my lips with commiseration despite the raised browed glances from that waitress. "I'm sorry. I promise this will be the last time."

"So how long you been using John Marshall as your alias? Is it because it sounds more English? You have to disguise your accent?"

"Something like that."

Bridget is a strong, tenacious woman, one that's difficult to lie to.

"I have to confess this is the second time I've followed you."

I regard her, astonished, my heart accelerating. "Why? Because you don't trust me or something? Is it because you think I might be having an affair?"

"Not at all. Besides, you've got too much to lose if you had an affair. That wee baby for one thing. I know even you wouldn't be that stupid to risk that."

I mutter a desultory, "thanks, Sis."

"I followed you because I care. You might be thirty years old, but sometimes you still behave like the sixteen year old kid I was still trying to keep out of trouble. Even after I got married. I'm sorry, I can't help worrying about you. I know I shouldn't put a trail on you."

"It's called a tail, Sis." I grin, despite the unease I feel that my sister might know far too much about me to be healthy. "You're right though. I don't like to be followed, not even by you. You must have suspected me of something. Since we're having this conversation, there is no one else but my wife. Those days are well and truly over."

"I'm glad to hear it, but I suspected you didn't really have to take someone to Scotland to account for your reason to be away. Caitlan might believe everything you tell her, but I don't . And if you had an affair I'd see to it personally that you were strung up by your testicles, mister."

"Jesus, I believe you would."

"You can count on it. It's this other business."

"What other business?" I ask, narrowly.

"This John Marshall stuff. Honest people don't need aliases. Are you some kind of... you know...?"

"Some kind of what?"

"It's useless." She sighs, and tuts in her customary Bridget fashion. "I can't discuss this here. Drink up. All I need to know is that I won't lose my brother to iron bars and a possible thirty stretch. Or worse."

I swiftly drain my coffee, while the guilt courses through me once more. Because of what this job might be doing to my family. I vow that it will be the last. I attempt to placate her that everything will be okay, while I maintain my fingers figuratively crossed.

"It doesn't stop me worrying about you. I worry about your wife and wee wain too."

"I can take care of my family. You don't need to worry about them. Now let's get back to the car. I have stuff to do."

"It's the stuff that worries me."

"Anyway I need a favour."

We return to the Cabriolet where I roll and light a cigarette, observing the streets for a while. Until breaking the silence which has sprung up between us, Brid gestures to the package I have now tossed into the back seat. "Is that a job?"

I stiffen, but have to admire her perception. "You promise you won't say anything to Caitlan?"

"I told you I wouldn't. Besides it's up to you to tell her. If you've got any sense you'll do that, or get out. It would send that poor child into a neurosis to find out that her husband is a hired killer. Because that's what y'are, aren't you, Aidan? Now this is where you have a go at me for watching too many movies or having an over-active imagination."

But I don't. When I turn back to her again, I am surprised to witness tears standing in her eyes.

"I guess by your silence that I'm right aren't I?" she asks.

I nod painfully.

Blowing her nose on a tissue, she shakes her head as if I'm a lost cause. "Och, Aidan, och, Aidan." She tuts and swipes at her eyes again. "I know Ruairi is aware of some of the stuff you do, but we love you too much to let anything happen to you. This will be your last job? Promise me." She grips my arm, and I brush the wetness from her eyes with the stark realisation that not only do I have a family who love me, but that I am hurting them.

"I promise. There won't be anymore. I'll tell Treveleyan as much."

"Just come home safely, that's all. Did you say something about a favour?"

"I might be away for a while."

"Out of the country?"

"It's in London, but it's undercover work. While I'm gone I want you to look after Caitlan and the kids."

"Sure I will. I promise I won't breathe a word of what we talked about. She's going to ask, isn't she? So is Patrick. What will you tell them?"

"That I have to chauffeur this guy around for a while."

"More lies, Aidan? I'll look after Caitlan and the kids, you know I will. In return you must do something for me."

I drag on my cigarette reflectively. "Sure, if I can."

"Don't shut me out. Keep me posted."

"You know I can't do that. When I'm undercover I'm not supposed to have any contact with my family. Not only that, but it could put your lives in danger."

Chapter Ten

Corrigan

I concentrate on a mental picture of Daniel Corrigan while perusing his photograph. Thirty five years old. He was born in Ballymurphy to Mairead Corrigan. Miss Corrigan was reputed to have hidden wanted Provos and IRA sympathisers in the seventies and eighties.

The photo is black and white. Corrigan's hair is relatively short, very dark and curly. He sports long sideburns that are shaped to the jawline. He is clean shaven, quite immaculately so. I am compelled to zero in on his eyes. They are so intense, deeply-seated and piercing, marginally eclipsed by a high, overhanging brow. The lips are full, almost feministic, yet pursed disdainfully. It is not difficult to deduce that Daniel Corrigan is one cruelly smug individual.

Maybe I should heed Brid's advice and get the hell out. Treveleyan has other operatives. Nonetheless 'the Great Man' seems most insistent he wants me in on this. "He will trust you because you are his countryman and a Catholic," he had argued when I suggested that these qualifications might not be enough to get me within speaking distance to the man, without him wishing to put a bullet in me.

"Oh he will, my boy. Believe me, he will accept you, as if you were one of his own," Treveleyan had retorted with such conviction. Still I can't help the feeling that I'm putting my head into the lion's mouth, and Treveleyan is the one who's opening the cage.

In reality, maybe I'm doing this because Dennis Mitchell and I go way back, to Maidstone jail where we shared a cell. Plus he's got me out of a few scrapes recently. I can at least try and discover what's happened to him. Maybe effect a rescue.

My brief outlines that I have been out of prison for almost a year. I've just returned from Ireland, where I learned from a friend in Dublin that Corrigan has a lot of fingers in a lot of pies across the water.

I carry my belongings because I've been evicted from my lodgings for non-payment. That my wife in Dublin had kicked me out. Something that I hope in reality will not come to pass.

Apparently, Corrigan frequents a pub in Clerkenwell called 'The Emerald Lady', which, unsurprisingly turns out to be an Irish bar.

I have been staring at Corrigan's picture for what seems an age, when the phone buzzes in my jacket. I pull the phone from my pocket to see Brid is calling.

"Sis?"

"I'm calling on Caitlan's behalf."

I jerk upright in my seat, Corrigan ultimately forgotten, my heart beating a crazy tattoo. "She's okay isn't she?"

"Don't worry, she's fine. It's just that she's had a wee bit of a shock, that's all."

"Shock? What about ? You haven't...?"

"No. Jesus, brother, what do you take me for? It's your bank account."

"My bank account? What about it?"

"Seems she went to the bank to draw some cash. You have a joint account?"

"Sure we do. Why?"

"She was taken into the manager's office."

"Why for Heaven's sake? I should have enough money in our account. I know she wanted some baby stuff..."

"It was because of the money," Brid interrupts.

"What's wrong with my money?"

"I was with her, and wondered too. How come a few weeks ago you could hardly afford the rent on your flat. Now, according to the manager, you have almost a million pounds paid into your account. If you haven't won the lottery, Caitlan and me wonder how you came by so much."

So Treveleyan's invested practically a million pounds into my account. All an incentive of course for my infiltration into Corrigan's lair. Now I'm compelled to explain it to my sister, who is obviously waiting for a response. Brid already suspects what I do and in all likelihood realises how lucrative the work is. But what to tell my sweet and trusting wife? More lies. It would break her heart to discover the truth. This will be the final time.

"I have the money now."

"Blood money!" Brid hisses in my ear. "But I'll not tell Caitlan that. So what do I tell her?"

"That I've worked for the Agency for almost a year, and they owed me money."

"Practically a million pounds? It might be easier to say you won the lottery."

"No, don't tell her that. She'll want to see the ticket and stuff. Just tell her what I said."

"Och, sure I'll try and convince her somehow. Otherwise she'll think you've robbed a bank."

So I have almost a million pounds in the bank. Nevertheless my pretence is to outwardly appear that I'm down on my luck.

In my old black leather coat, check shirt and ball-cap, I enter the 'Emerald Lady' a little after 7:30 in the evening. Treveleyan assures me that's when Corrigan puts in an appearance. The place is located down a backstreet, and where Corrigan can retain an incognito status amidst his own countrymen.

The place is crowded. The music emanates from a juke box

somewhere in the room where my gaze fails to penetrate. With
a rucksack containing my meagre belongings hefted onto my
shoulder, I pause to scan my surroundings. Moving to the bar I
wait to be served. Long benches, with accompanying tables, occupy
the majority of the olde worlde public house. Selecting a quiet
corner I resolve to head for that, to await Corrigan's arrival once
I've been served.

Middle-aged and greying, the barman enquires what I'd like
to drink. I order a beer, when I observe a woman, seated on a stool
across from the counter, staring me out. She's young, quite pretty,
and sports a pinkish tinge to her short bobbed blonde hair. Her
eyes regard me with an ill-disguised curiosity above the rim of her
glass. They are so darkened with mascara, that they are rendered
almost black. She must be about Caitlan's age, but all that shit on
her face does her few favours. My wife knows how much I hate
all that make-up and stuff. She's beautiful as she is and needs no
adornment.

The girl wears a striped tee shirt, over which she's thrown
a bolero-style jacket. She deals me a small, hesitant smile from
screaming red lipstick.

Not only am I married with a jealous wife, with the purpose I
have in mind I can do without any kind of entanglements, sexual
or otherwise. To hopefully divert my attention away from the girl,
I enquire of the barman what time Danny Corrigan comes in. He
stiffens, lowers his voice, so that it's barely discernible over the
noise. "Who wants to know?" he demands suspiciously.

Before moving away from the bar, I tell him that I'm a friend
of his from Ireland. Thankfully the answer appears to satisfy him,
and he duly informs me, "Mr Corrigan comes in most nights,
usually about eight, eight thirty. Except for Sundays when he's in
church." He's a man true to his faith.

The corner seat remains vacant, and I slip into it and take a
sip from my beer. It's warm and flat, but it'll do. The Pink Lady,
as I've mentally christened her, appears at my side. Despite the

over-abundance of make-up, she is quite attractive, and much younger than I had first believed. Perhaps no more than eighteen or nineteen.

"Is anyone sitting 'ere?" She indicates the facing seat.

"If they are they're invisible."

"Oh you," she laughs. I half expected her to be Irish, but her accent is pure East End. "Can I?"

"Sure. Feel free." I shrug.

"I ain't seen you in here before. I would've remembered you."

A nice chat-up line, I deduce, but I have other things on my mind. I hope she's gone before Corrigan arrives.

"I'm Zoe," she introduces herself before depositing her weight.

"Look, Zoe, I'm waiting for someone."

"You're Irish!" she exclaims, as if she hasn't heard a word I've said. "I thought you'd be Irish. You look Irish."

"Well I'm not wearing green, and I don't have a shamrock in my hair. So how did you know? Oh, I forgot, it must be the accent."

"And a comedian. So who are you waiting for? Your girlfriend?"

"No. I'm waiting for a guy."

"Aren't we all, ducks?" Her sigh is heavy. While I can't help but grin at her own comedic efforts.

"It's business."

"So it's not your girlfriend?" she asks hopefully.

"I'm married," I tell her and reach for my beer again.

"The best looking ones are. She isn't with you tonight then? You have a bag with you." She raises herself from the seat in order to obtain a closer look. "It looks full. Does that mean something? Has she chucked you out? You could buy me a drink. Or you could tell me to mind my own business. But I'm a good listener. If she has she's a...."

"You talk too much, darlin'." I interrupt her. "Maybe another time. Like I said, I have some business."

"With Danny Corrigan. I know."

I regard her in surprise. "How?"

"I have ears, darlin'." Her tone conveys a hint of mockery. "I heard you ask Frank the barman when Danny came in."

"You sound as if you know him. Danny I mean."

"Yeah, I know Danny." Her mouth visibly tightens. "I dated him once. What a fuckin' bastard he turned out to be."

"Why did you call him a bastard?"

"Because that's what he is. He's bleedin' good looking, and he fuckin' knows it. A lot of birds have fallen beneath his spell, me included. But he's cold and cruel. Sorry if he's a mate of yours. You knew him in Ireland?"

"Yeah, I... I knew him in Ireland," I lie, and hope she won't interpret anything in the hesitancy of my speech. Instead of wishing the girl would leave, she has aroused my curiosity. Simply because I need to know everything I possibly can about Mr Daniel Corrigan.

"Maybe I don't want to discuss him anymore." She folds her arms defiantly, an indication of the subject being closed. Not to be outdone however, and slipping a couple of fivers from my wallet, after all I am practically a millionaire, I press the money into her hand.

"What's that for?" She regards the money dubiously.

"Buy yourself a drink. Then you can join me."

"If you want we can..."

"Talk, sweetheart." Sipping my beer, I view her thoughtfully over the rim of my glass.

"We can talk, if that's what you want," she shrugs nonchalantly. "Look, Mister..." She fishes for my name, but I fail to give it. "I'll be honest. I find you attractive, and there ain't many good looking guys around, at least none that I meet."

"Maybe you've been looking in the wrong places. So why don't you get that drink and you can tell me about Danny Corrigan?"

She moves to the bar. An unwitting erection is in the ascendant. I think, 'not now'. I'm smiling to myself when she returns. Predictably she wants to know what I'm grinning at.

I encounter the question with a shrug, telling her, "nothing much," waving a hand dismissively.

"So tell me about Danny Corrigan."

"Maybe you know more about him than I do. So, have you just arrived from Ireland? Or have you been here a while?"

The question surprises me. Maybe she isn't all pink hair and mascara. Flicking my watch a cursory glance, I refer to Corrigan's arrival.

"Yeah, he comes in about eight, eight thirty. You still ain't told me your name."

"It's Aidan. So, Corrigan's cruel? Was he abusive toward you?"

"Not exactly abusive. I suppose he could be," she adds thoughtfully. "I wasn't with him long enough to find out. When we had sex he was quite considerate."

"You must have known him pretty well."

"Not really. Danny Corrigan isn't an easy man to get to know. He's sort of, what is it? Deep. The kind of geezer who plays his cards close to his chest, believe me, Aidan. I really like that. Aidan. You sure you wouldn't? Your wife doesn't have to know. Danny's nothing if not predictable. He won't be here until well after eight." She closes a palm over mine.

I instinctively pull away,and remind her that we were discussing Danny Corrigan. Her mouth tightens, she folds her arms and shrugs as if my rebuff is of no consequence.

"You had sex with him."

"Yeah. When it was over he just got dressed and slammed the door behind him without a word. When I asked him if he wanted to see me again, he said he did. Then I suggested we meet up somewhere. Do you know what he said?"

I shake my head.

"He just stared at me. Then he asked me who I was. When I told him, and asked him why, he pretended not to know me. He just told me not to bother him. That he didn't know anyone called

Zoe. What a bastard. Anyway, can I ask what kind of business is it you have with him? I mean he's into some heavy stuff, and you look too nice. You're not one of them Gardys, or what they call the cops in Ireland are you?"

"It's Gardai," I correct her with a smile. "No, I'm not a Gardai, or any kind of cop, honest. Like I said, it's business, and I can't discuss it. When he arrives I'd appreciate it if you'd make yourself scarce, sweetheart."

"You think I'm trying to make Danny jealous being with you? But I'm not. I really do fancy you."

"Sure y'do. But like I said..."

"I know." She prolongs a sigh of resignation, and rises to her feet. "I'm going now. It's nice knowing you, Aidan. Good luck with Danny."

"You think I need it then?" I ask, but she's already moved away.

I'm in the process of draining my last swallow of this disgusting beer. I'm trying not to make a face, when the door opening admits two men who saunter in. One of them is young, roughly my age. He is inordinately skinny, and sports a thick shock of wild, tawny hair, which happens to be fashioned into an outmoded kind of Elvis quiff. He is garbed in a rather nondescript grey linen suit, worn with a narrow plain grey tie and white shirt.

The photo fails to do justice to the man with him. My heart accelerates, because the object of my surveillance is now present in the flesh. His eyes are impenetrably dark as if he sleeps little. The lips are full-bodied set as if in a permanent pout. It isn't difficult to assess the element of cruelty that ostensibly borders on the sadistic.

Corrigan is immediately served by the nervous barman who stutters his enquiry, "Y...your...your usual, Mr Corrigan?" After which, Frank gestures to where I am sitting. Unfortunately, I am unable to comprehend what he says because of the loud music, and the ever growing crowd now lining the bar. Although the two men zero in on me instinctively.

His mouth twists into an unmistakeable moue as Elvis Quiff follows Frank's direction. Corrigan's black orbs flash my way with something that appears oddly akin to recognition. Or is that my imagination? Despite my lie to Zoe, Corrigan and I have never met before. He smiles, although it's a somewhat cynical inflection, as if he is unaccustomed to even that small feat.

Leaning leather jacketed elbows onto the bar counter, Corrigan rasps, "Just get the fuckin' drinks, Billy boy," in his reedy Northern Irish accent.

My heart performs a double somersault, worthy of a gymnast, because Corrigan is approaching my table. I half expected him to shrug his shoulders and totally ignore me as being of little consequence. Whispering something in the ear of the man he addressed as Billy, he accepts the drinks. Billy mutters, "But, Mister C, you don't know..."

"Just fuckin' do it, Billy," Corrigan growls ill-humouredly.

I observe Billy visibly stiffen.

Now Danny Corrigan confronts me face to face. He's not as tall as I imagined. Less than 5'10", I conjecture.

"So you wanted to see me." He nurses a whisky in a shot glass. His tone is surprisingly friendly when I expected him to growl at me irritably, the way he did to Billy.

"Sure I... I do." Jesus. Now I've developed a stammer. Raising my eyes to his, I can't avoid noticing there is an absence of the coldness I had initially anticipated.

"So can I join you? You want another?" He gestures at my now empty glass.

"No thanks. I'm alright."

Corrigan drops into the seat vacated by Zoe. Sipping at the whisky in his glass, he pauses interminably to study me above the rim. I detect something almost primeval about those steady black eyes.

"So you know who I am. And you are?"

A momentary hesitation on my part. Any longer and he'll

think I'm giving him a false name. I had referred to using the alias John Marshall for my confrontation with Corrigan. Or maybe adopting a pseudo Irish moniker, to which Treveleyan had strangely undergone an almost apoplectic state of astonishment at the suggestion.

"It won't be necessary to change your name, not this time," he had inferred. So here I am vouchsafing my given one.

"Aidan, hey?" Corrigan muses. "My half brother's name was Aidan." There's an odd poignancy present in his tone all at once.

"Was?"

"He was killed, so he was. Eighteen months old, would you believe?"

"Eighteen months old? Jesus," I echo in surprise.

"Anyway, we mustn't get maudlin must we? So, Aidan, you're from the ould place, Dublin?"

"Yeah, I'm from Dublin."

"So how long have you been in London?"

I lie that I arrived last night. Add that I can't afford a hotel, or even a guest house. "So I kipped in an alley like a homeless person."

"Jesus, I've been there myself. I can't see a fellow Irishman out on the street. You must have had a home in Dublin."

"So I did, until I sort of played away. My wife kicked me out."

"Aye, the women, hey?" He tuts and shakes his head. "Look, Aidan, what I know about women is, you get as far as marrying 'em, they'll take what they want. A man can't help having a roving eye. That comes as part of the package. If you fancy something else, you take it. You know what I mean?" He winks impishly. "No fuckin' guilt. That old saying, love 'em and leave 'em. That's my motto."

I think about Zoe with an element of regret for her treatment at this man's hands.

"It's not that simple. Not when there's a kid involved." Jesus, I'm actually becoming friendly with him.

"Fuck me. I fuckin' got a few wee wains scattered about the Province, I shouldn't wonder." He laughs. "Aye, and maybe in the Republic too. Even in the Big Smoke. Just like my old Da. He couldn't keep it in his pants either. Poor old boy." He shakes his head once more. His laughter ceases, as a darkness ostensibly descends. "He'd be sixty now. So what did you want to talk about?" There's a sense of dismissal, as if the mention of his father were far too painful.

Lowering my tone to a more conspiratorial level, I explain that I've been in prison for eight years.

He savours his whisky before tendering a response. "Aye, you have."

I regard him puzzled. When he says 'you have', it's almost a statement, rather than an exclamation of surprise. Almost as if he's aware of that fact. How can he know?

"I hear you're in business, if you see what I mean. I've been out a year and can't get any work. Another reason why my wife threw me out. There ain't much work out there for an ex-con. Especially for what I do."

"Why don't we go back to my place? You're talking the kind of business it ain't wise to discuss here. I live in Maze Hill. You got a car?"

"Sure, it's parked out the back. I was told about your…" I clear my throat, "business affairs from a mate of yours. Emmett Tooley. You know him?"

"Aye. Sure I know Emmett. Thought he was still in jail."

"He is. I've been in a couple of jails. Both here and across the water."

Slowly uncoiling his loose-limbed frame from his seat, Corrigan signals to Billy.

Propped up against the bar, Billy regards me with a barely concealed suspicion.

"Yes, Mr C?"

"Fetch the car round, Billy. Me and Aidan got some business to discuss. We"re going back to the house."

"Sure, Mr Corrigan."

"Your belongings?" Corrigan gestures to the rucksack I haul onto my shoulder.

"I'm afraid so," I tell him with a sigh.

"Leave your car here. I'll get Billy to collect it for you."

I'm amazed. Disbelieving almost, at how I've successfully managed to ingratiate myself so effortlessly with my target. Corrigan appears to have accepted me as easily as if I were a long-lost friend. He's even invited me back to his Maze Hill residence.

Nevertheless, I can't help but remain wary. While I'm glad of the .32 Walther I have secreted in my rucksack.

Chapter Eleven

Dashurie

Corrigan speaks precious little on the journey. Occupying the back seat of his elegant BMW, I endeavour to respect his silence. Engrossed in my thoughts, a small ferret gnaws away at my stomach now I am this close. When Corrigan reaches to the inside of his jacket, I catch a breath. I wonder if I'm about to confront a silencer-equipped pistol. From what I know of Daniel Corrigan he's a potentially dangerous man. Now he behaves as if he's my benefactor.

Producing a packet of cheroots, he extracts one of the thin cigars, and enquires if I've ever tried one.

"Not recently," I tell him, "but I'll try one now." I accept the cheroot and Corrigan flares a gold-plated Calibri.

"Can I have one of those please, Mr Corrigan?" Billy asks from the driving seat, only to be told by his employer to keep his eyes on the road.

"You know you have ideas above your station, Billy."

Billy grudgingly elevates his shoulders in a shrug of resignation, although his lips remain tight and set as he concentrates on the road. I observe that we're headed toward London Bridge. Dragging on the cheroot, I discover that it possesses a distinctive sweet aroma, making me wonder if it might contain some kind of narcotic.

Without preamble he offers to take me to his place. Although I continue to feel apprehensive, I promised to go along with this, if only to ascertain Dennis Mitchell's whereabouts.

"Alright is it?" Corrigan disturbs my retrospection. "The smoke?"

"Sure, it's fine." I prefer to glance out of the window rather than his way.

"We'll observe silence now until we arrive, with himself listening. He knows too fuckin' much, so he does. Don't you, Billy?"

Billy mutters inaudibly beneath his breath. It sounds remotely like, "Fuckin' hell I do."

"I didn't catch that, Billy." Corrigan leans forward in his seat. For the first time I am conscious of that familiar cruel twist to his lips.

"Nothing, Mr Corrigan." Like Corrigan, Billy's accent is Northern Irish.

"Give 'em a wee inch and they'll take a fuckin' yard, so they will. Ain't that right, Aidan?"

"I guess. But I have to say, you don't know who I am, yet you're taking me to your home. I could be an axe murderer for all y'know."

"Then you'd be a dead axe murderer, my friend. Besides I know who y'are. Anyone who tries to kill me, well a lot of men tried..." He breaks into a sing-song voice, and savours his words, "and a lot of men died. That's how the song goes anyway."

Why is his smile endowed with such cynicism? While his, "I know who y'are," leaves me with an all-pervading chill.

I drag on the cheroot reflectively. Maybe it does contain a narcotic. Or maybe it boasts nothing more sinister than pure tobacco. Whatever its ingredient I'm beginning to relax. The ferret is no longer churning up my guts.

Ultimately, the past unfolds before me. The long gravel drive. The beautiful red-bricked facade. This was once the home of Ray

Lamond. It has been a while since I was last here.

Billy parks the BMW. I accompany Daniel Corrigan and steer my gaze toward the familiar lead-paned windows of the ostentatious abode. The long red carpeted hallway stretches ahead. The vast staircase. Nothing has changed. Even the paintings are the same. The same Civil War art Ray adored so much hangs in his hallway. As if interpreting my thoughts, Corrigan says, "I've changed nothing since himself died."

"Himself?"

"Mr Lamond. Raymond Lamond. Now, Aidan, don't pretend you didn't know, or that you haven't been here before. Because I know all about you. It's that I don't want Billy to know too much. He's a nosey wee bastard, so he is."

I can't but help regard him nonplussed. I'm also entertaining a modicum of lightheadedness. I demand to know how come he knows all about me.

"Don't look so worried, Aidan. You're among friends now. I know you've been living in London for twenty years. Aye, since you came from Dublin."

"What do you mean?"

Corrigan chooses to ignore the question, however. He ushers me into the drawing room with a hand on my shoulder. The long-lost pal gesture. No way does this bastard deserve to be considered a friend.

"Look, Corrigan..." I begin.

"Danny, please. I don't call you McRaney." He pouts like a chastised schoolboy. The black eyes are downcast and inordinately chill once more. The look affords me the sensation, if I were to cross him, he would prove a dangerous opponent.

"You still haven't explained what you mean by friends," I remind him.

"I've known Ray Lamond a wee while. He spoke highly of you. Now, come through. My house is yours, Aidan." He throws open cream painted French doors with a sense of alacrity. I'm allowed sight of the sumptuous room. The black leather suite remains in place, plus the familiar marble topped coffee table. Deep burgundy pile carpet.

A woman rises from the leather chair. Although inspecting her more closely, I see she isn't more than an adolescent girl, who appears to be little more than fifteen or sixteen. Copious black hair spills to a tiny waist. Her eyes are darkened with mascara, her lips with a pinkish tinge. Her cheekbones are high, sculpted with rouge. She is undeniably beautiful. Her beauty enhanced by a blue silk Chinese patterned blouse she wears with a short black skirt. Sheer black stockinged legs, narrowing to trim ankles, spill into a pair of blue satin slippers. The girl reminds me of a Geisha, yet she is not Oriental. Her skin is pale, almost opalescent.

"Aidan, this is Dashurie," Corrigan introduces her, sliding an arm around her waist. I observe her stiffen slightly. All I can do is to offer her a smile. His head rests on her shoulder. He nuzzles her neck and suggests that she fixes us both a drink.

"Yes, Danny," she acquiesces almost humbly in a distinctive European accent.

"She's beautiful, isn't she?" Corrigan remarks, pride in his voice.

I can't fail to agree.

"Dashurie is here to serve my purposes, so she is." His tone is treacly and insipid. While he runs a hand through his black curly hair. "Aren't you, darlin?"

She says nothing but looks uncomfortable.

"When you've fixed the drinks you can go. Aidan and I need to talk." He slaps her bottom playfully, before turning his attention back to me." A whisky, Aidan? Chivas Regal is it?"

I wonder how he can possibly know that. From Lamond I'm guessing. Had the late gang boss told him everything about me? It is odd, but nothing appears remotely real about any of this.

The butterfly pours the whisky. That's what she reminds me of. A delicate gossamer-winged butterfly. She hands me the drink, for which I politely thank her. Her eyes remain downcast, although a shy, indecisive smile dances about her lips. The smile fails to reach the dark eyes, however. Instead they appear extraordinarily sad, almost poignant.

Dashurie exits the room with a cursory bow. Corrigan observes her departure with a lascivious lick of his wide lips, while those penetrating black orbs seem to shimmer with what I can only describe as an unholy light.

I ask him how old she is.

"Dashurie? What does it matter? Women are at their best at that age, and younger. Once they turn 25 the old looks begin to go, so they do. She's sixteen. Dashurie is a pleasure lady. Kept solely for a man's pleasure. Or a woman's if she's that way inclined," he delights to inform me.

Chapter Twelve

The Safe

"She isn't English, is she?" I ask the obvious question.

"You think I'd use Brit girls?" Corrigan exclaims in shocked tones. "Besides, Brit girls talk too fuckin' much. Dashurie is from Albania. Albania has some of the prettiest girls in the world." He pauses to regard the golden liquid in his glass thoughtfully. "If only pretty girls didn't have to lose their looks so early. You see, Aidan, I'm a collector." Once again he inspects the contents of a half empty glass. The way it catches the crimson glimmer of firelight in the crystal. I find myself automatically stiffening at the mention of the word 'collector', because I'm aware all too well of what he collects. "Lamond was a collector too. This room for instance..." He waves the glass, "that's why I haven't changed a thing. I love beautiful things, so I do. My late mother," he effects the Sign of the Cross briefly and raises his eyes Heavenward, "she loved beautiful things too. Maybe that's where I get it from."

I'm prompted to retort that the things this man chooses to collect couldn't possibly have met with his mother's approval.

"You see, I love beautiful women. As some people collect antiques and such, I collect women. The only stipulation is they have to be pretty and of a certain age. Like I said, even the pretty ones lose their looks early. And you, Aidan, do you enjoy the company of pretty women?"

I am about to tell him that I do, but the only woman I love is my wife, until he interrupts, "Of course you do," before draining the contents of his glass. "I know you like Irish girls. They've taken everything from me," he adds strangely, and shakes his head almost sadly.

"Who has?" I stare at him in puzzlement, uncertain of his meaning. "Irish girls? I don't understand."

"No. I mean the Brits."

Scanning the ostentatious room, it would appear to be the opposite. He happens to be living in their country, so what has he to complain about?

We confront one another in the familiar surroundings of what was once Ray Lamond's home. When his brother Frankie lived here I practically had the run of the place. I'd made love to Leanne in one of the back bedrooms. It's as if I've come full circle.

Nevertheless this isn't Ray Lamond. I really don't know Danny Corrigan. I regard him with speculation above the rim of my own glass. I explain that I've never been into any of that political crap.

"So why did you leave Ireland, Aidan? And don't tell me stuff about your wife throwing you out. That you've been to prison over there."

I freeze and stare at him in disbelief. He knows! He knows who I really am. Now what? Is all this friendly companionship about to turn sour? His next move will be to ring for that Billy character. He'll probably pull a pistol, because I can't imagine a man like Corrigan getting his own hands dirty. They'll either kill me or I'll be tarred and feathered like poor Jason Lang.

"You alright, Aidan?" Corrigan asks with concern. "Only you've gone a wee bit pale, so y'have."

"You know?"

"Oh come on. I know who y'are. I told you that. Sure I make it my business to know who I invite into my home. You haven't answered my question."

"I left Ireland because my Dad had to look for work across the water."

"Your mother. What was she like?"

The question surprises me. I regard him with a frown. "My mother? My mother was a lovely woman. She died when I was ten, giving birth to my youngest sister, who has also passed. She was killed."

"I know that too. The same as I know you killed the man who did it."

"What the fuck, Corrigan?" I half choke on my whisky. How many people know what I did? Half the population of London I shouldn't wonder.

"I make it my business to know things. Oh, don't look so worried. You did the right thing. If you don't look after your own, no one else is fuckin' going to do that, and I trust the Peelers about as far as I'd trust the Proddys. I would have done the same in your shoes. But that's all in the past. I do believe you're down on your luck. I can tell that by the way you dress. I reckon that old jacket must have seen better days. Can't have one of me own looking like a rag-bag can I?"

So he doesn't know everything about me then.

"What do you mean? One of your own? You mean an Irishman?"

"Aye, an Irishman." He smiles. The inflection is merely a transient flirtation of his lips.

"You said something about the Brits taking everything?" I change the subject in an endeavour to steer it away from myself.

"They took my Da. They seized a lot of my stuff. Any Irishman's bitter about what those bastards have done to their country."

"I'll stop you there!" I raise a hand. "Don't involve me in all that. This is the 21st century. We have to look forward, not back."

"He was murdered by the Brits, Aidan. At one of their fuckin' checkpoints. The wee bastards' occupation of our country was no different from the French occupation by the Germans in the second world war. Except the bastards had the fuckin' nerve to call it a peace keeping mission. There's never been any thing peaceable in their presence. Not in 1916 or in 1920. We lost some good people then, the same as we lost them in the Seventies and Eighties."

I sarcastically tell him that I flunked history at school. When Corrigan fails to tender a response, and I imagine tears stand in his eyes, I apologise for my flippancy. I enquire, a fraction more solicitously this time, if his father had done something wrong.

"Was he IRA?"

"He was fighting for his country and his beliefs, that's all." His voice rises to a crescendo. Lips tighten as his fist is visibly clenched against his leg. "I'm sorry. I can't discuss this anymore. It's far too upsetting."

"I'm sorry. You must have loved your father very much."

Swiping the tears away with the back of his hand, he shakes his head. "I barely knew him."

Considering the subject closed, he heads toward a Canaletto on the wall. Producing a small remote device from his jacket, he levels the remote on the painting to reveal a grey metal safe.

I recollect that this is where Frankie Lamond housed his own cash. However I am astonished to observe how much money the safe actually contains. Even in Frankie Lamond's time the safe failed to boast that amount. I make an effort to steer my gaze away, but it automatically returns to the two shelves that are liberally brimful of money.

Corrigan makes no pains to conceal the money. I wonder why he expresses so much trust in me. If he knows as much about me as he professes to, then he must know who I work for. Why I am here. What I do. I can't help but remain uneasy, expecting at any moment that he's about to pull a gun on me.

"That's a lot of money, Danny. Wouldn't it be safer in a bank?"

"Don't you think banks get robbed?"

"Not with such security these days. Anyway, don't they have insurance against your money if a bank gets robbed?"

"Och, I'm not talking ski masks and assault rifles here. A

bank can be robbed. Someone's personal account lifted by a clever person with a computer. I prefer to have my money where I know it's safe."

"The house could catch fire or something."

"The safe is fireproof. Bullet-proofed. It's also heavily alarmed."

"Why have you shown me? How do you know you can trust me not to pull a gun on you and rob you right now?"

His back is turned. He busies himself leafing through a pile of notes. "Because my boys would be in here faster than you can breathe. But I do trust you, Aidan. You said you were down on your luck. Here's a couple of hundred." He presses the money into my hand. Now things are really becoming a little surreal. Not only as he invited me into his home, he's actually offering me money. "Take it please," he urges on witnessing my hesitation. So I stuff the money into my wallet.

"So I'm guessing you sought me out because you want to work for me?"

"Sure. Something like that." I slip the wallet into my jacket.

"And because...?"

"Because what?"

"Just because." He shrugs. "Now why don't I show you your room? As y'know, I have plenty of rooms in this house. You are staying, aren't you?"

If Treveleyan could have seen me, he would not have believed how easily Corrigan has accepted me, when I had initially expected it to be difficult. That I would have to act my socks off to get him to even notice me. He's treating me like the long-lost pal again. I can but conjecture it's because I'm a fellow Irishman. What other reason could he possibly have?

"If you want me to."

"I wouldn't have asked, would I? So, what do you know about me?" He returns to his seat, his eyes darkening once more.

I think, treading carefully. "You'd taken over from Ray Lamond and his business concerns. If you know as much about me as you say you do, you'll know that I once worked as Frankie Lamond's minder."

"Sure I know all that." He waves a hand about him dismissively.

"And these businesses. What do they entail exactly? I mean, if you want me to work for you, I'd like to be put in the picture. If you see what I mean."

"I need to know how far I can trust you before I can discuss my businesses. A sort of initiation you might say." The familiar clinical, yet deceptively friendly, smile returns. Interlacing his fingers, the black eyes rake me over meaningfully.

Why do I swiftly detect the chill that now embraces my neck as if from an open window? "What kind of initiation?"

In response, he taps the side of his nose enigmatically. Closing the safe with the remote, the Canaletto slides into place. "We'll discuss that later. Let me show you to your room. I want you to make yourself at home. My home is yours."

When I rise to my feet, taking me by surprise, he grasps my arm. The sloe black eyes slam into mine. "It's good to meet you at last."

Chapter Thirteen

The Gift

Easing the heavy brocade curtains aside in the room Corrigan has allocated me, I peer into the grounds. It's dark now, a three quarter moon bathes the sprawling estate into an almost ethereal relief. Corrigan has invited me to make myself at home, to take a shower if I wish. Downstairs is the man I have been ordered to infiltrate and discover as much as I can concerning his rather unsavoury criminal activities. A simple enough instruction. If only he wasn't acting quite so friendly.

Like everything else about this place, Corrigan has changed little since the Lamond brothers owned it. The bed is double and spread with a red damask quilt, cream pillows. The decor is almost feministic. A thought occurs to me, one which I fail to divest myself of. If he knows so much about me, why am I still here? It's this that affords me a sense of impending unease. Have I fallen into the trap I had envisioned for Corrigan?

I'm in the process of unloading my rucksack of the few meagre items I pretend to possess. My hand closes over the Walther, when a couple of tentative raps sound on the door. I swiftly shove the gun into the nearest drawer, unwilling as I am to alert Corrigan to the fact I am armed. The taps issue again, and I prepare to respond, half expecting to find either Corrigan or Billy on the threshold. To my surprise Dashurie stands there. She's exchanged the top and skirt for an ankle-length blue kimono. The kimono is colourfully decorated with a birds of paradise pattern. Her copious ebony hair streams to her waist, and catches the light so that it appears to develop a bluish tinge.

"Dashurie is it?" I smile pleasantly. "So what does Corrigan want now? I take it he's asked you to fetch me."

"I not understand." Perfectly sculpted brows manufacture a frown.

"Didn't he send you to fetch me?"

"No...no, I come to you."

"To me? Why?"

Before I can prevent her, she pushes past me into the room. Left with no other choice, I usher her inside and close the door. First I ascertain that the corridor is empty, easing myself outside before returning to the room. I discover Dashurie depositing her weight, with all the grace of a beautiful butterfly, on to the bed. I'm beginning to get an uncomfortable feeling about all this.

"You find me attractive?" she enquires demurely. "I saw you look at me when you come in."

"Sure I looked at you. Then you rather caught my attention."

Uncoiling her slender form, the dress rustling with her every movement, she raises a hand to my face. "Danny send me to you as gift."

"A gift? What's that supposed to mean?" As if I didn't know.

"A gift. He choose me from other girls. Says I am the most beautiful. He thinks a lot of you."

"I hardly know the guy. He's sent you to me for sex, hasn't he?"

Before I can prevent her, or intercept her actions, she throws her arms around my neck. Because I'm a foot taller, she attempts to pull me down in order to reach her lips. As she does I can't help but catch an intimation of her perfume. It manages to assail my nostrils, subtle but strangely exotic, as if the scent embodies the sweetness almost of a narcotic.

When I disentangle the clinging arms, she appears swiftly

crestfallen.

"Yes, sex. I want to have sex with you. You find me attractive?" The red lipstick mouth pouts with disappointment.

"Sure I do, but you're sixteen, sweetheart. I'm thirty. Corrigan and me are much too old for you. Maybe you'd be better off finding a nice guy closer to your own age."

She appears close to tears, I guess at my rejection. Dashurie regards me nonplussed as I fetch a chair. I climb onto it with the intention of searching for bugs or wires because my thoughts are traversing uneasy lines. Maybe Corrigan's planted a hidden mirror or camera in the room, in an endeavour to catch me having sex with an underage girl.

"What you look for, Aidan?" she asks with curiosity.

"For bugs, darlin'."

"Ugh." She clutches herself and shivers. "You mean insects? Spiders?"

"No." I cannot avoid a grin at her logic. "Listening devices or hidden cameras."

I discover nothing untoward in either the lamp shade, or in any of the wiring. Climbing down from the chair, I can't help stiffening when she helps me down, a hand around my waist. "Corrigan's probably sent you to me as a plant, hasn't he?"

"Plant? Don't understand."

"That's because I'm Irish," I quip. "Maybe all this is making me a wee bit paranoid. And you," I tilt her chin with a forefinger. "You know I find you attractive. What man wouldn't? I took a young girl once. I've lived to regret it ever since. I have no idea what Corrigan has planned, but I certainly don't have sex with underage girls. But there is something I'd like to know."

"I want to kiss you. I not like boys my own age. They are so, what is word? Immature."

Thinking of my twenty two year old brother Ruairi, I can't fail to agree.

Stretching a hand to my face again, she traces the contours of my beard, before complimenting me on it. "I like man with beard. It shows strength."

"Or just proves that I can grow one."

It would be so easy to succumb, until all the images collate in my mind. Caitlan at home with my children. My sister professing to know some of the stuff I do. Danny Corrigan downstairs, no doubt laughing at the trap he has set. If I have sex with this girl, I'll probably be photographed or filmed in an endeavour to discredit me. After all, he knows that I killed Fitzwalter. I'm already beginning to feel trapped and uneasy. Dashurie's presence only adds to the apprehension.

Taking her hand, I regard her critically, simply because I need to make her understand. "You're a pretty girl, sweetheart, but I'm not going to have sex with you."

"But Mr Corrigan will send me back to the Palace."

"The Palace? What palace?" The only palace I know has to be Buckingham Palace. I can hardly believe for a moment that's where she means.

"The palace in the White Chapel."

The penny drops. "Do you mean Whitechapel?"

"White chapel." She continues to repeat the name as if it's two separate words.

"Yes. That's where they take me when I first arrive in England. The place called the White Chapel."

I urge her to tell me who took her there. Opening the drawer in the bedside cabinet, taking care not to allow her sight of the pistol, I remove the £200 that Corrigan gave me from my wallet. "So does Mr Corrigan expect your punters…" Observing her frown, I explain that I mean her clients. "Do they pay for sex?"

"Pay for sex? Oh yes, they pay. But Danny say I'm gift. You do not have to pay." She pushes the money away. "I do not take money from you, Aidan."

"What's so different about me? Is it because I'm the same as Mr Corrigan, Danny?"

"Same?"

"Nationality. We're both from Ireland."

"Ireland?"

"You know Ireland?"

She shakes her head as if I'm speaking in Gaelic. "Never mind. So tell me about the palace in the White Chapel. What is it?"

She affords her familiarly delicate smile. "The palace for pleasure. There are girls there. All nationality. Danny say I am the most beautiful."

"I guess y'are. So how old are these girls?"

"Old?"

"Their average age. You're sixteen. Are they older? Younger?"

"Why do you ask these questions? I only want you to love me, not because Danny ask me to. You a good looking man. A lot of men, and women too, come to the palace. They put down money. Choose girls. Danny good looking but not like you."

She really is trying hard. Offering herself this way. I'm further surprised when she unfastens the kimono, allowing the drapery to fall aside, revealing her nakedness beneath it. Again that exotic perfume assails my nostrils so predominantly, the room is almost pervaded by it. It's as if she has bathed herself in the scent before coming to my room. Firm, youthful breasts embody the early nubile blossoming of a woman, yet still a child. Her stomach is toned and flat the way Caitlan's used to be before I gave her a baby.

The erection pulsing against my jeans is becoming almost too difficult to resist. The headiness of the perfume, the pure alabaster of her white skin is conducive to making me a fraction dizzy, as if I've imbibed some strange exotic drug. That it would be so effortless to pluck that still ripening body. Nevertheless I bring myself to my senses with an effort.

"Whether you're a gift or not I'm still going to pay you." Her eyes shimmer with pure excitement, and I wonder why. "Then you will have sex?" She moves into kiss me again. Although it's against my better judgement, because she has no idea what she is doing to me, or maybe she does, I press a finger to her lips preventing her.

"It's not going to happen, sweetheart. I want you to tell me who runs this pleasure palace as you call it. Whereabouts in Whitechapel is it?"

She pouts. She seems to be good at that.

"I not want to talk."

"Please, gorgeous, indulge me." I can pout too. "Then maybe I'll let you kiss me," I cajole.

"I not know what street it is. The palace is big house. What is it Mrs Ryan call it?" She pauses to recollect.

"Who's Mrs Ryan?"

"Lady who runs it. I not like Mrs Ryan much. She said I must pleasure men and women when they want me. That they pay good money for me because I am young."

I mutter, "Jesus," beneath my breath, while I experience an odd glacial chill the length of my backbone. I ask her why she doesn't return to Albania and get away from all this. Why did she come to England in the first place?

"My family very poor. I see advertisement in paper. I learn English because Danny say I have to. Not all girls learn English. Danny say I could be model or actress because I so pretty. That I have to start at Pleasure Palace. I earn money there until I become model. I send money back to my family."

"So do you keep all the money you earn?"

"I give half to Danny in exchange for meals and room in his lovely home."

"This Pleasure Palace, you know it's a brothel?"

"Brothel? I not understand this word."

"It's okay. So is this broth...I mean Pleasure Palace. You say it's in a big house?"

"It has lots of rooms. A lodge?" I nod my understanding. "I have one. I not share, but spend time with Danny when he send for me. He choose me from other girls. Now tonight I pleasure you."

"I'm married, darlin'." I make my voice sound deliberately

flippant, assuming a lackadaisical attitude, otherwise I shall drown in that anomalous perfume. "I have two children."

"But you say your wife give you kick."

"Kicked out." I can't help but smile at her turn of phrase. If Caitlan saw me with Dashurie she probably would kick me out. "But that doesn't mean I want to have sex with you.

"I not stay at Pleasure Palace all my life. I will be model. But it helps my family."

To prostitute herself in order to feed her family. I trace the sculpted cheeks with a palm, which she presses with her own.

"You want to stay in England? I mean not at the Pleasure Palace. You should be doing something better with your life."

"But my family..."

"Study hard and get a good job. You speak good English. You can still help your family. Sorry to be harsh, sweetheart, but do they know you're prostituting yourself? Because that's the way it looks to me."

She pulls away swiftly as if I have struck her physically. "I'm not prostitute. I pleasure lady."

"Sure, have it your way," I thought, "but a prostitute you surely are, no matter how many pretty words you use to dress it up."

At the impatience of two sharply delivered raps on the door, Dashurie jumps startled, while I hiss for her to get into the bed. I have no desire to see her get into trouble, if Corrigan discovers that she hasn't had sex with me. Needing no second bidding, naked, she slips beneath the covers, which I pull over her. I instruct her to stay there.

"Easy to imagine having sex with you. I imagine when I saw you."

I ask her what the perfume is that she's wearing. Its pungency, instead of lessening, seems to become progressively stronger.

"It is called Erotica," she whispers sotto voce. "It is to bathe in. Not to wear."

"Course it is," I effect a cursory mutter, and peel open my shirt.

I'm in the process of re-buttoning the garment, when I answer the door. Only to discover a lasciviously smiling Billy standing there. I maintain the door partially closed, so that he shouldn't be compelled to peer into the room. I growl, "What do you want?" in an impatient tone.

"Himself wants to see you in the basement." He gestures his Elvis quiffed locks in that general direction.

"The basement?"

"Aye, I'll take you there."

From what I remember, the basement once housed the Lamond brothers' wine cellar. I had often been sent down there to select the finest red or white. The cellar is reached by a lengthy flight of wrought iron stairs. Slipping a key from his jacket, Billy twists it into the lock. I wonder why the door is locked, although I refrain from mentioning the fact. I am more interested to discover what Corrigan wants with me in the cellar. Billy's lack of response to my question only serves to increase my apprehension.

The door squeals on its hinges noisily. I am greeted by a room that is partially shrouded in darkness. The only relief emanates from a shadeless bulb that swings from a dingy ceiling. I suggest that Billy precedes me. I don't trust the bastard to not push me down the stairs.

A further shrug, and with a muttered, "suit yourself," Billy moves ahead of me. Initially I hear hushed voices. Corrigan sounds as if he is reprimanding someone.

"What did I fuckin' tell you about bringing your lunch down here, Pug? It's himself who'll be hungry." He appears to be in an ill-humour.

The bulb swings as if from an unseen draught, but is enough to illuminate the man on the bed. I detect a smell that lingers strong in the air. The unmistakeable stench of blood.

Apart from the bed, there is a single chair, one from which a stockily built young man eases his bulk; nothing remains of Frankie Lamond's once well-stocked wine cellar.

Somewhere into his late twenties, the man yanks down a baggy green sweater, which he wears over equally baggy jeans, as if in a vain attempt to conceal his ample proportions. Corrigan addresses him as Pug. Well the name seems to fit. Pug rakes a big hand through tousled mousy hair indecisively.

Corrigan drags on a familiar cheroot. Pug swipes tomato sauce from wide lips, and swallows uncomfortably.

"Ah, Aidan!" Corrigan enthuses with a smile. There is an almost excited animation in his voice. "See the man on the bed?" The black eyes glint over me with a peculiar enigmatic light.

"What the fuck is this, Corrigan?" I demand, while the little ole ferret in my guts pops up to say "hello".

The bulb swings above him, so that the light falls directly onto the bed. Although from what I can see the light fails to bother him unduly. His clothes are ripped and shredded, exposing his chest and his bare legs, from which blood has long since congealed. His boots are also caked in blood. Both of his arms hang limply at his sides. The merest undulation of his torso indicates he's barely breathing at all. The thick tawny down of chest hairs are also badly matted with blood. His features scarcely recognisable. I can just make out the tawny beard that contours his jawline. Somehow the man is strangely familiar. One of his eyes is closed shut with congealed blood. The other hardly blinks. But continues to stare upward, as if that too is sightless.

"Is... is he dead?" I enquire in a voice I scarcely recognise as my own.

"Not yet," responds Corrigan, producing a .357 Magnum revolver from beneath his jacket.

"What's that for?" I regard the gun uneasily.

He urges me to take the weapon. "You wanted to work for me you said. This is your initiation, Aidan. The man on the bed. I want you to kill him. The coup de grace." He holds his smile. It's equally as cold and clinical as those demonic black eyes, as if this man is spawned from Hell itself, or as if he is possessed by the devil when he says, "I chose a revolver because it fires but six rounds. There's only one slug up the spout. So make your shot count, you know what I mean."

I accept the pistol reluctantly, almost as if those cold, incalculable demonic eyes are compelling me. The wee ferret is now joined by a couple of pals. Because when I approach the bed, I realise that the man who lies there more dead than alive, is none other than Dennis Mitchell.

Chapter Fourteen

The Coup De Grace

"Mitchell!" I exclaim, my heart crashing against my ribs so painfully, that it's getting harder to breathe.

He continues to stare at the ceiling, as if he has little knowledge of my presence.

"Who...who did this?" I find my voice, listening to my own shaking timbre.

"I did," Billy declares, as if he's proud of the fact. "Me and Pug," he adds as an afterthought.

Pug merely growls, but is more interested in polishing off the remains of his burger.

The surge of anger inside me makes me wonder if one shot might embellish its trajectory and kill all these inanely grinning bastards. Dennis Mitchell was not merely the guy I once shared a cell with for six years, or now as a work colleague, but also as a good friend. I recollect how he rescued me and shot my assailant when Caitlan's ex, Shaun Blackwood, almost blinded me.

From somewhere in the distant haze that is my subconscious, Corrigan says, "If you want to know why, it's because our wee man's a fuckin' British agent sent in by that other fuckin' wee Brit bastard Sir George Treveleyan."

LJ had related the reason why Dennis had volunteered for the job, because I have a wife and young family.

"The war is over, Corrigan. It's been over for a while. We were children at the time. Besides, you are in their country. You claimed to have known Ray Lamond. He was a Brit wasn't he? He was from Essex. That's in England, man."

"Aye, sure I know that. But Ray was a man of vision."

"Meaning? What kind of vision?"

"The vision to bring the Brits down from the inside. Not with bombs or doorstep assassinations. You're right, Aidan. That part of the war is over. There are other ways."

"Is that why you're behaving so fuckin' pally with me? Because I'm Irish? If you think I want to hurt these people, then you've got another thing coming. Sure I hated their schools when I first came to London, but since you seem to know so much about me, you know that I've been here a long time. How are you going to bring the Brits down from the inside? How?"

"Where it hurts the most. Soft targets my friend. It's always been soft targets." That clinically cold smile is firmly in place once more.

I can't help but express an involuntary shudder at what he intimates. Soft targets. Children. So this is what he plans then. He intends to keep the war alive in his own inimical fashion.

"And the man on the bed?" I ask.

"He's half dead. The wee bastard's been knee-capped amongst other things. He don't have much longer. It'll be a mercy killing. As a nationalist I'd thought you'd like to do the honours. That's a .357 Magnum."

"I know what it is," I snap. "And if I do this?"

"If you do this?" Billy demands, his eyes narrowing with suspicion.

Corrigan rasps, "Shut the fuck up, Billy," irritably.

"I need to do this alone."

"You ever killed before?" Pug wants to know. "I mean if you ain't..."

"Like the boss says, shut the fuck up," I retort.

The fat man glares at me treacherously. I think, "you're going to be next, you bastard." That obese frame will probably require more than just a few rounds.

Once they have left maybe I can rescue Mitchell, and get the hell out. At least, if Corrigan hasn't lied, I have one slug up the spout. I check the chamber. He's right. One slug. That's all it takes. My brief is to discover all I can with concern to Corrigan's operations. I am already aware that he is into white slave trafficking and murder. What else do I need to know in order to eliminate the bastard?

Tonight. It has to be tonight. I'll take Mitchell out of here, and return with LJ plus an entire arsenal of weaponry. We'll also take Dashurie with us.

"I don't like to work if I'm watched," I tell them.

Corrigan lays what I imagine is a friendly hand on my shoulder. "Ray said you were good. That's why I saved that wee Brit bastard for you. It'll teach that fuckin' pompous bastard Treveleyan a lesson. You ever hear of him?"

"Who?"

"Treveleyan. Sir fuckin' George," he spits a large globule of saliva which drops to the floor, narrowly missing my boots. "Some wheelchair bound bastard who thinks he knows it all. He's friendly with some of those pompous-assed officials who sent their agents to the Province during the Troubles."

I lie that I don't know Treveleyan, and check the .357 once more.

"I understand, Aidan. Take your time. Our wee man ain't going nowhere," he laughs, and is joined by Billy and Pug. The sound is harsh and grates on my already strained nerves.

Corrigan ushers a reluctant Pug and Billy ahead of him. The former mutters something about being denied the pleasure of seeing the wee man putting a bullet through the Brit's head.

Corrigan admonishes him about showing some decorum. They have gone, and I find myself alone with Mitchell. I wonder if

Corrigan has planted any bugs in the room. I have no time to find out, however. Wedging the Magnum into the back of my jeans belt, I ascertain if anyone might be listening. I whisper his name.

"What the fuck they done to you, man? It's Aidan. Your old pal McRaney."

"I know who it is." His words are barely audible. I am practically holding my breath in order to catch what he says. When he finally deigns to speak, I'm astonished to observe the blood that bubbles up through his teeth, dribbles from his dried cracked lips. "I can tell by your voice who it is."

"Look, Dennis..." I placate, touching his shoulder. I recoil a fraction when my hand comes away sticky with blood. Running the palm down my jeans, I attempt to reassure him that I'll get him out of there. As there is one bullet I can't take them out right now. I explain that I have a pistol upstairs, that I'll be back tonight.

He grasps my arm. "For pity's sake, Aidan. I can't walk. My knees have gone. The bastards. My eye is gone. All I can make out is that fuckin' light above me. You're just a blur. I can't see properly."

"Maybe I should have gone in anyway. For some strange reason Corrigan appears to be pretty pally. It's because we're of the same nationality and religion. I realise now that his intention is to keep the Irish War alive. You shouldn't have gone in because you're British."

"I... I," He is barely able to speak, and slicks a blackened tongue over cracked lips. "I don't think being Irish has anything to do with it. I think it's something else. What, I don't know. I can't talk anymore." He lapses back onto the solitary stained pillow. "Get out of here tonight, Aidan."

"Oh, don't worry I'm going to. And I'll fuckin' carry you as big as y'are, Dennis."

"No...no, Aidan. Kill me. That's what they want you to do. I want you to kill me to. I'm blind. I'm crippled. Nobody's gonna miss me. Not my old lady. My sister's disowned me. Her and that pompous old man of hers. You got that nice little family. I... I can't hold on much longer. Kill me. I'd rather you did it. You're my friend, ain't you?"

"You know I am." The words are practically choked out of me. "But I... I can't..."

"He's given you a gun. Fuckin' do it!" He rasps, closes his eyes. His hand falls away. I can barely hear him, except when he repeats his request for me to kill him. "Just fuckin' do it, McRaney!"

Tears wash my eyes so that I can barely focus, when I slip the Magnum from my belt. Level the weapon at the man on the bed. My eyes are so blinded by tears now, that everything is reduced to an unfocussing blur.

"You got a fag, McRaney?" The nights he would whisper in the semi darkness after lights out

"I'll fuckin' get him, Dennis, so help me I will," I promise.

But Mitchell fails to respond.

Easing back the hammer with a trembling finger, I press the trigger. The entire task is performed with closed eyes. There is no silencer.

The reverberation of the shot rebounds around the room with a sort of hollow echo.

A stifled sigh emanates from the bed, as if with relief that I have put him out of his misery.

"Farewell old friend. May God have mercy on your soul." I know I should have gone to church more.

My eyes remain closed. It's a while before I open them again. Unable to look at Mitchell, I have no way of knowing if the single bullet has found its mark. I guess it has because there is no sound emanating from the man on the bed.

I freeze instinctively as a hand presses my shoulder to find Danny Corrigan regarding me with a look of pure self-satisfaction etched on his face.

"He's dead, Aidan. I need to talk to you," he says.

So what the hell does he wish to discuss with me now? I've

done exactly as he asked. I've killed my best friend. Probably my only friend outside of my family. My heart has turned to stone. While the little ole ferret grows ever adventurous as it gnaws happily away on what remains of my insides. I am undesirous of staying here any longer to listen to that man rabbit on about a war that has long been over. I long to yell at him to cease fighting his one man war, using innocents in order to do it. Besides there is a girl in my bed whom I've practically forgotten. But sex is the furthest thing on my mind. Only revenge and getting hammered remain uppermost.

Nevertheless I trail blindly in Corrigan's wake, while he plunges on about us being of the same nationality. Freedom for the Irish and all that. How the war is never over. That it's still going on. I shouldn't be deceived by the Brits. That the politicians are doing a pretty good job of bringing their country down from the inside. How the Brits were either too blind or stupid to realise it.

I am familiar with this house however. I know exactly where I am, while I make a mental note of my planned escape. He escorts me to the dining room. Motioning me to a set place at the table, Corrigan proceeds to carve from a piece of roast beef resting on a large oval platter.

He's not alone. There is a woman present. I judge her to be somewhere into her fifties. She helps him serve the food. Her hair is dark, but slightly tinged with grey and bobbed at the neck. The woman sports an immaculately white apron over a high-necked black dress.

"This is Phoebe." Corrigan introduces the woman. "She's a grand cook, so she is. Phoebe was once a member of the Cumann na mBan."

Unwilling as I am to display my ignorance, I have to ask to what he is actually referring.

"The Cumann na mBan is the female wing of the Paramilitary," she declares proudly, speaking for the first time.

Now why doesn't that surprise me? So is this the woman

Dashurie mentioned, Phoebe Ryan?

"When you've finished, you can leave us, Phoebs," instructs Corrigan. "Aidan and I have a lot to talk about."

"About the fact I've just killed a man?" I throw into the mix.

Phoebe Ryan and Corrigan exchange, what I can only describe, as self-satisfied grins.

If I as much as entertained a modicum of appetite it has clearly deserted me now. Especially when I see that amidst the platter of vegetables on the table, Mrs Ryan is serving Colcannon. Colcannon is a particularly Irish dish which consists of mashed potatoes, bacon, kale and onions. A well is made in the centre into which she has added what appears to be cream and butter. I loathed the dish when my mother used to serve it, which was frequently, and mainly because it is inexpensive. When Mrs Ryan spoons a large amount of the stuff onto my plate. In the wake of Mitchell's demise, I'm beginning to feel physically sick again. And I push the plate aside.

"Not hungry?" Corrigan asks. There is precious little acrimony behind his words, merely concern.

"I cooked that special because you asked me to, Danny." Phoebe Ryan's expression is filled with a thinly disguised disdain. Obviously my reluctance to eat her food has pissed her off somewhat, but that Colcannon does appear distinctly unappetising.

Corrigan presses Phoebe's hand affectionately. A spectacle I find particularly disturbing. As if they share some unwarranted kind of intimacy. "Not really. I'm still trying to get the taste of blood out of my mouth."

To my surprise Corrigan nods sympathetically. "I understand how you feel. But that man. He meant nothing to you, did he?"

He was only my fucking best friend, that's all. I merely shake my head, and respond numbly. "No, he meant nothing to me."

"Good." Corrigan beams, and waves a hand about him indiscriminately, as if a man's death is of precious little consequence. Except I would have preferred to have expressed my grief for Dennis in tears. However, I'm aware that if I do Corrigan will think that not only am I a wuss, but that the former meant more to me than simply another job.

"Phoebe's a friend of my late mother's, aren't you?"

"Aye. Poor Mairead." She shakes her head regrettably.

"So what happened to your mother?"

"She had cancer, Aidan."

"I'm sorry to hear that. Guess you can't blame that on the Brits."

"I blame everything on the Brits," he is quick to retort. "Now I'll call you when I need you, Phoebes. It was a lovely meal."

"Sure, Danny." Phoebe Ryan practically delivers a curtsey to Corrigan. I receive but a cursory glance. Probably because I refused to eat her Colcannon. She exits, and I'm curious to discover why he should blame his mother's cancer on the British.

"Worry, Aidan, worry. You see my ma, God rest her soul..." He quickly fashions the sign of the cross over his chest. "A devoted Catholic lady. When I was growing up I spent nearly as much time in church as I did in school. Like Phoebe, Ma was devoted to the Cause. Ma didn't join the Paramilitary because she had a small child, but she found other ways to do her bit for her country. She housed the men on the run. Aye, and the sympathisers too." He pauses to pour gravy from a white ceramic jug over his food. Even this simple act is accompanied by a flourish of contemplation, as if he has all the time in the world. Nothing should be rushed. Aware of my hesitation, I merely toy with my food. He urges, "eat your food. Don't worry, we haven't poisoned you."

Heaving a sigh of resignation, I practically drown the Colcannon with gravy. Now it appears even more unappetising, merely a slushy mess.

"She was constantly worried that she'd be lifted by the wee bastards. As you rightly pointed out, I'm in their country. In fact, truth be known I've been here a wee while, so I have."

"Don't you ever talk about anything but that war?" Although I continue to play with my food, I have to admit that the beef tastes pretty good, and is cooked to perfection.

When he fails to respond, I add, "Course I never really grew up with the war. My dad used to watch it on the news. When we lived in Dublin it never interfered with our lives too much. Though I knew the Troubles were still going on when I was born."

"Let me stop you there!" Corrigan's tone rises to a crescendo. When he raises a hand I quickly glance up from my food, wondering what's coming. "Your parents were more involved than you think."

Chapter Fifteen

A Startling Revelation

The wee ferret that negotiates my guts has invited his pals to a disco, with strobe lights and everything.

"You didn't know my parents. My father was never in the 'Rah. What, Dermot? That's almost laughable. He is an Irish Catholic, but that's about it."

"Aye, sure I know that. To my knowledge, no, your Da was never in the 'Rah. From what I heard he was but a humble painter and decorator."

"He had his own business. So what you driving at, Corrigan?"

"Please, Aidan, don't let's be at loggerheads. I'm merely stating a fact here. I heard your Da worked with a man named Padraig Keenan on a house at Tallaght, right?"

"I don't fuckin' know," I growl uneasily. "Sure. I remember Padraig when I was a kid."

Pop used to take me with him in the school holidays. Paddy often gave me a sandwich from his lunchbox, admonished me about not eating the crusts . He'd joke that I probably had enough curls already. My attempt at a smile fades at the recollection. A little over twenty years ago. But it could have been an entire lifetime since I left Dublin. "I still don't understand what you're getting at. And I don't think Paddy Keenan was in the 'Rah either."

"I'm not talking about Paddy Keenan. I'm talking about the

wee man who came to your house."

He can't be referring to Michael Docherty, can he? The man my father killed when he discovered that my mother had an affair with him. When a body was discovered in a shallow grave outside Dublin, the Gardai had come to Dad to hopefully eliminate him from their enquiries, satisfied that this old man had nothing remotely to do with Docherty's death.

"Like I said, you don't know anything about my parents. How could you? Unless you've obviously been checking up on me.If you've got a point to make, then fuckin' make it. Because I get the feeling that all this pally-pally shit doesn't hide your real reason for bringing me here, making me as welcome as you have."

"You were the one who came looking for me. That must mean something."

"Oh sure it does. It means that I've been hired to kill you, pal." Naturally I refrain from vocalising my thoughts. Instead I say, "Because I was told you hired people to work for you, particularly if they're Irish."

"As an assassin. That's what you're asking isn't it?"

"It's what I do cos maybe I can find no other employment. My life is already fucked up. So why do I get the feeling you're going to fuck it up even further?"

"I'm not a fool. I know why you're here. I think it's time you and I laid our cards on the table."

I observe him on the conclusion of his meal. The action is almost delicately perfected before he tosses the napkin down, that's tucked bib-like over his shirt.

"What's that supposed to mean?" God, that Colcannon now even more resembles an unholy mess that someone's regurgitated. While I attempt not to grimace at the sight of it.

"Sure, I know that part of what you told me is the truth. You are an assassin. That's why you are here. The same as I know you work for that wee Brit bastard Sir George Treveleyan."

I stare at him in a kind of glacial silence, when the only

movement is my brain working overtime. It urges me to get out while I still can. Then what is it that compels me to remain and listen to him rabbit on? His subject is invariably the British. He's off on his usual diatribe. This time his grievances purport to the Royal Family, plus the underserving people who are indiscriminately knighted, before he adds, "Architecturally England is a lovely country. It's all that fuckin' pomp and fuckin' circumstance that spoils it. If it were a Republic there would be no fuckin' class system. People would be either rich or poor, depending on how you worked for it. The way it is in America. And not because they've been born into it, and sod to the rest of the populous."

"Maybe I agree with you for once."

"You do!" he echoes, surprised. "Sure if some of the Brits don't feel the same way. Old Noll had the right idea, even if the wee bastard ran their parliament."

"And desecrated the churches. But, I'm not here for a fuckin' history lesson. You know who I am, you said, and who I work for."

"I'm not about to pull a gun on you. See, I'm unarmed." To confirm that fact, he eases his jacket aside. "At least not yet anyway," he adds with a wry grin, albeit that particularly crooked grin does little to alleviate the tightening knot that twists and writhes inside me. "Sure I know exactly who you work for."

"Is that why you wanted me to kill the guy in the cellar?"

"Ah! Mr Mitchell. I'm getting to that. I shouldn't have put you in that position."

"Then why did you? "

"I needed to know where your loyalties lay."

"He asked me to kill him."

"He asked? Jesus! Did he really?"

"Don't sound so fuckin' surprised, Corrigan. Your hoods did him up pretty good. Okay, since you know everything about me," I prolong a sigh of resignation, "you knew I worked with Dennis Mitchell, you bastard. So what happens now?" I think of Caitlan and my children at home. My family. I realise that I've entrapped myself, or rather that bastard Sir George Treveleyan has. So is this what he plans for ex-cons? Expose them to other criminals, as if it were a game. A kind of sport. Let them fight it out. After all we're expendable. Now I've stupidly fallen into the trap that Treveleyan has set.

Corrigan's expression remains unchanging and oddly expressionless.

"You think this is where I call one of my boys, or hoods as you call them. That's a wee bit American, isn't it? They'll take you for a ride, and blow you away in a deserted field somewhere?" The bare inflection of a smile lingers briefly about his mouth.

"The thought had occurred to me," I say, almost nonchalantly, which belies the way I really feel. Cold. Scared too. I'm at no pains to admit that. The perspiration that seeps through my shirt has little bearing on the heat of the room. Plus the fact the anger that surges through my insides isn't totally directed at Corrigan. No, Sir George Treveleyan has a fucking lot to answer for. All I can hope for, despite LJ's doubts to the contrary, is that he'll ascertain that my widow is financially secure. The only salvation I have is LJ knows where I am. That she can hopefully effect a rescue.

"Come on, Aidan." The grin widens. He waves a slim brown hand about him indiscriminately. "I wouldn't do that to you. Not..." He pauses to clear his throat, as if he has something stuck there. Closes his eyes as if composing himself for what he is about to say. While I can't avoid the uncomfortable sensation, the next words that issue from his lips will sign my death warrant. "Not to a brother," he adds at length.

"Brother? I'm not your fuckin' brother. Not in your fuckin' politics. Just because I'm Ir..."

"As I was saying," he interrupts so forcefully, that I'm compelled to listen, against my better judgement. "First, let's have a drink. I see you didn't finish your meal. Phoebe is a good cook y'know."

"I don't doubt it. The beef was cooked to perfection."

Corrigan eases himself from his seat, moving to a mahogany cabinet. Opening the cupboard, he retrieves a bottle of Bushmills. Holding aloft the latter, he enquires if I'd like some. Now that's something I cannot fail to refuse. Hauling the bottle onto the counter, he pours from the whiskey into a couple of glasses, before passing one across to me.

Accepting the whiskey, I afford him a cursory gratitude. Those black eyes, ones I can only describe as intimidating, appear to follow me avariciously as I take a sip. It's been a while since I've drank Bushmills. I detect a slight undertaste, but one I fail to remark on. It's probably because I'm used to Chivas.

Corrigan wants to know if the drink is okay. When I tell him that it is he's there with the bottle, topping me up.

"Where was I?" he asks. Composing himself, an arm resting on the table, he toys with the whisky in his glass, his expression thoughtful.

"You mentioned something about brothers. I was going to say that I might be an Irish Catholic, but that's as far as it goes. I'm not into any fuckin' brotherhood shit."

The whiskey begins to warm my insides. I'm imminently desirous of getting drunk right now, except I need to keep my wits about me. Nevertheless, all that goes out of the window when Corrigan declares, "But you are, Aidan," enigmatically.

"What's that supposed to mean, for fuck's sake?" A frozen hand swiftly encompasses my insides, while I frown at his meaning.

"As I was saying, your Da and Paddy Keenan were doing up a house in Tallaght when a man, a plumber, turned up. This plumber was suspected of being in the Provos. Your Da, being the good Catholic that he is, couldn't turn the man away. This was in 1981."

"How should I remember that? I wasn't born until 1982."

"Och sure I know that. I was only four years old myself. This man told this to my mother in '81. He had black curly hair like yours. He was also married with an 18 month old son. Funny that, but his son's name was also Aidan."

"Sure, Corrigan. This is all fascinating stuff. So Aidan is quite a common name in Ireland."

Strangely, as Corrigan continues not only his narration, he also holds his smile. Yet it isn't difficult to perceive, the smile is oddly not one of humour but, dare I imagine, of something akin to satisfaction. His features have developed an odd sort of blurry edge. The kind Caitlan, a migraine sufferer, refers to at the onset of one.

Corrigan continues as if he hasn't heard me, while I wonder if I actually uttered the words myself.

"The UVF had this man high on their list as a suspect. That's why he had to move around a lot. He had left his wife and came to Ballymurphy. My mother hid him out for a while. In 1976 he had an affair with her. I was the result. After that he went to Dublin where he figured he'd be safe if he crossed into the Republic."

"So is this going anywhere?" I ask wearily. Realising how tired I'm beginning to feel, I run a hand over my eyes.

"Your da, Dermot McRaney," he continues again as if I haven't spoken, "brought this man to his house. I don't think that even your Da realised, when his wife was too tired for sex, and himself too drunk to perform his conjugals, that she was having an affair."

I freeze in spite of my erstwhile weariness when I realise what he's saying. I swiftly rise from my chair, my heart crashing angrily.

"Jesus, Corrigan, that's my mother you're talking about! How the hell do you know all this?" I gesticulate with my arms wildly, half stumbling against the chair, so that I manage to knock it over. As before there is barely a flicker of emotion in those penetrating black orbs. The drink has fuelled the impassioned wrath inside me, while a crazy sense of lightheadedness washes over me. Coupled with the anger, the blurry outline that encapsulates Corrigan's features seems to increase. I move to the door, or maybe stagger would be more appropriate. "She's dead, Corrigan. My mother is dead!" I rasp angrily, almost in tears now. "My mother loved my father. I don't need this." I clench a fist hard against my leg with an idea of striking that evil smile from this bastard's smirking face. If only I didn't feel quite so tired all at once. "Who is this man you keep talking about?"

My outburst appears to leave Corrigan completely unfazed however. His tone remains as softly spoken as before. "Your mother told this man to leave when she discovered she was pregnant, but my father said he would know his child when it was born. Marie knew that Dermot would reject her if he found out, and so would his family. The child was a wee boy, but Marie was worried that her lover would turn up to destroy what she had. So she contacted the authorities. My father was accosted by the Brits at a Crossmaglen checkpoint and shot dead.

"You see, Aidan," he pauses momentarily, and as if to savour his words, "you see, we're half-brothers, you and I."

My head spins, likewise the room. Whether from the drink or his revelation, I have no idea. My breathing is harsh, belaboured, as if I have been running hard. I half collapse against the framework of the door, when I hear myself ask, "Who... who is this man?" numbly.

"His name was Connor McMartland. Sure I know it's a lot to take in. Apparently you were born at the very hour of his death. Midnight on the 21st June, 1982. Spooky isn't it?" he adds with an involuntary shudder.

Chapter Sixteen

Honey Trap

With a somewhat girly reaction, I have little choice than to fling myself from the room. I can leave of course. Corrigan assures me that I'm not a prisoner. Then why don't I?

When I enquired what his plans are regarding the removal of Dennis Mitchell's body, the cruel lips snarl with an almost gleeful response. "Oh, it will be delivered to Mr Treveleyan with our compliments." As if he were sending flowers.

Does nothing, no matter how evil, deter this man? In the wake of that rather revealing conversation, confessing that Connor McMartland was my father, Corrigan has ultimately signed his own death warrant. The fact that Corrigan and I are half-brothers cannot possibly be relayed to my family. Bridget, Harry, Ruairi and Dermot are my family. The latter is my father. My mother, the beautiful woman whom I have loved and worshipped, missed these past twenty years. To even remotely suggest that I am a Provos' son by a man with whom my mother had an illicit affair is inconceivable. Yet the most startling revelation of all is that Sir George Treveleyan must have known! The reason why he wanted me to work for him in the first place.

In the room upstairs, I lean my head against the door. Allow the tears to fall. I wondered, was Dermot so bad? He was never the happiest of men of course. That all he did was spend time complaining. But surely that wasn't sufficient to explain why my mother should be desirous of flinging herself into the arms of the first available man.

Or is Corrigan merely playing some convincing mind-game? A clever ploy? Or is it the last vestige of desperation? Because he's aware that I will ultimately destroy him. It's either him or me now. The anger remains. Except I'm far too weary to do much about it. Sleep practically overcomes me as I hit the pillows.

Without bothering to remove my clothes, apart from my boots, I drop onto the bed, where I swiftly descend into slumber. Before I do, however, I'm marginally conscious of two things. Dashurie continues to lie in my bed. Her hair is spread in a raven-wing curtain against the contrasting white. Plus the fact the phone is ringing in my jacket. Both of which I choose to ignore.

My sleep is punctuated with so many dreams. Dreams which ostensibly blend, intermingle. Mostly of Caitlan and my children. The cold fear I entertain that I might never see them again. That I have consummately placed myself at Corrigan's disposal. I dream of our wedding day. How sweet and delicate my bride in her white lacy dress. The way she smiled up at me on reaching my side at the altar. Except – the way it is with dreams – when I lift her veil, I can't avoid recoiling. It is Judy who stands there, a cold smile etching her face as if to say, "You'll never escape me. No matter how many other women you have in your life."

It is this which brings me partially awake. Or is it something else that begins to stir me? Gentle fingers are softly probing when they coil around my penis. I can't help but whisper Caitlan's name. My eyes remain closed. Because in my disorientated, drugged state, I believe that I am home in my own bed. That Caitlan lies next to me, and I revel in the manipulative pressure of her palms as they caress my balls. Straddling me, she undulates herself almost rhythmically. The experience is one akin to euphoric. Half asleep, barely awake, I reach for her. My penis hardens inside her. The searching fingers rove across my chest. I murmur my wife's name once more, because I continue to believe that she is the one who manipulates me into arousal. It is only when I feel the touch of her hair falling into my face, her cries of ecstasy arousing me into full wakefulness, that I realise the woman making love to me isn't my wife!

Fully awake now, I exclaim, "What the hell, Dashurie?" in shock and disbelief. I'm further astonished to observe she's removed my jeans and shorts, and peeled open my shirt.

"Please, please, I want to make love," Dashurie starts to protest. As naked as the day she was born, her small breasts are unfettered and swinging free.

"Jesus, Dashurie! Get off me!" I yell at her, and struggle to raise myself from the bed, while admonishing myself for enjoying it, as my organ deflates.

She's reluctant to leave. I am left with no other choice but to push her off. It isn't my intention to inflict hurt on her, but she falls back onto the bed. Long black hair curtains her face so that I am unaware of her expression momentarily. Pushing her hair back from her face with irritation, I'm conscious of the tears standing in her eyes. Anger negotiates her lips into a tightly strained moue.

"I only want to make love to you." She attempts to blink back her tears.

"While I was asleep?" Easing myself over the edge of the bed, I reach for the shoes and jeans she had tossed onto the floor.

"I can tell you were enjoying it by your expression." She traces cool fingers the length of my back. They feel like talons scratching at my flesh beneath my shirt.

"Sure I was enjoying it. I thought you were my wife." Dragging Levis over my hips, buttoning into them, I confront her squarely, angrily. I'm aware of her face crumpling because she knows how much she has upset me.

Dashurie shrinks from me, appearing almost scared.

"You're a Honey Trap aren't you?"

She regards me, mystified at the question. "Honey Trap? I not understand."

"I bet you don't, sweetheart," I mutter. "Somewhere around here," I pause to scan my surroundings reflectively, "Corrigan has placed some bugs. I couldn't find them before. But I know they are around here somewhere."

"You not like sex with me?" She slides from the bed, as delicately as this beautiful butterfly accomplishes everything else.

"I'm sorry." I adopt a more conciliatory tone, and place a hand against her cheek. "But there is only one woman in my life. I've got so much. I can't take the risk of losing it all. You know how to please a man, but get yourself out of here and find a nice boy your own age. I'm not the man for you, okay?"

In the process of locating my boots, I'm about to slip them on when Dashurie, an expression of unbridled anger negotiating her face, and with an animal-like whimper, flings herself at me. With such ferocity that I am caught unawares. When she rakes my cheek with her nails, I entertain the sensation of blood welling up. I angrily demand the reason why. Touching a finger to the cut, it issues crimson with blood.

"You rejected me!" She wraps the kimono about herself, hugs into it.

A palm dabbing at my bleeding cheek, I rasp for her to get out, but she merely stands there unmoving, before deciding to approach the bed. Stretching a hand to my face, she effects a mock innocence.

"I am sorry, Aidan. I was angry."

"So am I, Dashurie. Just go, okay?"

Aware of her hesitation, my command issues more stridently.

Shrinking from me, she moves to the door. Swiftly yanking it open, she exits, slamming the door behind her.

Guess she'll complain to Corrigan that I've rejected her. But somewhere in this room, though they are obviously well hidden, there are strategically placed cameras. I'm certain of it.

So is that Corrigan's game? To use Dashurie, and others like her, as Honey Traps? For blackmail? What else? Although he fails to admit it, maybe he is aware of all the money that I have in the bank. Therefore is it his intention to film Dashurie and me having sex to show Caitlan, in order to extort money? He knows how much my wife and children mean to me.

I dab at the sliver of blood with a handkerchief. The cut isn't deep, more of a scratch really. I half expect Corrigan, or one of his acolytes to demand the reason why I treated Dashurie the way I did. No one does, however. Slipping the phone from my jacket, I patch through a call to LJ.

Corrigan has obviously laid his intended plans expressively well. The drugged whisky. Dashurie coming onto me.

LJ invariably responds as soon as I call her. Not now it seems. I hear her phone ring, but no LJ. Wary as I am of raising my voice an octave, I hiss, "Please pick up, LJ. Where are you? It's important." There is an unmistakeable crackling noise the other end, as if someone's either snatched the phone away, or maybe she's dropped it. This is our main contact telephone, one that is used solely by the Agency operatives. We are instructed to maintain the phone on our person at all times. So why the hell isn't she picking it up?

Prolonging a resigned sigh, I close the communicator reluctantly, after making a last futile attempt to contact her. Maybe she's out riding. Perhaps she's dropped the phone, and the horse has trampled on it. Or she's in bed with someone, and doesn't wish to be disturbed.

My name automatically comes up on the screen. Maybe she's pissed off with me for some reason. Women don't always let you know when they're angry with you. They just scratch your face. But this is work. Personal feelings shouldn't come into it.

I promise myself, this time, that I'll be prepared for Corrigan. Yanking open the drawer where I keep the Walther, I freeze instinctively. The gun is missing. A further search of the drawers, including the wardrobe, yields no better results. While I was rendered non compos mentis, someone had entered the room and taken the pistol.

Chapter Seventeen

Lady Snow

In spite of being in the throes of a splitting headache, I resolve to vacate the room and ascertain Corrigan's whereabouts. The time is a little after midnight. Maybe the wee bastard's in bed tucked up with Dashurie, thwarted at not reaching a sexual climax with me. But I have vowed that those days are well and truly over, when I involuntarily gave in to my highly-charged sexual urges, and fucked any woman who offered it to me on a plate. Now I have far too much to lose. Having a child does that to a man. The guilt that automatically prevails, because of the way I had turned my back on my son ten years ago.

Making yet another inspection of the room for hidden cameras, although I discover nothing untoward, I fail to contain my unease. I wonder what the drug was that Corrigan had obviously administered in the whisky. Not only has it left me with a throbbing head, which refuses to lessen my temper any, I'm also in possession of an inexorably dry sore throat.

The house appears uncommonly quiet. I descend the stairs with a measured tread, and pause to listen to the various night sounds. Only silence returns my eavesdropping. Although the stairs are carpeted, unwilling to announce my presence, I creep down them minus my boots. Checking my watch, I note that I've been out for more than seven hours. I reason that anything could have happened in that time.

I could use a coffee. Therefore my first port of call is to the kitchen, halting in my tracks when I discover Danny Corrigan. His back turned, he fails to hear my approach. He's wearing a black quilted drape-style smoking jacket with a pair of black trousers. He sits at the large oak table. His hair damp, as if he's recently showered. He snorts the unmistakeable white dust, reminiscent of softly fallen snow, in front of him. So engrossed in his task, he fails to glance up until I say, "Don't you know that stuff fucks up your life, Danny?" with heavy sarcasm.

"Aidan!" He jerks up his head instinctively. "What the fuck?"

My appearance has obviously taken him by surprise, because he manages to spill some of the coke down his clothes. "Do you have to creep about like that?" He brushes at his jacket with irritation, traces of guilty colour negotiating his face.

"Caught in the act, hey? So you snort coke? Why don't that surprise me? So what other drugs are you into? And what the hell did you give me? I've been out over seven hours."

"Maybe you needed your sleep?" he responds nonchalantly.

"Sleep? That whisky was drugged and you know it. And why send Dashurie to try it on with me? She was a fuckin' Honey Trap wasn't she?"

"If you've finished." The erstwhile mask composes once more.

"So what did you put in that whisky, Corrigan? Or has Bushmills developed a new brand?"

"I'm sorry, but I needed..." He attempts an apology of sorts.

"You needed me to keep out of your way. Then to film me with Dashurie. That ain't all. You took something that belongs to me. It's called stealing.

Before he can snort another line, I grab him by the wide lapels of his jacket, and propel him unceremoniously from his chair. Corrigan is slightly shorter than I am. At 6' 2" I tower over him. Irrespective of the power this man ostensibly brandishes, I pummel him hard against the kitchen wall so that he can't help but ouch aloud with the pain, as his back is slammed into it.

"Is this what you're looking for?" The Walther springs immediately into his hand from somewhere in the depths of his jacket and I find myself staring down the barrel.

"Let me go, or I'll pull the trigger. I've released the safety." As to illustrate his intention, his finger crooks in that general direction. I am reluctantly compelled to relax my hands.

"That's better. You've got a powerful grip, so y'have." He adjusts his jacket.The cruel black eyes traverse me with a look I can only describe as self-satisfied, while that glacial smile flirts about his lips once more. "I might have known you'd be carrying a gun, that you wouldn't have come here unarmed." He pauses to examine the weapon, his expression thoughtful. "A Walther PPK. Very James Bond. Is that how you see yourself? As a sort of Irish James Bond? Though from what I've seen of your wee man, you ain't exactly dressed for the part."

"Fuck you, Corrigan," I retort,but have to smile at the comparison. "No I don't see myself as James Bond. I could use a coffee. Then you can tell me why you drugged me."

"Help yourself." Corrigan waves a hand in the general direction of the numerous cupboards.

I recollect my time spent at LJ's home. She'd fixed me coffee. We talked. I discovered she was Leanne's sister. Again I wonder why she hasn't answered her phone. When Corrigan eases a hand behind his collar, I am immediately conscious of the red wheal left by the imprint of my fingers about his throat.

While I wait for the kettle to boil. Corrigan asks if I'd like to try a line.

"I told you that stuff fucks up your life. Where's Dashurie?" For my own peace of mind I avert my gaze from the compelling snow-white trail scattered in front of him.

I wasn't averse to trying cocaine in my late teens. The coke had afforded me a high I have scarcely forgotten. One I had fully intended to experience again, but not in this man's presence.

Sober, I refuse to trust the bastard. Stoned, God knows what might happen.

"She's taking a bath. To wash away your rejection, she says. You're the first one who's rejected her. You notice I didn't say 'man'." Corrigan savours his words. While the lurid black coals scan my face with something that is close to licentiousness.

"What's that supposed to mean in that devious mind of yours?"

"A lot of women are partial to Dashurie. Her beauty is incredible, isn't it? Surely you're not blinded to that? Maybe if you took off that band of gold. Don't tell me a man like you can be faithful to one woman."

"What do you mean, a man like me?"

"Some men only stick with one woman because they can't get anyone else, and vice versa. But people like you, me, Dashurie and my father, can take their pick."

"Sure. I used to be like that. But not anymore. I love my wife and children. Though I don't see as it's any of your business."

Corrigan counters my reproof with a cursory shrug, and an, "it's your life. Dashurie do that to your face did she?" The smile returns in all its self-satisfaction.

I nod affirmatively. He adds, "Sure, if that wee girl can be a wildcat at times."

"You don't have to tell me that." The scratch, already beginning to heal, feels jagged beneath my touch.

"It's okay, it won't fuck up your good looks. Look, Aidan, you're right, she was a Honey Trap. I confess I wanted to film you and her engaging in y'know...." He allows his words to trail, as if he's embarrassed.

The kettle boils. In the process of pouring water into the white china cup, a sudden idea occurs. The boiling hot kettle remains poised momentarily. I reason that I could surely do some damage with that.

As if he has interpreted my thoughts, the Walther springs into his hand, and I am once more staring down the barrel. "You were going to throw the water weren't you? You do that and I'll squeeze the trigger. What will that do to your wee family if you are dead, hey?"

Prolonging a sigh, I pour the water into my cup. My back is turned, unwilling as I am to look at the man with the gun, fully aware that he's volatile enough to pull the trigger anyway. In an endeavour to change the subject away from my immediate demise, I refer to his previous intention to film Dashurie and me having sex.

"I wanted to film a beautiful couple. And you and Dashurie make such a…"

"You're one helluva bastard, ain't you, Corrigan? You said I'm not a prisoner, I can leave anytime." I remind him.

"To return to Treveleyan and report on everything you know about me? Sure y'can. If that's what you want."

Reclining in his seat, he finally returns the Walther to his jacket. After which he begins to rap out a monotone rhythm on the table. His action prompts me to enquire where Pug and Billy are, convinced as I am that he's about to call them.

"They're not here. They're doing a wee job for me, so they are. Nothing for you to worry about. It's just you and me. Sure you can go anytime, Aidan."

"I can't help feel there's a distinct but in that sentence."

"I just need a wee favour first." Once again the word 'savouring' emerges as if it were a delicious meal. An inflection I've come to associate with this man when there's something he wishes to impart that ultimately bodes ill for me.

"A favour?" I echo disbelievingly, and taking a sip from my coffee, I hope he hasn't drugged the Nescafe jar. But the coffee is palatable with no evidence of an undertaste. If only my stomach would cease to churn with both unease, plus the omnipresent anger I can't help in this man's company.

"I won't do you any favours, Corrigan."

"I think you'll do this one."

I round on him swiftly, my senses reeling. The tone of his voice contains a barely disguised sense of intimidation. "Why should I do anything for you?"

The pistol is replaced by a plain white cotton handkerchief, with which he blows his nose.

The black orbs snap wide, and regard me speculatively.

"I want you to bring Sir George Treveleyan to me."

Chapter Eighteen

The Bargaining Tool

The request that I bring Treveleyan to him has me practically choking on my coffee, the way it is in comedies, when someone poses an incongruous question.

Patting the seat next to his, he invites me to join him before I choke myself.

"What the fuck did you expect? Bring Treveleyan to you? Jesus, it would be easier to pluck the moon from the sky. For a start, the guy rarely leaves his apartment. When he does, it's always with Harland, his manservant, as his chauffeur, in his Merc. There's a motorbike escort in tow. The guy lives in fear of assassination. hardly surprising in the kind of business he's in. The only place he goes is to his club. I'm not telling you where that is. You try snatching him, there would be a hue and cry all over the show. He isn't called Sir for nothing. He's been knighted by the Queen." I impishly decide to throw the latter into the mix, aware of his feelings in that direction.

Predictably he mutters, "Anyone that woman's laid her fuckin' sword on should be put up against a wall and shot. Aye, sure I know all that. I know his pals too. A particular one who just happens to be Detective Chief Superintendent Duncan Sandford. I know he and your wee man were at Police College together in the seventies."

Now there's a familiar name. Duncan Sandford. The guy who bought the painting of Leanne Harlow that I had sold while in prison. I had met his daughter Caroline after Laurena was murdered.

"You know I can't do what you ask, Corrigan. For what reason do you want Sir George anyway? Or can I guess? So that you or one of your hirelings can put a bullet in him? So he can be a manipulative bastard, and sometimes I could throttle him myself, but to others he's just a frail old man in a wheelchair."

"There's nothin' fuckin' frail about that wee bastard. His mind is stronger than a man's half his age. It'd be easy for you. All you have to do is enter the Agency premises.

"Night is the best time. Himself has to sleep some time. You must know all the security codes and alarms."

"You're forgetting that Treveleyan has a team of security men all armed to the teeth, and dressed like Ninjas. They are also SAS trained," I tease.

As before, the colour drains from his countenance. Swallowing, it's a while before he speaks again. Aware of the raw nerve I've touched, it's my turn to smile at his obvious discomfort.

"You do it on purpose, don't you? You know that word sets my teeth on edge."

"What word? The SAS? See, they hold no terrors for me. My brother was in the British Army."

"I won't hold that against you. You're not a true McRaney."

"For fuck's sake, I'm a McRaney through and through. My name isn't fuckin' McMartland. So don't start that brother crap again. My mother wouldn't have an affair with a Provo. That's ridiculous. And no way, I'm not going to bring Treveleyan to you, like a lamb to the slaughter. So forget it. Nothing doing, mate. So when are you going to let me go?"

The smile is firmly restored, ultimately conducive to leaving me uneasy once more.

Elbows resting on the table, linking his fingers, he searches my face thoughtfully. He remains like this for what seems an age, making me uncomfortable further. "Oh, you won't refuse me, Aidan," he emphasises so strongly that the uneasiness grows almost tangible. "Sure you'll do exactly as I tell you."

An omnipresent anger washes over me, until it becomes difficult to restrain myself. If I hit him and take the Walther, I won't hesitate to kill him. "I'm not your fuckin' puppet, Corrigan!"

Holding that insidious smile, Corrigan motions at me with a beckoning finger. "Follow me, Aidan. I have something to show you that will make you do everything I ask, as if I really am a puppeteer and you're my marionette."

Observing my hesitation, he indicates with the Walther that I precede him. I manage a reluctant sigh, but add, "Since you and my pistol ask so nicely, I'll go with you. But nothing can make me change my mind. I don't want Treveleyan's death on my conscience. So go on, shoot me, if that's your intention."

"Shoot you? Only as a last resort. You're far too valuable to kill. You don't know how much. You must know it's been Treveleyan's plan all along, for you to infiltrate my affairs. He knew you were Connor McMartland's son."

"I told you I'm not McMartland's fuckin' son. My father is Dermot McRaney. But you're right about one thing: I suspect Treveleyan thought I was McMartland's son."

"He knew that if you came to me that I'd readily accept you. Aye, and I'm pleased to do it. But Treveleyan's wee plan has misfired. You'll bring him to me. You see, you don't really have a choice."

So why do I do as he asks and follow him? A natural curiosity on my part, I suppose. Maybe it is this that compels me other than the presence of the gun. I'm surprised when Corrigan returns to the basement. A place that now serves to hold a veritable sense of dread. It was there that I'd been forced to kill my best friend when he asked.

"So who do you want me to kill now?" I bitterly enquire.

"Don't look so worried. I'm not asking you to kill anyone. Just the opposite, in fact. If you do as I ask, you could be saving someone's life."

All of which leaves me inordinately puzzled. Corrigan's smile parallels the cat who's licked at the proverbial cream. While he savours his words as if they were his favourite dish, he taps on the wooden framework. I hear a man's voice from behind it demand to know who it is.

"Don't be fuckin' funny, Jimmy," he growls. "You fuckin' know who it is. Aidan's here and we'd like to come in."

I wonder why the door is locked. What untold horrors lie concealed behind it? Even with the door closed, there is the unmistakeable stench of putrefying blood, as if the glutinous bodily fluid has seeped into the very surroundings.

"So why have you locked the door? What have you got down there?"

"All in good time." He raises a palm before sweeping the hand through his hair. I'm surprised when it comes away damp with perspiration. "Is everything secure, Jimmy?" he calls through the door.

"Sure it is, Danny." The accent is Northern Irish. Another comrade no doubt.

"So what the fuck's down there, Corrigan? A monster?"

"Hardly," he responds enigmatically.

The door is finally opened. Then only ajar. A man, I judge to be somewhere into his early fifties, appears on the landing. The man's features are heavily gnarled, seasoned with deeply seated crags. In spite of this, his eyes, however, are sharply piercing, as they rake me over with an acute speculation. He wears a crumpled suit that's obviously seen better days. His hair, although marginally tinged with grey, is otherwise quite long and thick, spilling the collar of a grubby once-white shirt.

"This him?" he asks, squinting quizzically in my direction.

I demand to know what all this is about, while a sensation, one that is lethally glacial, manages to trace surreptitious fingers the length of my backbone.

Ignoring me, the man addressed as Jimmy mutters, "I can see the resemblance."

"Resemblance to who? Not this fuckin' brother shit again? I'm not his fuckin' brother," I add, gesturing at Corrigan contemptuously.

"We're not talking brothers here, Aidan."

Jimmy ushers Corrigan and me into the room, while I entertain the sensation of both the Walther jammed into my back and Jimmy's startlingly clear blue eyes, as hard as gemstones, boring into me.

The bed is still there. Poor Dennis's body has thankfully been removed. Only that fetid stench remains. I observe the small figure who squats in a chair in the furthest corner of the room. This time my breath catches because the meagre lighting serves to throw the figure into a watery, unfocussed relief. Because of the tears that involuntarily spring to my eyes. His hands are bound behind him to the chair rungs. Duct tape secures his mouth. The familiar dark forelock of hair falls into eyes that are immediately raised to my face, while tears slither unchecked. He struggles to mouth the one word from behind the gag.

"Daddy."

My heart ceases to function momentarily on witnessing the terror that is reflected on my son's ashen face.

Chapter Nineteen

Jimmy

The bed remains. There has been no attempt to clear away the bloodsoaked sheets. Blood continues to hang fetid and heavy. The glint from those piercing blue eyes is cold and calculating in the depths of the craggy features, serving to intimate the depravity this man is capable of.

I breathe my son's name, while tears wash my eyes. The anger that surges through me is so tangible, that I almost taste it. "That's my son!" I explode, turning my attention back to Corrigan. "What the fuck you done to him?"

I'd enjoy nothing better than to swipe away that infernal smile that continues to play about his lips. Nevertheless, my main concern is with my son. He appears so small sitting there. His child's hands bound to the chair, his feet are anchored to the rungs by rope and tied together. His breathing issues faint and slightly belaboured, as if he is in the throes of a mild asthmatic attack. Although, as far as I know, he has never suffered with asthma before.

I yell at the two men to release him. Oblivious to my own sense of danger, I make a move toward my son, when Jimmy positions himself behind Patrick's chair. "Please release my son." I'm begging now, helpless and consumed with such guilt that I feel physically sick over what I've put my beloved family through these past two years. Feeling sorry for myself I can only wish that I had remained in prison. Perhaps it's where I have always belonged. Only then would my family be safe.

Regardless of my own fate, I reach to remove the tape from Patrick's mouth. The serrated edge blade flashes in Jimmy's hand from the sheath concealed inside his jacket. The scintilla of steel glides across Patrick's throat. His eyes are so profoundly large, terrified in the ashen pallor of his face. I catch a breath, my stomach knotting.

"You come any closer and I will slit the kid's throat. But before that I'll enjoy..." Jimmy allows his words to trail when Corrigan presses a cautionary finger to his lips.

Patrick's still wearing his school uniform. There's a suspicious stain of wetness, serving to indicate that he has peed himself. The two men fail to take a great deal of notice. I demand that at least they change his trousers. Corrigan responds with both a cursory shrug, and a nonchalant, "We don't have anything in his size," as if he's some world-weary shop assistant.

Corrigan leans against the doorframe and inspects his nails. Easing away, he retorts, "Jesus, what do you think this is? A fuckin' creche?"

"You don't have kids do you, Corrigan?"

"Like I said, none that I'll fuckin' lay claim to."

"I hate having to beg to you bastards, but you can't do this to a child. Let him go. I'll do everything you want."

"Sure, I trust you about as much as I trust the Peelers and those fuckin' Brit bastards that have been trampling over our country for the past eight hundred fuckin' years. No, the kid's insurance that you'll do as I ask. And if you don't bring Treveleyan to me, the kid suffers. You'll only have yourself to blame. Oh I forgot to mention that Jimmy's an ex-con too, ain't you, Jimmy?"

The craggy face breaks into the semblance of what passes for a smile. Although it issues more of a grimace in those unprepossessing features. "Aye. Twenty years on and off."

"So is he another of your Long Kesh terrorist pals?"

"Jimmy's no terrorist. That ain't what he was inside for. You see," Corrigan pauses, before savouring his words once more. "Jimmy spent time in prison for kiddie fiddling. As I like young girls, Jimmy's rather partial to young boys, ain't you, Jimmy?" Corrigan licks his lips salaciously. "So how old is he?" He gestures at Patrick. "Nine, ten?"

"He's eleven." My words are frenzied, almost bordering on a hysteria that demands release. Once again my hands manage to wrap themselves about Corrigan's throat. I'm pummelling his head so far back against the wall, I hear the thud of his skull as it connects to the framework. I want to go on slamming his head up against the wall until he's fucking dead.

Now I'm half choking him, so that his breathing issues muffled and strained. His face has transformed to an unhealthy shade of puce. Perspiration beads his brow. A testament to the fear he entertains at the hands of a man who knows how to kill without the use of a weapon.

"I'll fuckin' kill him! Let him go!"

The knife blade catches the light, half blinding me. He threatens to slice it across Patrick's throat. I know he's not bluffing. The man's a fucking paedophile . The words echo and rebound in the reverberating acoustics of the cellar. The sound fills my brain until I entertain the sensation that it will burst right through it.

As if to verify his intention, the gnarled fingers inch toward Patrick's shirt buttons, about to loosen them. My son has little choice than to sit there, frozen immobile in a wasteland of silent, incalculable fear. Raising his eyes to my face he silently implores his daddy to release him, yet I am powerless to do so. The crawling fingers, reminiscent of a poisonous spider, begin to peel the first two buttons.

Uncaring now what happens to me, I rush headlong, blindly, my arms flailing wildly, screaming at this man for mercy, to leave my son alone. "Please, Corrigan. If you believe that I am your brother, then remember Patrick is your nephew. He's my blood. I know how much blood ties mean to you, the same as they do to me. So if there's any pity left in you."

At a signalling nod from Corrigan, Jimmy eases his hand away from Patrick's clothes, albeit reluctantly, judging by the tight expression etching his face at being outdone from his insidious pastime.

"Okay, Jimmy, he's his da after all."

I wonder what Judy would have to say if she could have borne witness to the way our son is being treated. I'm glad she's in America. After this I doubt she will allow me any access at all. I stretch a hand to my son's hair. They appear to allow me this much. Guess it must have struck home my reference to Patrick being Corrigan's nephew. Although a chill rhapsodies my vertebrae when I dare dwell on the fact that someone like Connor McMartland should have been Patrick's grandfather.

I ask Corrigan the obvious question. How he managed to snatch my son.

"Oh, that part was easy enough. I got Billy and Pug to do it when your wee boy was in the school playground. That stupid wee bastard didn't know which was your boy at first. I warned him if he brought the wrong kid I'd fuckin' kill him, but he had a photo. There was another boy with him. He wanted to help when Billy told your son that his dog was missing. An old trick I know, but your wee wain fell for it, didn't he? Then my boys bundled him into the back of the van. The kid put up a fuss, started kicking and thrashing about, just like his da. He wasn't having any of it."

My stomach knotting as I demand to know if they have touched him.

"Apart from tying him up, no. Himself don't just look like you, he's a wee wildcat too, ain't he? He's safe... for now."

"When I do this, bring Treveleyan to you, you'll let us go."

"Just bring the Brit to me. Then, and only then, will we discuss it. Now let's talk about how you're going to do it."

I hazard another uneasy glance toward my son, and to the paedo with further suspicion.

Corrigan says, "Don't worry about Jimmy. He won't touch your wee boy unless something goes wrong, or you do something like contact the authorities. Like I said, your son will pay for your mistakes. Cos once Jimmy's finished with him, the boy will never be the same again."

Chapter Twenty

A Sense Of History

I pace and smoke profusely in Corrigan's kitchen. He too drags on one of his familiar cheroots, reminiscent of the late Ray Lamond.

Corrigan declares that we have to formulate a plan. While a modicum of unease serves to undulate his tone, he observes the wild, raging animal who metaphorically paces his cage. In fact, anger scarcely bears contribution to the way I truly feel. Although I am mad enough to kill, there is nothing that I can possibly do even if I were in possession of a weapon. Corrigan's made that perfectly clear, as he discusses timings, of how the operation has to be conducted with but a ten minute delay. Meaning that if I'm ten minutes later than scheduled in bringing Treveleyan, Jimmy – I learn that his surname is Brennan – will exact certain unspeakable acts on my son. He'll slit his throat no doubt. Perspiration saturating my back has forced me to strip to my tee shirt. I fail to tender a response but continue my agitated pacing, before pausing at the window. Twitching drapes, I peer into the darkness.

Corrigan has cleared the table. A map of Lambeth now replaces the notorious white powder. He scribbles on an artist's pad. "Talk to me, Aidan. Sure, I know you're angry, but you're wearing out the laminate, so y'are. The sooner we get this over with, the sooner you'll be with your wee boy."

I cease my pacing eventually to confront Corrigan. "You'd

better get out of the country when this is over. I don't mean across the water. Australia and New Zealand might not be far enough away. Maybe a deserted island somewhere would be safer. Because I'm mad enough to come after you."

"Don't worry, I plan to get away as far as possible after this. Now tell me about this Agency building in South Lambeth. I need to know the kind of security it has. I reckon that has got to be sewn up pretty tight."

"As tight as Fort Knox. Maybe tighter. You're right about one thing: you'd never get beyond the door before those SAS guys jump you."

"Nothing a wee bit of Semtex wouldn't take care of."

My heart begins to race erratically at what he intimates; I wonder if he can hear it. I have positioned myself behind him in order to study the map. Not to mention within strangling distance. "There'll be no need for explosives. Jesus, I won't be a party to that."

"If you come through there'll be no need for explosives. Besides, I'm not stupid enough to blow up an entire building. I'm only after lifting one man. It's to be done with stealth, not bluster."

"Alright. I know the lay-out pretty well I suppose. The voice-activated security recognises my accent. I know the key codes and the like. No one needs to get hurt."

"You'll be the one going in. Whether or not anyone gets hurt is up to you. I'm guessing there's a few security cameras dotted about the place." His eyes are partially slitted from the cigar smoke. The very atmosphere is laden with both the smoke and the heavily scented aroma of the tobacco. He waves a palm about him indiscriminately in an endeavour to clear it.

"Of course there is. What do you expect?"

"I'm guessing they're CCTV. They record all those who enter and leave the building?"

"Sure they do. So what you getting at?"

"They'll show you were the one who took him out. You'll have to cover your face. And you'll be pushing his wheelchair?"

"No, I'll be giving him a fuckin' fireman's lift. Yeah, course I'll be pushing his wheelchair. The guy can't walk. I still reckon it would be easier to lift him when he goes to his club."

"You know, if I do that, I'll run the risk of getting shot?"

'I think, that's the fucking general idea, Corrigan.' Although I refrain from a response, except to suggest that his plan is a ludicrous one. "I'm already beginning to feel like Judas. As I said, Treveleyan can be a manipulative bastard, but there's no way I wish him dead. Because that's your plan, isn't it? Or is there a ransom involved?"

"Sandford will be contacted. I want a million euros for the safe return of himself."

"A million euros? Fuck me!" I whistle tunelessly, and think of the £800,000 I have in my bank, but only momentarily. That's for my family. For the landscape business I intend to develop, hopefully, once this is over. "You don't do things by halves, do you? Though I can't help feeling the ransom is merely a bonus. I'd like to know that once the ransom is paid, that you'll let Treveleyan go free. Somehow I have my doubts."

"You're a very perceptive man. A lot of our countrymen have died at the hands of the Brits. I'm not just talking about my da in the eighties, but over the years..."

"For fuck's sake, Corrigan," I interrupt, running a hand over my face with exasperation. "Not that old chestnut again. You seem to forget what the 'Rah did to the poor folk they murdered. Innocents. So what other reason can you possibly have for wanting Treveleyan brought to you, other than for a ransom? Has it to do with the history lesson? You should have been a fuckin' teacher."

"It has to do with a man who was crippled with a bullet in his leg, who the Brits forced to stand up against a wall so they could shoot him." At this juncture, Corrigan's lips are clenched so tightly, with his vehemence, they are rendered practically non-existent. "He must have been in so much pain," he adds, shaking his head sadly.

"Well he wasn't in pain anymore if they killed him was he?"

"Do you have to be so facetious, Aidan?"

"Well all this fuckin' history lesson is beginning to get on my nerves. What do you expect?"

"Me to kill you if you disrespect Irish history anymore, so help me I will."

"Yeah, you kill me, and Treveleyan remains where he is. Okay, I'm sorry, I know how you feel about these things, but it's all in the past. Ireland is a multi-cultural country now."

"It was men like James Connolly who put Ireland on the map."

Oh sure it was, Corrigan. With his little gang of rebels throwing their weight around, drawing the attention of the authorities, and getting themselves shot for their pains. Nevertheless, although I won't admit it to Corrigan, I'm not averse to siding with Connolly and the like. If only for the simple reason they lay down their life for their country, and the ideals in which they believed.

"What's Connolly's fate to do with Treveleyan? Because Sir George can't walk? You're not suggesting you prop him up against a wall, and put a bullet in him? To do that would be downright murder."

"Aye, and wasn't it fuckin' downright murder what they did to our countrymen?"

I think, shit, for allowing myself to fall into the ignominious trap of having to suffer another discourse of history.

"Jesus, I wonder where your sympathies lie."

"My sympathies lie with my family. I'm not condoning what was done to Connolly and his little band, but we've moved on since then. Or at least," I add sotto voce, " some of us have." I say it with an element of derision, which appears lost on a man so eaten up with revenge for an event which happened practically one hundred years ago. "What do you intend to do to Treveleyan once Sandford pays up?"

"I shall conduct a court."

"A court?" A sense of unease pervades my insides at his words. "What do you mean? As in trial? You're not suggesting what I think you are? A kangaroo court?"

"If that's what it's called." Corrigan edges. "Where he'll represent all the bastard Brits who have..."

"Now I know you're fuckin' crazy. Jesus, Corrigan, do you know what you're saying, man?"

"Sure I know. And I'm not crazy. Don't you ever say that." He bunches a fist, as if to strike. I'm prepared for it. However, all he does is emit a weary sigh.

"Sure you'll find him guilty of course. Guess that goes without saying. Treveleyan doesn't deserve your blind justice. You don't have the power over life and death, or the jurisdiction to hold this crazy court."

Corrigan holds a mobile phone in his hand. "You've said enough. I told you. I only have to call Jimmy..."

"Okay, okay," I acquiesce with resignation, hands raised, my breath issuing ragged with exasperation. "I'll bring Sir George here. You can conduct your ridiculous kangaroo court, if that's what floats your boat. All I ask is you don't let that fuckin' paedo touch my son."

"That's better." The familiar smile of satisfaction returns. The composure restored. The mobile disappears into his jacket. "Hey, what is it with kids and pregnant women that make a strong man go soft? And y'are a strong man, there's no denying that."

"It's called love, Corrigan. Something you wouldn't know anything about."

Chapter Twenty One

Nightwatch

I leave Billy hunched over the wheel of a stolen Toyota van, a knitted hat plastering the recalcitrant Elvis-style quiff. A cigarette signposts his lip, an omnipresent fixture. I subsequently learned that Billy's surname is Symondy. He is armed, and spares no pains to reveal the big Sig Saur automatic nestling in a holster behind his jacket. To my utter amazement, Corrigan has returned the Walther. What is even more surprising is that the gun remains loaded. "In case the Brit gives you any trouble. Although I prefer him alive, as himself will be useless to me dead, at least for the time being. If you try to turn the gun on Billy, or not return in the scheduled time… well you don't need me to tell you what will happen to your precious wee son."

I enter the Agency building alone. I could of course alert Treveleyan's Security, or contact the police. However, Corrigan's a clever bastard, because he's aware that my hands are tied.

The vast marble floored entrance hall stretches before me. I pause to scrutinise the position of the security cameras. Positioned high into the wall, the cameras are surreptitiously concealed in strategically placed wall sconces. To all intents and purposes, to the untrained eye, they appear as nothing more inquisitive than innocent candles. Because of the presence of the CCTV, in an endeavour at disguise, I too have donned a knitted hat; a bandanna scarf conceals the lower portion of my face.

Thankfully I have encountered no one. Nevertheless it fails to prevent my heart from beating far too erratically. Perspiration forms along my back, until I entertain the sensation that I'm bathed in it. Reaching the lift, I realise that it's going to make some noise as it descends. My only alternative is to use the stairs. All five flights of them.

First the key codes, then the sensitive pad on which I rest first one palm, then the other. After that, the voice-activated machine. This one is affixed to the first inner door. Without the machine recognising your voice, you can never get beyond that. Another key-pad. Similar to the rest of Treveleyan's tight security, the pad flashes a red warning light. This connects to the central alarm system. Immediately this triggers a deafening klaxon-like sound enough to wake the dead. Naturally this brings the security guys. You really don't want to mess with these highly-trained commandos. Not much scares me, except them.

I haven't lied to Corrigan when I explained how these black-clad Ninjas, heavily armed with Enfield SA80 assault rifles are so threatening. Therefore I'm all too conscious of the kind of danger I am putting myself in. Maybe it's thoughts of this. Because when I vouchsafe my name, I listen to the slight tremble present in my voice and hope that I won't be refused entrance. Inestimable minutes later, which feels more like a lifetime, I am told, "Security recognises the voice of Aidan McRaney."

Raking up the scarf once more, I breathe a fraction easier. I console myself that I now have an immediate access to Treveleyan's private suite. First I have to conquer those five long flights, which right now appear little different from the north face of the Eiger. I hope that, not only am I fit enough, but all my physical training as one of Treveleyan's operatives has paid off. I'm doing this for an eleven year old boy. Guilt washes over me, deservedly so, because he's probably blaming his father for placing him in such a predicament.

"Hey, mate, where the fuck do you think you're going?"

My gloved hand hovers over the banister as I stiffen involuntarily at the sound of his voice. I retain my attention on the stairs. They are the old fashion kind, wide and half-carpeted. My back arches. I am all too conscious of the presence of the Walther's cold metal behind my jacket, and wonder if I should afford it daylight. Naturally that depends on my adversary. I half expected him to be similarly clad as the other security guards. On easing myself around I'm further surprised that this guard wears a dark blue uniform. There's a badge denoting him to be a Night-Watch Guard emblazoned on his shoulder. A peak cap plasters his hair, greying wisps peering below the cap, like wiry duck-feathers. His stomach is paunchy, testifying to the later advances of middle age. While the wide leather belt, anchored to his waist, contains nothing more formidable than a night stick and a mobile communicator. Thankfully no gun, or at least none that is visible. His jacket is fastened and smart.

Of course I'll only produce the Walther as a last resort, and hope that it doesn't get that far. My explanation is that I'm one of Treveleyan's agents and I've left something behind upstairs. I didn't want to use the lift for fear that I might wake up either Treveleyan or Harland. My explanation manages to convince him. I add that it's nothing for him to worry about. I tell him to go back to his business, and hope he gets the message.

Instead he fumbles for the night stick, then the mobile. Raising the latter, he moves toward me, threateningly. "I'll have to call security."

"Look, mate, put the phone away. There'll be no need to do that."

"People don't mask their faces just to retrieve something they've left behind." Small, blue orbs squint up at me quizzically, from beneath his hat. "I reckon you're up to no good. Anybody creeping about at this time of the night has got to be reported. It's more than my job's worth." Flicking up the mobile's case, he is about to speak into it. I've obviously not succeeded in convincing him then.

It seems that I'm left with no other alternative. I ease the Walther from behind my jacket, with the realisation that I need further back-up. He finds himself staring into the barrel.

"A gun! You've got a fuckin' gun!" he exclaims, and practically falls over his feet in an attempt to escape its presence.

"You don't report anything, understand? What's your name?"

When he regards me obtusely, I repeat the question more sharply.

"It… it's Freddie. Freddie Watts. What do you fuckin' want to know that for? Why you got that shooter, mate, if it ain't to do some mischief?" His bravado returns a little, although his tone remains wary.

"I'm an agent. I'm allowed to carry a gun."

"But why the mask? What you gotta hide? You look like one of 'em outlaws."

"Yeah, maybe I'm an outlaw."

"Is it… is it a robbery then? You know I only gotta call…"

At this juncture I realise that I have to think quickly. The last thing I intend to do is to fire a shot. Minus the silencer, the sound of a bullet will resonate throughout the building, reminiscent of a thousand jungle drums. It'd mean exacerbating the chance of signing my death warrant. Beside, I am undesirous of injuring a man who's obviously only doing his job. Grabbing the mobile, beneath further protestations, I dash the phone to the floor and crush it with as much belligerence as I can muster, beneath my boot.

"You shouldn't have done that, mate."

"Then you shouldn't have interrupted me," I retort and add another cursory glance at my watch, noting I have but fifteen minutes to get Sir George out of his bed and into the van. The trouble is I hadn't reckoned on being intercepted by an astute security guard.

"Look, Mister… Freddie," I soften my tone. The pistol motions him toward a connecting door.

Aware of his hesitation, I'm compelled to drive the gun into his back. He moves reluctantly ahead, and I open the door that leads into the TV room.

He demands to know why I've put him there, and what I'm going to do. I derisively suggest that he could always watch TV. After all, Treveleyan has a vast collection of the old movies he seems to enjoy.

I am anxious that the moment I leave him the guard will escape and alert Security. I'll find myself forced to the floor by the rifle toting Ninjas, which can only result in leaving my son to the mercies of the ugly paedo.

Having no rope to hand, amidst his further protests that I'll be in trouble when security discover what I've done, all I can do is suggest that he remove his tie.

"You going to tie me up then?" He states the obvious. "Them security geezers will be on you faster than you can piss."

"I don't doubt it, but you're not going to tell them, are you?"

"Anyway," he mocks, "the tie's a clip-on. In this game you don't give anyone a chance to grab…"

"Your belt then," I demand impatiently, gesturing with the Walther at his hesitation. "Come on, I don't have all fuckin' night."

"Alright, alright, keep your bleedin' hair on, Jesse James," he mutters. Sliding out the belt, he hands it to me grudgingly.

I push him into a hard wooden chair and secure his hands behind him to the rungs with the leather.

"And you fuckin' talk too much." After some fumbling around in the guard's clothes, I manage to locate a none too clean handkerchief. Glad I'm wearing gloves, I fashion the handkerchief about his mouth, amid further outcries of how he won't be able to breathe. His eyes begin to bulge with discernible terror when I level the gun inches away from his face.

"You tell them nothing, understand? Or I'll come back and find you, Freddie. And I will use this." I indicate the automatic with a gesturing nod.

Unable to talk, all Freddie can do is nod his agreement.

Chapter Twenty Two

The Judas Complex

Although I am familiar with practically every inch of the Agency building, I have had no occasion to find myself in the Great Man's bedchamber. Another flick to my watch informs me that I don't have much time. Hope the old boy won't give me any trouble. I'd hate to have to render him unconscious.

With all that has occurred, I realise that I have forgotten about Bridget and Caitlan, and either one of them invariably collects Patrick from school if I'm not there. They have obviously realised that Patrick is missing, and has been all night. With what I know about my wife, she'll already have succumbed to paroxysms of both guilt and apprehension because she's supposed to be responsible for her husband's child. Barely ten years older than my son, my wife is still a child herself in some ways. Whereas Bridget is made of sterner stuff, and no doubt will have marched into the nearest cop-shop by now in order to report a missing eleven year old boy.

There is precious little time in which to dwell on that, however. While I have no idea how long the belt, secured about the guard's arms, will hold. He's rather burly, and capable of breaking loose from such a flimsy restriction.

Upstairs, I hear the muted sound of the television. Treveleyan once suggested that a bedroom is for sleeping in and not for watching TV, or those pretentious computer games. Therefore

I deduce the sound emanates from Harland's quarters. The penthouse contains three bedrooms. One has to belong to Treveleyan.

I have less than ten minutes. Time enough to let myself into the room, hoping it is the correct one, I hazard a final glance at the landing. Half shrouded in darkness, the watchful gaze of the oil paintings ostensibly issue a warning from their cold glints. We know what you're up too.

Sir George Treveleyan lies in his bed, snoring sonorously. The trick is not to alert Harland to my presence. An old fashion lamp with fringes remains on, and shimmers with a meagre illumination, throwing the archaic furniture into a shadow-huddled relief. Facing the bed, a large oak wardrobe, patterned with vines and leaves that trail the length of it, while in the wardrobe's heart, a full length mirror. The mirror reflects the man on the bed. Although he snores, at times his breathing develops a sort of rasping, wheezy sound, as if his lungs are tortured. Making me wonder, although it was thirty years ago, how much damage that bullet must have done. It's a wonder he has lived this long. I think of what Corrigan has planned for him, and find myself shivering involuntarily. If only there was another way. I have a gun. Nevertheless, if I should attempt to turn it on Symondy, and he doesn't arrive at the allotted time, I'm aware how inconceivable the danger is to my beloved son.

Adjacent to the bed is a dark oak cabinet, which matches the wardrobe. The unit boasts the lamp and a glass of water in a plastic beaker. A rose patterned tray contains an assortment of pills, mostly painkillers, allowing the guilt to wash over me once more. The old guy on the bed reminds me more than ever of some kindly grandfather. Adjacent to the pills, however, I'm surprised to discover the grandfather's secret bedtime companion is an old Webley revolver. Checking the weapon I discover there are four slugs up the spout. Maybe the gun might come in useful. Aware of Treveleyan's wheelchair by the window, I conceal the weapon in there, covering it over behind a woollen blanket.

Now to wake Sir George. I begin by prodding him, urging that he wake up. He really does appear frail, and I have no desire to break a bone. My dad is ten years older, but even he seems more robust pitted against Treveleyan. I guess thirty years spent in a wheelchair does that to someone.

He finally stirs, murmurs something that sounds remotely like, "What... what is the time, Harland?"

"It's not Harland, Sir, it's me, Aidan."

"Aidan? What?" He blinks his eyes a couple of times,as he makes an attempt to wake. A frown creasing his brow, he scans my face as if with recognition, and I lower the scarf. "Aidan, what are you doing here?"

Much against my better judgement I'm compelled to place a hand over his mouth. Above it, his eyes widen incredulously, while the frown continues. "Keep your voice down. We don't want to alarm Harland, do we?"

"Where is Harland?" His tone fairly bristles with suspicion.

"It's okay. Harland's fine."

Stretching a hand toward the table, Treveleyan fumbles about sightlessly for awhile. I'm fully aware of what it is he's searching for. Unable to locate the weapon he murmurs, "Where's my...?" uneasily.

"Your revolver, Sir George?" At his barely perceptible nod, I explain that I placed the gun in his chair. That I have my reasons at his obvious question. "I didn't know you took a gun to bed."

"With all that's happened to you, don't you then?"

"You don't have a wife who would freak out if I kept a gun on my night table."

"You know I live in fear of assassination. So what are you doing here, Aidan? Has something happened?"

"I can't talk right now, Sir George. But I do have to get you out of here. Your life is in danger." Quick thinking, McRaney. Or is it Judas Iscariot?

"What!" The grey orbs snap wide awake now with incredulity. He pushes himself up in the bed. For the first time I clock that he wears one of those old-fashion nightshirts. The kind I believed had gone out at the turn of the century. The 20th that is. If I wasn't quite so anxious over my son, then the situation would be oddly laughable, because Treveleyan reminds me of Scrooge, the way the Dickensian character is invariably portrayed on TV and in the movies. The same grey beard, the nightshirt wrapping his scrawny body. Certainly a far cry from the formidable Agency boss.

"Corrigan. Is it Corrigan?"

All I can do is respond with a nod.

"Is Corrigan planning to kill me? Have you escaped? And LJ, where is LJ? I haven't been able to raise her. Do you know if she's alright?"

"I don't know, Sir. I'm sure she's fine."

"What about Harland?"

"No one must know but you and me. You can't tell Harland. Look, I'll help you into your chair. Wrap the blanket around you."

"What about my clothes?"

"You don't have time to dress."

"Where are we going?"

A good question. Guilt overwhelms me that I'm putting this man's life in jeopardy. However, when I think of the frightened boy, helplessly bound and gagged in the filthy cellar, at the mercy of a heinous paedophile, I reason that I have little choice.

An old man or a little boy.

He pats my hand affectionately, informing me that I'm a good boy to display such consideration for his life. How he considers me the son he never had. If only he knew.

Treveleyan really is quite helpless, although he is capable of walking a few yards, and makes it from the bed to his wheelchair. I help him into an outmoded green wool robe. It's the least I can do. It is now a little after one. The air is piercingly cold. Wracked with guilt, I bundle the blanket about him. Afterward I commence a search of his wardrobe, to regard the collection of uniform grey suits inside, with derision. Each suit is fashioned from grey flannel. One for each day of the week no doubt. Five grey marl pullovers. Plain white or grey shirts. Dark blue, black and grey ties. In the process of my search, Treveleyan wants to know if we are going to a safe house. I lie that we are.

"You know I trust you maybe more than I trust most of my operatives. You and LJ of course."

My heart sinks at his kindly words. I long to confide the real truth of where we are going, and why. If I do, however, and Corrigan discovers it, my son will be irretrievably lost to me.

Chapter Twenty Three

Betrayal

I help Sir George into his chair and I fuss over the blanket that's wrapped around him, and I ascertain that he's comfortable. I check his comfort for two reasons. Firstly I'm so wracked with guilt because I've led him into a trap, plus the Webley is there. The last thing I intend is that Symondy should be aware of it.

It's practically 1:30 in the morning; Treveleyan is fully awake and apparently intent on conversation. Resting a liver-spotted hand onto mine, he refers to the fact that no other operative would be so considerate of his life. He tells me how he wished that I really was his son. While I think that I seem to have enough fathers already, idiotically. That I was a 'a young man to be proud of'.

"We had our differences at the beginning, but that's all water under the bridge now. The impetuousness of youth." He spoke of how, before he was crippled at 28, and, "confined to this monstrosity," he mouths between clenched lips. He was quite impetuous too. "Hard to believe now of course." His tone is a poignant one before changing the subject, and enquires where the safe house is.

"I can't tell you that. Not right now. It's best if we keep it a secret." Truthfully, I have no idea of the location myself. I have my doubts that we'll return to Maze Hill. I could have left a note for Harland. But if I had, the manservant would in all likelihood contact the police. Heaven only knows what fate might befall my son if the law should be swarming all over the place.

"Of course," he agrees, but there's a thinly-veiled suspicion in his voice. A suspicion that increases when he enquires why I feel it necessary to mask my face.

"Because of the cameras. It's best whoever looks at them shouldn't know who has taken you out. This has to be conducted covertly. You should know that better than anyone, Sir."

"Well that's as maybe, but I am pleased for anyone to know the identity of the man who saved my life. There could be a knighthood in this, you know, my boy."

Sir Aidan and Lady Caitlan. Oh she'll love that, although I reason that Sir Judas might be more appropriate. No wonder he killed himself. The old boy trusts me to such an extent that it's becoming almost painful with this overwhelming guilt, so that I ache to confess the truth.

Thankfully he changes the subject, and enquires if I've seen Mrs Allardyce.

"No, Sir. I tried calling her. But she didn't pick up. Maybe I've pissed her off or something."

"LJ is a professional. She allows nothing to interfere with her work. You should know that, Aidan. The last I heard from her was that she had a lead on something she intended to follow up. I called her house. Her brother answered. He was quite rude you know. You ever meet him?"

"I met Luke once. He seemed okay." Although he certainly displayed his dislike of Treveleyan.

The lift finally bumps ground. The solitary ping as the door opens sounds, in the unutterable stillness, like a thousand bells all ringing at once. I stiffen, hoping it hasn't alerted Treveleyan's team of Ninjas.

We arrive at the entrance hall and he wants to know where Freddie is.

"Freddie?" I feign innocence,

"Fred Watts, the night security. He's a friend of Harland's. They were in the Army together. I know he's only one man, but Freddie knows how to take care of himself."

But not as well as you think, Sir, I consider.

"Can't say I've seen him," I lie, and hope simultaneously that we'll make it out of there before Freddie manages to slip his moorings.

"I should have told Harland where I was going. I'm worried about him."

"There was no need. He isn't the target. Look, I'll make certain he knows once we get there. I'll call him myself." How effortlessly the false promises slip from me. I observe Treveleyan attempt to suppress a shiver. Further adding to the guilt that has become almost a physical pain.

"You haven't told me much."

Do I detect an element of suspicion in his voice?

"Corrigan wants me dead? I know all that. I know enough about that man to understand that I'm just one of the Brits he has on his kill list. So you have a vehicle?"

" A...a van. It's outside."

Conscious as I am that he will pick up on my hesitation, Sir George Treveleyan is an excessively astute individual. Maybe all the questions he tosses at me are deceptively probing, rather than in an attempt at simple conversation.

I'm in the process of punching in the security codes, and tender our voice patterns. Sir George asks me what the point of the mask is when I've just furnished security with my name.

A good question. So get out of that one, McRaney. Like a bird awaiting a crumb, Treveleyan expects a suitable response.

"You know your policy, Sir. That we don't meet other operatives because of the undercover work. Not everyone knows my name, but they may know me by sight."

"I've obviously taught you well."

Reaching the outer doors, I pause. I pretend to straighten his blanket once more. As before, I possess the urgency to confide the truth. The way he has about him, when those perspicacious grey eyes lock mine, is like an attempt to interpret my thoughts. I wonder if he realises that I'm about to betray him. I turn away, straightening to my full height as the doors swing open, letting in the cold night air. Once again I catch him shiver and I wrap the blanket tighter, while he murmurs a grateful, "Thank you, my boy."

So no security. Our movements remain unimpeded. I'm intrinsically aware, however, that all Treveleyan has to do is to press the button located in the arm of his wheelchair and I'll find myself surrounded. A semblance of relief is only allowed to wash over me when we finally make it outside. Lowering the scarf, I roll and ignite a much needed cigarette. With the smoke in my mouth, I wheel the chair toward the waiting van.

Symondy remains hunched over the wheel, drumming gloved fingers impatiently. Clocking our approach, and discarding his cigarette, he jumps agilely from the van.

"You took your fuckin' time, McRaney," he growls irritably, and checks his watch. When his gaze travels over Treveleyan, a cynical smile appears on his face. "This himself then? He ain't nothing like I expected."

Before I can tender a response, Treveleyan indignantly exclaims, "Aidan, who is this?" He obviously looks to me for an explanation. "I thought you were alone. This man is Irish. What is he to do with this?"

"I'm sorry, Sir George..." I allow my words to trail, while I can't help but lower my head shamefacedly, sickened to the stomach.

"Who are you?" Sir George addresses Symondy. Now I detect a semblance of unease in his voice.

"What the fuck has it to do with you? You ain't nothing but a fuckin' wee Brit bastard. Just get him in the van."

"Fuck you!" I hiss, and move to assist Sir George, who's already blustering his demands and asking what the hell is going on. All the while his right hand hovers over the button located under the arm of his wheelchair. Symondy has no knowledge of its existence of course.

Thankfully I do. When a slender finger inches in that direction, I reluctantly warn him against it with a gesturing nod. Sir George directs me the cold reproving stare of a man betrayed by someone he believed he could trust.

I am left to assist him into the back of the van. While Symondy, holding his gun over us, demands I return the Walther. Prolonging a sigh of resignation, I ease the weapon from behind my jacket. Passing the gun butt first, his reaction is somewhat nervous, as if he imagines I might turn the pistol on him. Oh I would believe me, if my son's life weren't at stake.

Sir George wants to know if I'm working for them now. I emphatically explain that I am not.

"For pity's sake! Don't you know who I am?" Treveleyan, an element of composure seemingly restored, turns his attention back to Billy Symondy.

"Aye, we know who you are alright. That's why you was snatched."

"So you're Irish. What's this, the Real IRA?"

"Not anymore. This is a new faction." Symondy retorts, but without elaborating. His tone is no less irritable. "And don't listen to McRaney. He's one of us now. He's a fuckin' Irish Catholic, ain't he?"

Maybe I'm feeling too tired to protest my innocence, to try and convince Treveleyan that I'm doing this under duress.

Symondy slides into the driving seat. I join Sir George in the rear of the van. At least he's allowed him to remain in his chair. Treveleyan has fallen ominously silent, his head lowered. He refuses to look my way, which only serves to fuel the guilt. Occupying the seat facing him, uncaring of Symondy's presence, I have to explain that I'm certainly not one of them. "They're holding my son," I blurt.

"They're what!" The grey eyes widen, first in astonishment, then disbelief. "I'm the one who got you into this. Now they have your son. Oh, Aidan…" There's such a poignancy underlining his words that I half expect him to break down. "I'm so sorry."

"Jesus, can't you two fuckin' bastards shut up? You'll have me in fuckin' tears in a minute." Symondy guns the van's engine ruthlessly. "Och, almost forgot. Boss's orders."

I had initially noticed there was a grubby sort of bag on the front seat. Symondy tosses the 'bag' at me now. I demand to know what it's for.

"Hood him."

"What the fuck?" I gasp, astonished. "You can't…"

"I can, and I fuckin' will. And no back chat from you, McRaney. Remember that kid of yours. Right now Jimmy's just waiting to get a crack at his…"

"Fuck you, you bastard!" I'm out of my seat, and flailing my arms at him angrily. My gaze drops to the Webley concealed in the blanket Sir George is sitting on. Catching my intention, however, Treveleyan swiftly blinks a warning look. "So help me!"

"You lay a finger on me, McRaney. I only gotta call Mister C. We've spent enough time jawing. I told you to hood him."

"Another thing." I return to the hard wooden seat reluctantly.

"What the fuck's that?" Symondy swings the Toyota out of the drive. I hear the crunch of gravel beneath the wheels. Street lighting picks out Sir George's features, which are partially shrouded in shadow, serving to accentuate his already ashen pallor. I can't help my heart going out to him.

"I'm sorry, Sir George," I placate him with as much conciliation as possible. I feel every struggle that emanates from his paralysed body when he allows me to slip the hood over his head. I enquire if he is okay. Initially he fails to respond. I guess that maybe he's angry with me. Once again I apologise for my actions. Only when I repeat my question, he nods his head, a grotesque figure beneath the grubby hood.

"My family, my sister and my wife. Either one will go to collect my son from school. I imagine by now they will have contacted the cops, to report a missing eleven year old boy. Don't you think?" I turn my attention back to Symondy, my voice dripping sarcasm.

"You don't need to worry about stuff like that."

"If you've touched any other members of my family, you bastards will be fuckin' sorry."

"They're quite safe for now."

"What the fuck's that supposed to mean?" I crush my cigarette vindictively into the dusty van floor.

"It means that Danny told the school, and your sister, you had taken your son out for a while. You had gone to Ireland."

Rage surges through my insides at what he intimates. "Jesus! To Ireland? For fuck's sake, surely they knew the call wasn't from me."

"Don't you think Danny can't fake a Dublin accent? It's all set up you see. Your precious family think you've taken your kid to Ireland. There's no need to tell the Peelers now is there ? Danny was pretty convincing."

All I can do is to prolong a resigned sigh, lapse back against the cold interior, and close my eyes. All the while an unerring disregard for my own safety is enough to plunge me into a maelstrom of revenge and the prevalent desire to kill.

"And you, McRaney." Symondy's reedy voice breaks into my retrospections. "The scarf you're wearing."

"What about it?"

"Wrap it around your eyes."

"What the hell for?"

"So you won't see where we're going, course."

"I can hardly do that. I'm sitting in the back of the van."

"But you can still see out of the back of the van."

"So we heading back to Maze Hill?"

"Sure, right where they can find us? No, we gotta nice place lined up. Now cover your fuckin' eyes. I'm losing patience with you. See, I only gotta make a call…"

"Okay, okay." I reluctantly acquiesce and bind the scarf around my eyes.

Every sound magnified now, in the interim stillness of the night.

Billy Symondy's grating voice. "That's better, McRaney. Now you fuckin' bastards don't know where we're going."

"My son, will he be there? Wherever we're going," I dare to enquire.

"Sure he will. He's the insurance you'll do everything that's asked of you."

"Haven't I done that already?"

My only response, however, is the noticeable silence. A silence punctuated only by Sir George Treveleyan's erratic, belaboured breathing.

Chapter Twenty Four

Destination Unknown

I'm robbed of sight. All I can hear, despite the muted sounds of the night and the incessant rattle of the van, the one sound predominant above all else: Sir George Treveleyan's shallow breathing. I note the way it appears to crescendo, until his breathing is the only viable sound, with its almost guttural resonance. He's not as young as I am.

I suggested to Symondy that I would wear the hood, that Sir George might be better off with the blindfold. I receive a grudging response of, "Mister C don't want you to be inconvenienced more than you have to be. That's his words, not mine. For some reason he trusts you, fuck if I know why."

I imagine that I hear Sir George mutter something which sounds like, "I know why," but can't be certain.

So we lapse, at Symondy's suggestion, into silence. I would have preferred to have spoken, say anything, even nonsense. Simply because that breathing seems to have increased in dominance, until I am unable to concentrate on anything else that takes my mind off it. That somniferous breathing reminds me of a story I had once read. Of a man who had a late night visitor. It transpired that the visitor passed away during the night. Long after the body was removed the man continued to hear the breathing emanating from the room where his friend had stayed.

We must have finally arrived at our destination, because the van shudders to an unexpected halt. I hear the door squeal open. There's a smell that's easily detectable as fish. I wrinkle my nose. Definitely fish.

"We're here, gents," Symondy declares with alacrity.

"Where is here?" I ask.

Predictably the question fails to extract a response from the taciturn Symondy. I raise a hand toward the scarf to untie it when he snaps, "Not yet. I want you inside first. I'll guide you."

The van shudders a fraction as he jumps aboard, grabbing my arm.

"It's okay. I'll make my own way, so just fuckin' get off me. Just take that hood off Treveleyan. He has trouble breathing. He's not a young man."

In the wake of the van's engine being shut off, I realise that the breathing has become stilted, a little less predominant. I stretch a palm to his shoulder, enquiring if he's okay.

"He's still alive if that's what you're worried about," declares Symondy. "Hi Pug." He's obviously joined by the fat man. "You brought him then? The Brit."

"Aye, I brought him."

I move to where I figure the rear of the van is located.

"You alright, McRaney?" Pug wants to know. Although I can't see him it isn't difficult to deduce that the fat man is chewing food from the distortion of his speech.

"How the fuck do you think I am? Cramped up in that van, unable to see. So where are we?" I ask. Although I sense the question hangs loosely on the air. Nevertheless I'm certain that's definitely fish that I can smell, but not fresh fish. The air practically reeks of the stale odour. The cold is sharply piercing, that I feel it permeate into my bones. There's even the lonesome cries of circling sea birds. I want to know if we're close to the sea.

"Sort of I suppose," Pug mutters, only to be contradicted by Symondy.

"This ain't exactly the fuckin' sea. Just some out-of-the-way Brit shithole, but it's the perfect spot. Mister C had all this well planned. He's good at that."

"Is this Romney Marsh?" Treveleyan asks.

"It ain't called Romney," Pug replies. "It's K..." His words are swiftly interrupted by Symondy. Although I'm quick enough to pick up on Pug's reference to the single letter 'K'.

Possibly Kent then.

"Shut your fuckin' mouth, you fat bastard," barks Symondy irritably. "And what the fuck you eating now? You're always feeding your fat face."

"It's a scone. What's wrong with that?"

I hear the rumble of the wheelchair. Symondy grumbling that the fucking thing needs oiling. The wheelchair squeaks protestingly. The two men start swearing at it all over again, because the wheels seemed to adhere to the kind of ground I can but describe as shingle. If only I could see. My senses, however are overly acute, and I tense when Symondy suggests lifting Treveleyan from the chair. If they do, the pistol will be discovered.

Judging by the stench of stale fish, maybe lobster or crab, the piercing coldness, this is some kind of seaside resort. Pug almost gave it away that we are in Kent. Ramsgate maybe, or Margate. Alternatively, there remains an absence of the normal kind of sounds a seaside town invariably produces.

If this is a seaside town, then isn't there a distinct possibility that we'll be discovered. A Brit shithole, Symondy had described it. Guess any place in England, with someone of Symondy's proclivities, could easily be described that way. Therefore we could be anywhere.

I pride myself on knowing Kent quite well. Not quite a seaside town, and yet the smells are notably similar. The cry of seagulls. That familiar fishy smell. As if it were a while there has been any fishing. Definitely shingle. The crunch hard and faintly slippery beneath my boots. If I had to hazard a guess, I would suggest that we weren't too far from Dover. I was recollecting the nights I had driven Frankie Lamond to the docks to intercept the infamous drug dealers with whom he would rendezvous.

Innumerable raps on a wooden framework are cautiously delivered before I recognise Corrigan's growl, "Who the fuck is it?"

"It's us, Mister C. Danny. We got him."

"Well fuckin' come in. And Aidan?"

"He's here too," Symondy replies.

"Where else would I be?" I interject bitterly. "You're holding my son."

"You can go in now," Pug mutters. I find myself pushed inside, but not without a retaliatory retort of, "Don't fuckin' touch me. I'm going. Let me take off this blindfold, for fuck's sake. You'd better not have hurt Sir George or my son."

"They're safe for now." It is Corrigan who responds. "You can take off the blinkers I'm sorry about that, but just in case you manage to escape or tell anyone then you won't know where we are."

On the removal of the scarf, adjusting my eyes, I'm allowed an initial sight of my surroundings. It is now early morning. Pre-dawn. Already fleeting grey shadows hit the grimy, once white plaster. After the grandiose abode of Corrigan's Maze Hill residence, the place is, surprisingly, more descriptive of a hut. Rough and faded gingham curtains embellish a less than aesthetic addition to the grimy fly-specked windows. The furniture is mottled and sparse. A shabby green sofa occupies a dingy wall, while a low ceiling, grossly stained with damp, accommodates a shadeless low wattage bulb.

Sir George is wheeled in, and the hood subsequently removed. I'm astonished to observe that the men are wearing camouflage uniform. The addition of holstered pistols anchored to webbing belts, girthed about their waists. Despite my predicament I can't fail to sarcastically remark, "So what's this? Fancy dress, Corrigan?"

His features remain impassive, however. Unlike Symondy who raises a hand toward my face, his lips clenched whitely at my facetiousness. I hiss, "Don't even think it," at him.

Symondy lowers his hand reluctantly, but only at Corrigan's command that he mind his manners.

"So this is a wee bit of a comedown from what you've been used to, isn't it?"

Scanning the room I note there is another partially glimpsed through an archway.

"It suits our purposes," Corrigan says.

I demand to know where my son is, but entertain an already surfacing anger when the smile returns to Corrigan's face. It is one I could so easily swipe off. Not while my son's life is at stake of course.

"Calm down, Aidan. He's fine for now." The black eyes zero in on Sir George Treveleyan. The blanket remains wrapped about his knees, making me wonder how comfortable he might be because of the Webley's presence. Sir George is aware that I'll be the one to use it at the opportune moment. Admittedly there's only four bullets up the spout, but enough to blow these bastards away. Hence the presence of the gun serves to fuel my bravado.

Treveleyan's pallor has grown ashen. His hands, resting on the blanket, appear to tremble slightly. Only the intensity of the grey orbs return Corrigan's stare as formidable as before. "Now you've had me brought here, you can let Aidan and his son leave. You don't need them anymore." Those same eyes bore into Corrigan's with their familiar perspicacity. Treveleyan has a way about him, one which is capable of influencing others. He has often tried it with me, as if hypnotically drawn into their depths. Corrigan, averting his gaze, snaps, "I'm the one giving the orders around here, Brit. You think I'd let them leave to tell the authorities?"

"You surprise me, Sir George Treveleyan." Corrigan stands over his chair. The man is crippled. I hadn't realised how badly until I was compelled to assist him the relatively short distance from the bed to his chair. His lower limbs are totally useless. The guilt assails me as an almost tangible entity. So the old boy can be a manipulative bastard at times, but he scarcely deserves this treatment. That cruelly glacial smile lingers about Corrigan's mouth leads me to conclude that it bodes ill for the Agency boss.

"Why should I do that, Corrigan?" There is a surprising strength behind Treveleyan's words. Initially he'd displayed an understandable fear. Somehow, unless it's the presence of the gun under his blanket. Because all his erstwhile trepidation seems to have disappeared, reflected in the intensity of the grey orbs as they move over the three men.

I position myself in close proximity to Treveleyan's chair. Not that I dare try anything at this stage, not when that ugly paedo is holding my child hostage.

"Cos I heard you was a powerful wee bastard. You just look like a frail old man to me."

"Appearances can be deceptive, Corrigan," I interject.

"What the fuck's that supposed to mean?" hisses Symondy, bringing his face up close to Treveleyan's, both hands pressed onto his wheelchair arms.

"Nothing, nothing," I shrug, much against the better judgement that wills me to start an argument. In truth, I'm not afraid of these men. It's what they can do that scares me. With the threat to my son's life, hanging like the sword of Damocles over my head, I'm powerless to do anything. While the ache to wrap my hands about Corrigan's throat grows ever stronger.

Instead, I avert my attention to the grey walls and the way the early morning sun struggles to penetrate the grimy windows. The curtains are practically diaphanous. Enough to allow me a meagre insight to the desolation beyond.

"Now can I see my son?"

"All in good time, Aidan. I told you he's fine," Corrigan offers.

"He'd better be, or so help me, Corrigan... I'm not going to be palmed off. I want to know for certain that that bastard hasn't touched him. Cos if he has..."

I can't help it when my temper asserts itself. I'm aware that my anger is clearly visible, because Treveleyan's hand is latching my wrist. He counsels, "Not now, Aidan."

Except I no longer care. My son's life is threatened, and damn Corrigan for holding out on me. For the second time my grip around Corrigan's larynx is one that I barely realise. Sometimes I'm not always aware of my own strength. Although I'm fairly wiry, I'm athletically muscular, certainly enough to beat the crap out of Corrigan. I bounce him unceremoniously up against the wall. I feel the impact as his head makes contact with the plaster, regardless of the stunned expressions of the others. Neither Pug or Billy make any moves to rescue their leader. From my peripheral vision I'm aware of their expressions filling with fear.

"For fuck's s...sake," Corrigan gasps as if it were his last breath. "Get... get the kid."

"Do as he says. Now!" I rasp at the two men, who continue to stand there, unmoving. "I will fuckin' kill him, do you understand?"

Symondy moves from my periphery finally. I assume it's to fetch Patrick.

Nevertheless, while the inherent anger remains with me, I continue to feel the flesh of Corrigan's throat beneath my fingers as they endeavour to close off his final breath. A strategic squeeze and he's a dead man. He continues to struggle, to free himself from the iron grip. One hand attempts to pull mine away. The other fumbles for the gun at his waist. Intercepting his action, I grasp his hand, pushing it belligerently against his chest, restraining him. The man who's all bluster and history is seemingly powerless against my strength. He begins a strangled plea for his life. His reassurance that Patrick is fine falls on deaf ears as far as I'm concerned. Only when I see my son, will I be satisfied that he's okay and I'll release him.

I barely hear the softest footfall behind me. I don't even have time to turn before something indefinably sharp and piercing is thrust into my right shoulder. I can but emit a cursory exclamation of pain, and turn to confront, with something akin to disbelief, Dashurie. The Albanian girl's eyes are darkly chill, her lips tight, almost shrewish. All I can recollect is the blue colour of her dress, which is oddly tinged with a blurry edge. In fact everything appears to have developed the same white, blurred outline. As my strength ebbs simultaneously I loosen my grip about Corrigan's throat, before an unaccustomed blackness overwhelms me.

Chapter Twenty Five

The Ransom

The darkness has passed. I wonder how long I've been out. Judging by the throbbing pain that emanates from my right shoulder I had succumbed to some kind of sleeping draught, administered by injection. My momentary glimpse of Dashurie indicates that she was, in all likelihood, the one who gave it to me.

I discover that I'm sitting in a high backed chair. My hands, stretched out in front of me, are manacled to the arms. "What the fuck is going on?" I listen to the roar of urgency, admixed with desperation in my voice. "Fuckin' untie me, Corrigan, you bastard!"

Whenever I make an attempt to ease my wrists free of the manacles, they only succeed in cutting deeper. The manacles are attached, like bracelets, to each wrist. They're fashioned of a gunmetal grey, about five inches wide. My wrists hurt like hell with each attempt to break free. It's then I realise that the manacles are locked.

To hopefully take my mind off my position, I pause to survey my surroundings. I observe that this particular room is a basic dining area. There's a wooden table, plus four similar chairs to the one I'm tied to, pulled up at the table. The table top is layered with a fine film of dust, and set for three places.

I realise that Treveleyan is in the room. Seated in his chair, his head is lowered and he clutches the blanket draped over him tenaciously. "You okay, Sir George?" I enquire, unable to keep the guilt from surfacing in my voice. "At least you're still alive."

"It would seem so, at least for now." Grey eyes rise to my face forlornly.

"Where are they?" I whisper.

"Seems we are to be served dinner." His gesturing nod indicates the spread table.

"Or we are to be dinner." I make a feeble attempt at humour, to which Treveleyan reacts with both an uneasy smile and a tightly clenched mouth.

"Sorry. Guess it just popped into my head."

"Our Mr Corrigan might be a lot of things, but I think even he would draw the line at cannibalism."

"So why the fuck am I manacled to a chair?" I make another futile attempt to wrest my hand free.

Judging by the drizzle of blood seeping down my arm all I've managed to do is to lacerate my wrists.

"Because you tried to strangle me again." It is Corrigan who responds. He appears by my side as if teleported. "Jesus, you're a strong man. We could use you on our side. You're like a bloody grizzly when you're angry, ain't you? The sleeping draught in the needle was the only way to calm you down."

"So where did you get the drug from? Nick it from a hospital, did you?" I ask sarcastically.

"You've guessed right. Midazolam. You've been out for several hours. Any side affects?"

"Fat lot you care, Corrigan. I feel sick if you must know."

"It'll pass if you stop screaming and shouting. The drug was enough to restrain you."

"Well I'm fuckin' restrained now."

It's odd, but do I detect Corrigan's discomfort? He's sweating, and the room isn't particularly warm. A semblance of perspiration beads his brow, over which he runs a spotlessly white handkerchief.

Nevertheless, he is not the kind of man to lose equilibrium quite so readily.

I have been stripped down to my jeans. My chest is bare. My boots and socks have also been removed. Obviously Corrigan intends for me to freeze.

"What the fuck you done with my clothes, Corrigan?"

"It's cold out there. You try getting away..."

"I'm hardly likely to do that am I?" I manage to elevate a hand slightly in indication.

"I'm still not prepared to take any chances. You're a formidable man, Aidan. I hadn't realised how much until now."

Corrigan sports a green paisley cravat at his throat. One which appears oddly incongruous with the camouflage. Easing the former aside, he adopts a suitably pained expression. The holstered pistol remains anchored, to where he follows my gaze.

"Oh you'd like that wouldn't you?" Corrigan smiles evilly. How this man enjoys savouring his words, and delivers them as if they practically trip over themselves. "Oh, we found this." Whereupon he pauses to open a drawer in the table, and the Webley appears, as if by magic, in a gloved fist. "Bringing a gun with you. How fuckin' stupid do you think we are?"

At which point, Sir George portrays the look of a man who's been told he has a terminal illness. He passes a hand over first his beard , then his eyes. No longer the man I have come to know all these months. The kindly grandfather or the staunch leader of men. He is none of these things, simply a defeated old man. His last vestige of hope, in the shape of the old Webley revolver, is diminished. When Corrigan crashes the back of his hand hard against Sir George's face, I am swift to retaliate about leaving him alone, particularly when Treveleyan gasps for his pills. The ones I did not fail to bring with me.

I duly inform Corrigan that they can be found in the wheelchair. Sir George places a hand to a rapidly reddening cheek, the grey eyes blazing with a venomous light above it.

Locating the bottle of pills, Corrigan, unscrewing the lid, empties the pills into his hand. I figure at least Corrigan does possess a small element of compassion in his make-up. Sir George requests a glass of water with which to take the pills.

Corrigan waves the small white tablets before Treveleyan. Curling his fingers over his palm, his face a vindictively clenched line, he crushes the pills belligerently within his gloved hand.

"No! No! Oh my God, I have no others." Sir George makes a vain attempt to rise from his chair.

"You fuckin' bastard, Corrigan!" I yell at him, angrily commence to kick around in the chair, as if by some miracle, the manacles will sever. But all I can do is lapse back against the headrest with both a painful shoulder, plus two sore and bleeding wrists. "What the hell did you do that for? He has a heart condition. Jesus, don't you have any fuckin' compassion in you at all?"

"Compassion for a Brit?" he scoffs. "Fuck off."

The last remaining ounce of bravado Treveleyan ever entertained had deserted him now. A bowed and broken man, I ache to comfort him, placate that we'll escape from this situation somehow. That I'm so sorry I should have got him into this in the first place.

"I need you to make a phone call," Corrigan addresses me nonchalantly. As if a man's distress, the likelihood of him having a heart attack, is of precious little consequence.

"I can hardly do that can I? In case you haven't noticed I'm a wee bit restrained right now."

"Don't worry, I've figured that out."

"Then you'll release me?" I dare to ask.

"Don't be fuckin' stupid. So you can attack me again like the wild animal y'are? So why don't you just keep quiet? The more you try freeing yourself, you'll only make your wrists bleed."

"I'd figured that out for myself," I retort. "So if you don't like me screaming at you, why don't you fuckin' gag me? Be done with it."

My question merely counters a shrug, however. "There's no point. Anyway, you can scream and shout all you want, no one will hear you out here."

"Where's here anyway?"

"All I'm saying is it's a wee desolate spot. That's all you need to know."

"In Kent?"

"Don't push me, Aidan, or you'll get the same as your wee man here."

"Fuckin' bring it on, you bastard. It's not that I haven't had my face smacked before. Anyway, this phone call. A ransom is it?"

"So who are you going to ask for the ransom?" Treveleyan asks. "But you won't get far, you and your cohorts. No matter where you run."

"Shut the fuck up, you wee Brit bastard. You want another one?" Corrigan raises a hand to strike again, until I tell him to leave him alone. "Can't you see he's had enough?"

The hand is finally lowered, albeit reluctantly. "Sir George fuckin' Treveleyan. What the shit did you do to be knighted? Nobody ever knighted us."

"They don't knight murderers, Corrigan," I interject.

Once again the familiar semblance of humour rises from him. "Oh sure they do. What they did to our people in Ireland, they were only defending what was theirs from the British Invasion. That MRF? What the fuck was that but a murder squad?"

I mutter, "Not that again." Something that Corrigan is swift to pick up on. He levels a leather encased finger in my direction. His gaze is downcast, surmounted by that low, overhanging brow.

"And you, Aidan. You know you're a fuckin' traitor, both to your faith and your country. And you know what we do to traitors."

"And it's people like you, Corrigan, who make me sometimes wish I wasn't an Irishman."

Where that came from I have no idea. Except, maybe it's

because Corrigan and his fucking history lessons are beginning to piss me off.

"That sounds like traitorous talk to me," Corrigan retorts with blazing eyes.

"Please, please, gentlemen..." Treveleyan opts to intervene. Corrigan paces the floor, his lips pursed, his expression one of disdain. "You're both grown men. No one's a traitor, Mr Corrigan," he adds, his tone both respectful but authoritative. Corrigan pauses, before spinning around to confront the man who has spoken. Surprisingly, Treveleyan holds his gaze, even when Corrigan raises a hand to strike him. I command him to leave Treveleyan alone.

As if thinking better of it, he merely hefts his shoulders nonchalantly. "We've done enough jawing," he says at length. "There's a phone call to be made. A ransom to be demanded."

"So who are you going to ask for that?" asks Treveleyan curiously.

"Duncan Sandford, of course."

"Duncan Sandford!" Treveleyan echoes, disbelief negotiating his words.

"He's a wee pal of yours, ain't he?"

"Yes, but you'll be putting your head in a noose, Corrigan. Sandford has a lot of influential friends in high places. Whatever you're planning is doomed to failure."

"Well, it'll show you who your friends are, won't it, Treveleyan?" hisses Corrigan. He claps his hands. The sound appears to resonate throughout the room. He only has to do it once when Dashurie appears, reminiscent of a genie produced from a lamp.

I see her properly. She wears a loose fitting robe, which does precious little to accentuate her curvaceous young body. Immediately her eyes travel in my direction. I attempt a conciliatory smile, but her expression is fixed and chilling. She averts her head. I freeze because a rapidly swelling bruise is conducive to marring the once perfect alabaster cheekbones. Tears stand in her eyes, so that my heart goes out to her.

"What the fuck you done to her?" I demand, simultaneously affording myself another futile attempt at easing my hands free from the restraining manacles.

"She dared to answer back. No one does that to me. Especially a woman. Now the phone call. Time's wasting." He gestures to the mobile Dashurie clutches between trembling fingers.

"It might have escaped your notice, but I'm a little tied up right now, or rather manacled."

"The manacles are there because I think you'd be strong enough to escape from normal ropes like fuckin' Houdini. Dashurie will hold the phone in one hand. She has a card in the other. Your instructions are to read what is written on it."

"We are holding Sir George Treveleyan. We're asking for a ransom of one million Euros for his release."

"One million! Jesus! Corrigan. You don't do anything by halves do you?" I mock.

"Just read the note."

"Okay." I heft a shoulder in a painful shrug because of the restraints. "Plus free access out of the country. If you refuse to comply with our wishes, Sir George Treveleyan's life will be terminated. This is the NIRA."

"NIRA? What the fuck's that ?" I regard him with raised brows.

Corrigan snatches the paper from my hand. "You don't have to act so damned facetious about this. You're lucky that I've been lenient with you."

"Lenient? You call this fuckin' lenient?" I stretch a restricted hand in indication.

"Believe me, Aidan, that is lenient. If I could be certain you wouldn't attack me, I'd turn you loose. But as we're half-brothers…"

I regard Corrigan in disbelief, but avoid Treveleyan's speculatively raised brows when the former continues to refer to our family ties. "I'm not your half-brother, Corrigan. You're not my family." The large globule of saliva I spit his way lands at his feet, and he moves toward me threateningly. "Go on then. I'm trussed up here, I can hardly do anything can I? Not like the kind of damage you've done to Dashurie. She doesn't deserve that." I rake her over pointedly in the hope that she'll speak to me, but she chooses to say nothing. "Don't let him treat you that way," I tell her.

"It's nothing, Aidan." She lowers her gaze demurely . "I... I speak out of turn. So I am punished."

"Fuck you, Corrigan. I doubt she could have said anything to be punished for. You're just a fuckin' bully, when it comes to it."

I really am trying to free myself, if only in an endeavour to come to Dashurie's aid. Blood courses down my arm, which congeals in the hairs. My wrists throb with the pain. Reminiscent of a caged animal, I am frantically desperate.

"Come on, Corrigan. If you believe that I'm your half-brother then fuckin' undo these damned things." I attempt a last vestige of pleading.

"I know you're my half-brother, but it don't mean to say I'll set you free to come at me again. Wild animals have to be fettered and chained. Look at you with your wild hair, and your muscles straining at the leash. Calm yourself,or you'll burst a blood vessel."

"I'm not reading that fuckin' note to Sandford. The fuckin' NIRA? Jesus. You can fuckin' spit."

"Please, Aidan, do as he say. Or he will have your son killed," Dashurie interjects.

Treveleyan has chosen to say nothing. This man who had once been so formidable now appears dejected and filled with hopelessness. He is hunched and crumpled in his chair, appearing closer to eighty than sixty.

"Okay." I breathe a sigh of resignation. "I'll read the damned note. So why me? Is it that I can be implicated in all this?"

"Why else? They'll think you've joined us. After all, you have the two qualifications we need."

CHAPTER TWENTY FIVE

"Being an Irish Catholic doesn't qualify me."

Dashurie holds the phone close to my ear, when Corrigan dials the number. I ask Corrigan where 'Elvis' and the fat guy are. Adopting a puzzled frown, he demands to know to whom I refer.

"Your two henchmen. Cos that's what they are."

"'Elvis'? I guess you mean Billy. Him and Pug are busy right now." Corrigan ostensibly shares the joke, before lapsing into threatening mode once more. "Now the paper, read it. I only have to contact Jimmy."

Perspiration courses in rivulets down my bare chest, while I focus on the paper. Dashurie's hand shakes so much, that I request she keep it still. The phone is held to my mouth, and before I can speak into it, a female voice informs me, "The Sandford residence. Caroline Sandford speaking."

Caroline Sandford. She had been the Detective Sergeant in charge of the investigation over my sister's death. I discover my throat is inordinately dry. I slick my tongue across lips that are also beginning to feel uncommonly sore.

I clear my throat innumerable times before managing to blurt, "Is DCI Duncan Sandford there please?"

"He is. But can I ask...?"

"Just fetch him, will you?" I interrupt, before softening my tone. I repeat my question.

"He's watching television. You sound familiar." There's a thinly veiled suspicion in her tone. After all she is a police detective.

"Just bring him to the phone please."

"Daddy normally doesn't like to be disturbed."

She's in her late twenties and still calls him 'Daddy'. Jesus. If I called my old man Daddy he'd think I had reverted to childhood. Guess that's posh folk for you. "Perhaps I can take a message. Is it about work?"

Work? Momentarily I have no idea to what she refers. Besides I'm feeling so incredibly tired all at once.

"I need a name, Mister..."Caro breaks into my thoughts.

Oh yeah. If I confide my name, all kinds of ignominious questions will ensue. "If I could talk to him please."

She clears her throat a couple of times. "I understand. I'll fetch Daddy. I won't be long."

I'm left to wonder why the sudden change of heart, before the penny drops with the realisation with the failure to vouchsafe my name. In all likelihood, she's under the impression that I'm a snout, a grass.

Sir George rests his head against his chair. His hands lowered are recumbently in the lap of the faded green robe. No one has sought fit to dress him in the suit I have brought. He barely glances my way. While I long to wrest myself from this chair, I placate him that I'll get him out of this. I possess no weapon. Corrigan referred to my sheer brute strength. That's all I have left to me now, the ability to kill with my bare hands.

Corrigan has draped his slender frame onto the edge of the table. Lips pursed, dark eyes downcast.

"Is that you, Fishy?" The stridency of Duncan Sandford's tone returns me to the present with a jolt.

Fishy? Who the fuck is Fishy? Whoever he is he must be Irish.

I echo the name obtusely, without looking at either Corrigan or Treveleyan. Only Dashurie fills my vision, with her bruised cheek and partially swollen eye. I deal her a small commiserating smile. She averts her head, her lower lip trembling.

"Fishy Pilcher. You don't sound like Fishy."

"That's because I'm not. Am I talking to DCI Duncan Sandford?"

"You called my house. Yes, I'm DCI Sandford. So what do you want? Caro reckoned it was something to do with work."

"You know Sir George Treveleyan?"

"Georgie?"

I cringe both at his calling Treveleyan 'Georgie', plus the harsh command of his tone.

"Of course I know him. Why? Has something happened to

him? Is he alright?"

"For now." God, I hate having to do this. Corrigan watches me avidly from his perch. Treveleyan is slumped, appearing so hopeless and frail. Dashurie, still a child, yet a grown and damaged woman, attempts with a sheer resolve of will, not to make eye contact, while she clutches the card before me.

"What the bloody hell's that supposed to mean?" He blasts my eardrums, his voice bordering on the crescendo.

"It means you have to listen." I maintain the timbre of my own voice deliberately levelled.

"We, the NIRA…" I can't avoid an element of derision. To which Corrigan predictably pats his jacket pocket that I'm aware houses his mobile. "We have Sir George Treveleyan. If you want him released unharmed, you'll collect one million euros for his safe return."

"What the bloody hell?" he roars with such vehemence, I figure he's liable to burst a blood vessel. "The NIRA? Is that the bloody Irish at it again."

I attempt not to grimace, both at his bluster, and his detrimental reference to the Irish.

Undeterred, I continue however. "You pay the money and the NIRA will ensure Sir George's safe return."

"Whenever have the bloody Irish kept any bloody promises?" God, this is one angry guy. Deservedly so in some respects. But his vindictive reference to the Irish is unwarranted.

"Just get the fuckin' money." Much against my better judgement, I can't avoid my own anger, while Corrigan looks on, brows raised with speculation.

"Alright, I'll get the money, you bastard," Sandford hisses. "So where's the bloody pick-up point? Not that I haven't had to deal with you fucking Catholic scum before."

Jesus, now he's insulting my religion. Just because I am of that persuasion, it doesn't mean to say I practise it.

I read from the card. As much as I hate to admit it, Corrigan is an exemplary strategist. I inform Sandford that he is to drive to Bromley Park.

"Which bloody park? There's quite a lot."

"The outskirts of Covet Wood. There's a trash bin. Leave the case of money there. You don't hang around. Just drive away. Or Sir George Treveleyan will be delivered to you in a body bag."

"But he is alright?" The bluster has evaporated now. His tone is subdued, and filled with concern. "He has a heart condition."

Swiping a finger across his throat, Corrigan motions Dashurie to kill the phone.

Chapter Twenty Six

The Connolly Retaliation

"Now, are you going to let me see my son?"

"I told you, all in good time. He's fine. That's all you need to know." Corrigan sighs with both exasperation and an impatience that refutes me to argue.

"If I promise not to try and strangle you, will you let me out of this chair?" I demand.

"I want you to stay put. You're too powerful to have wandering about. The Brit can't walk. You can't move." He chuckles annoyingly. "The way I want you. So Sandford got the message?"

"Oh sure he did. After a lot of cursing of course."

"Fuck. What's a wee bit of cursing when it gets us that money."

Corrigan's features are simultaneously wreathed in smiles when Pug and Billy, minus Dashurie, appear. "Okay, boys," he addresses them, his expression thoughtful.

"Yeah, Mister C?" Pug enquires eagerly. I'm certain he's undoubtedly anxious to please because if either of the two men chanced to disobey him, Corrigan would ultimately have them killed. I think they are aware of that fact as attested to by their sheer subserviency.

A khaki sweater, large enough to accommodate two men, appears to fit Pug's ample proportions quite snugly. Both men have pistols holstered to their belts. I'm aware how ridiculous they seem. If I wasn't made so anxious over my son's welfare, I could see the funny side to their mode of apparel.

Unlike his acolytes, Corrigan carries himself remarkably well in the uniform. Billy Symondy, however, would be ostensibly more at home with a guitar strung across his middle and singing 'Suspicious minds'.

I can do little more than lay my head against the hard wooden chair rest. My wrists throb painfully, as does my shoulder, which is the result of the injection.

I also have no idea what Corrigan plans now. Even his two henchmen stand around with puzzled expressions. Sir George's grey eyes wander uneasily to each man in turn. Corrigan paces the dusty floor with an almost measured tread and ominously without a word. All of this serves to add to the already pregnant silence. There is obviously something on his mind. In this disquieting solitude, he ignites a familiar cheroot, and drags on it for what seems an age. It isn't difficult to conjecture something is about to ensue. What it is I have no idea, but I'm unprepared for Corrigan's next move. Not even in my wildest dreams.

He positions himself before Sir George Treveleyan's wheelchair. The latter regards him with an uneasy frown, which encompasses his every movement.

"Sir George Treveleyan," Corrigan declares. The snap of his words louder than a pistol shot.

"What now, Corrigan?" The old man asks wearily.

"You have been tried and found guilty," Corrigan announces, his tone coldly impersonal. Billy and Pug exchange uneasy glances. While the former runs a hand through his neatly coiffured hair indecisively.

"Tried for what? I don't remember any trial," Treveleyan rises to his own defence.

"Tried for murder, of course," Corrigan declares with an almost ribald humour.

"What the fuck you talking about, Corrigan? Who's he supposed to have murdered?" I exclaim. I attempt to free myself from the manacles once again, although I'm aware how useless it is.

"Loads of people probably, but we got to make examples for the execution of my countrymen. The noble Connolly for one."

"You mean James Connolly? Jesus, Corrigan, that was in fuckin' 1916. What do you mean, 'an example'?"

Sir George has gone noticeably paler. He regards me with imploring grey eyes. This old man looks sick and so incredibly tired. Nevertheless he dares to demand of Corrigan, "What do you mean? James Connolly? I don't understand. I might be older than any of you in this room, but I can assure you that I wasn't born until 1954." There's even a subtle hint of mockery in his tone.

I discover myself stiffening with fear for him. You don't antagonise Danny Corrigan. I sense that he is no longer the selfsame relaxed man I initially knew.

Now there is something almost crazed and wild about him, which further testifies to my theory when he adds, "I know how old y'are. Like I said, examples have to be made. No one has ever, to my knowledge, been punished for Connolly's, or the other patriots' deaths. If you don't know, Connolly was wounded in the leg. He was imprisoned in that ill place of misery, Kilmainham gaol. Even today that place holds so much sadness that will never leave that foul prison because of what those evil people did to our countrymen." Corrigan is practically crying with his impassioned diatribe. Even Billy and Pug regard their leader with an undisguised concern. This man who is so eaten up with revenge and retaliation for an event which occurred practically one hundred years ago.

"Jesus, Corrigan, don't you ever quit?" I retort. "You should have been a teacher. You know so much about Irish history."

I'm unprepared for the resounding crack he delivers to my jaw from the back of his hand. The blow practically sends me reeling hard against the wooden headrest, and leaves my skull throbbing with pain as it connects.

"I'm sorry I had to do that, Aidan, but you're beginning to annoy me with your backchat."

"Is that your answer, Corrigan? To hit out at anyone who dares to answer back. Isn't that why you hit Dashurie? What do you intend to do with Sir George?"

"Whatever it is, I suggest you get it over with. What about the ransom you've asked for?" Treveleyan enquires defiantly. "Surely you need me alive."

"You're stupider than I thought. We don't need you. We just have to collect the money. One million euros. Then get the fuck out of this Brit shithole." He addresses himself to the frail grey man. "You're scheduled for execution. To die the way Connolly died."

The news of Sir George's impending death leaves me with such an overwhelming guilt and fear for him. So he and I have argued in the past. He's often referred to me as a hot-headed young Irishman with an inherent temper that will always incur trouble. While I've considered him a manipulative bastard, I have often accused him of burning down the club, which was consequently my livelihood. So that with the club's demise, I had little choice than to work for him. Now all I can entertain is the sadness that I have brought him to this. He says he understands. My son has to come first. There's no need to reproach myself.

I only hope that Corrigan is bluffing, that he has no intention of setting Treveleyan up as an example for an event which happened almost one hundred years ago. I'm aware that our history is upsetting. Most of which I have learned courtesy of my father. I left Ireland when I was nine.

Minus my boots, shirt and jacket, Corrigan is aware that I cannot get far without freezing to death. The weather is cold. In the absence of central heating there's a small guttering fire in a small battered grate; I'm frozen already. Yet if there was the chance to escape, I'd take it. In bare feet if necessary.

After Corrigan's initial outburst in the sentencing of Sir George for termination, he has left us alone, Billy and Pug disappearing in his wake. Treveleyan and I are the sole occupants of the room. With the silence that has sprung up between us I long to speak to him, to promise that I'll get him out of this somehow. His head is resting against the back of his chair, his eyes are closed, but I sense Sir George is feigning sleep simply because he feels it unnecessary for much conversation.

I also wonder about Patrick, how he is. Corrigan promises that I can see him when I have calmed down. I'm calmed now, almost resigned to my fate. I'm certain that Corrigan, despite all the half-brother shit, intends to kill me too.

But not my son. An innocent young boy.

Unable to commiserate with Sir George, I lay my head against the hard wooden chair's backrest, close my eyes, and entertain an initial squeeze of tears from lowered lids.

It is only when Sir George says, "If only LJ were here. She would know what to do," blinking back the tears, I regard him through a watery, unfocussed vision.

"You said you hadn't heard from her," I remind. Nonetheless I wonder if maybe Lorna Allardyce isn't waiting her chance to rescue us. This lady is highly trained in weaponry.

Maybe she's just preparing her chance to burst in, an assault rifle blazing lead, to waste Corrigan and his associates. The way it is in movies.

But this isn't a movie. Both Treveleyan and I can only await the outcome of a mad man's nefarious intentions.

"Not for a while. It's not like her, you know. Lorna always reports in. Perhaps she has done so now and she'll find Harland who'll tell her that I'm missing."

"What do you think she'll do then? Come in and rescue us?"

Treveleyan's smile is a cursory one. "Contact the police I hope. I don't think even Lorna, as headstrong as she is, would burst in to rescue us, all guns blazing. I guess we all have our fantasies, even me. Leather-clad heroine, guns holstered on her hips, blasting away with an AK47 at the baddies."

"I wish you hadn't put that thought in my mind, especially when I need to pee."

Despite everything I manage to quip. Even Treveleyan sports a small, wry smile. I guess we can both visualise LJ in that role.

To hopefully take my mind of what's occurring in my nether regions, I refer to the ransom.

"Do you think DCI Sandford will come through?"

"We can only hope, Aidan." He lapses subdued once again. Our moment of hilarity passed. Neither of us dare to refer to Treveleyan's imminent demise.

From what I had learned from our history, plus what Corrigan had invariably delighted in informing me, James Connolly was executed by firing squad. Surely even Danny Corrigan isn't that insane or barbaric enough to perpetuate such a crime.

The creak of a door opening has me practically jumping out of my skin, which does nothing to lessen the pain in my wrists. Sir George, too, darts wary eyes in that direction.

I manage to relax with something akin to relief when Dashurie moves into the room, "What are you doing here? Where's Corrigan?" I ask her.

Her black hair is pulled back into a ponytail, fashioned with a white bow. Despite the bruised cheek and partially swollen eye, she remains a beautiful child, scarcely deserving the way Corrigan treats her.

"Danny is busy at moment."

"Doing what, may I ask?" I say sarcastically. "Cos whatever it is it can't be anything good. What's the water for?"

"To bathe your arms. I have salve for your wrists."

"Your idea? I doubt it was Corrigan's."

"I make request and he tell me I can do it."

Her eyes are reminiscent of enormous saucers in her ashen pallor. A far cry from the honey trap who had come to my room at the Maze Hill house.

Resting the bowl onto the table, she begins to squeeze out a flannel, before tracing the warm water, which I find expressively soothing, along the length of my arm. Her action is gentle, as if she is afraid of inflicting more hurt than has already been done. Her attention is purposely diverted, until I suggest that she look at me. "Why do you let that man do this to you? You don't have to stay here."

Still she refuses to glance my way. I repeat myself and that she finally raises her eyes to mine.

"Because I know no other life. Danny is cruel man. I know this. If I disobey he not just hit me." She pauses, swallowing uncomfortably.

"He'll what?" I long to comfort her, but my hands are tied, literally.

"He threaten to kill me."

"Jesus, I can't let that happen to you. We have to get away. Corrigan's going to kill Sir George. My son is in that cellar with that ugly paedo. I haven't seen Patrick since I've been here. If you can get a key to get these manacles off we can all escape and contact the authorities."

The black eyes flash dangerously with fear in my direction. "No, no, Aidan! He will kill your son if you escape, go against him."

"But I can prevent him if I'm free. Corrigan knows that. That's why I'm manacled to a chair. You can't stay with him. He's a total madman now. Gone crazy."

"But I cannot escape. Not now."

"What do you mean not now?"

"Because..." She swallows uncomfortably once more, averting her head again. "Because I expect his child."

Chapter Twenty Seven

False Promises

With Dashurie's departure, both Sir George and I exchange disbelieving glances, although no words pass between us. What can we add to that, except maybe to share a single thought? How could this woman, barely a child, allow a man so evil to entrap her. l know she really can't return home with her shame.

I protest long and hard enough that I am bursting to take a pee. The last thing I'm desirous of doing is to wet myself. Bodily functions scarcely cease, even if you are manacled to a chair. The undignified thing being that Pug has to accompany me to the toilet, at gunpoint. Both the latter, and Billy – even Corrigan – appear to extol a certain wariness in my unfettered presence.

Momentarily left alone with Pug I dare to enquire what Corrigan has in store for Patrick and me. The question encounters a nonchalant shrug, one that is only embellished with, "I think Danny got other plans for you, but don't ask what they are. You ain't a Brit, like the other one."

"And my son?"

"He's your son, ain't he?"

My only plan now is of escape, rescue my son and take Dashurie and Treveleyan with me. Night has descended and I'm re-manacled to the chair. I had previously entertained the notion of swinging around on Pug and disarming him. Nevertheless I have allowed the moment to pass. I was allowed one hand free in order to feed myself, when Dashurie offered to do it for me. All I can do was to growl at her that I don't need to be fucking spoon-fed like a baby, for which I apologised, The poor girl has enough to deal with without me adding to her problems. She allows me to wipe away the tear that falls from her eye.

I was soon to discover that the sixteen year old girl is no cook. Beans on toast or cheese on toast has been our staple diet for the time I've been here. Because I only have the use of one hand, the toast is cut into squares. When Sir George complains about the food to Corrigan, I tense expectantly, waiting for Treveleyan to receive another backhander.

Corrigan's only response is, "That's all the stupid wee bitch knows how to cook," acidly. "She don't understand there's men here."

"Maybe you could ask one of your hirelings to cook," I suggest. "Course, you get in some proper food, like steak. I can cook you know."

"Don't try to be fuckin' funny. I'd have to turn you loose."

"Sure you would." I fashion a crooked smile. "I can't do it with my feet now, can I?"

"Besides, it's women's jobs to cook," Corrigan remarks. "That and keeping their man happy. That's all those wee bitches are here for. Why do you cook, Aidan? Don't your wife do all that stuff?"

Unfortunately I am compelled to admit that Caitlan is not much of a cook either. Anyway I prefer to do it myself.

"That's the trouble with menfolk today, they make women too fuckin' lazy."

Neither Treveleyan and I wish to continue with Corrigan's defamatory regard for womankind. I enjoy doing things for my family. Caitlan has our daughter to take care of, and is a good mother. I'm perfectly content with that. I wonder what ever happened to Corrigan to squeeze even the remotest element of love from him. Is he so eaten up with anger and revenge for something that happened sixty years before he was born, he is incapable of allowing an emotion such as love to intrude?

Things have noticeably changed for Dashurie since leaving the Maze Hill house. There Corrigan treated her like a princess in her beautiful clothes. Now she wears unflattering dresses. She maintains her unwashed hair pulled back. Her head remains lowered while she keeps her eyes averted from mine purposely. Corrigan threatens her with another blow if she disobeys him. Chancing to overhear their conversation, he remarked how she was stupid enough to get herself in the family way. So what was it then, an immaculate conception? He must have helped a wee bit somewhere along the line.

Corrigan paces the floor, the Generalissimo inspecting his men. Pug sports a decidedly uncomfortable expression, while his unwashed body sweats profusely. Unlike his companion, Billy Symondy appears ostensibly hyper with anticipation. He blows his nose interminably, while his eyes are rendered glassy and distant. The facts tell their own story; Billy's been snorting some of the white powder Corrigan favours so much. Maybe their leader has himself succumbed to the temptation.

For the first time since I've been here, I must have dozed. Dashurie has bathed my wrists, so they are less painful. The muted sound of hushed voices and dragging footsteps alert me enough to jerk me awake. I discover Pug and Billy supporting Sir George Treveleyan as they pull him, barely struggling or protesting, from his wheelchair as if he is already dead.

"What the fuck you doing to him?" Blinking into full wakefulness, I observe that it's already dawn. The seeping grey of early morning dances vague shadows on the dingy walls.

"Shut your fuckin' mouth, McRaney, or I'll..." Symondy's gloved hand is wrapped about a Glock pistol. Corrigan hisses at him to put the gun away, that he was to focus. I wasn't going anywhere.

"Sir George!" I shout at him. "You can't let them do this!"

Sir George Treveleyan fails to respond. The once manipulative, imposing figure whom we called 'The Great Man' because of the power he automatically yields, is reduced to little more than a limp rag doll. His legs drag uselessly behind him. He fails to even dig in his heels. I notice too how thin and shrunken his wasted muscles are after thirty years spent in a wheelchair. Now the Great Man is rendered little more than a marionette as he is dragged away.

All I can do is yell and beg them not to do this, and undo all Dashurie's work of bathing my wrists. With the raging efforts of pleading to these men, all I've succeeded in doing is allowing the blood to run down my arms. The pain is unbearable, but I no longer care. Tears burn my eyes too, with both the anguish of the lacerating manacles and the infinite guilt that overwhelms me.

I realise, stemming from Treveleyan's unresponsiveness, they must have drugged him. Corrigan moves into the room, thumbs anchored to the webbing belt. He appears every inch the soldier. "You gotta know it ain't just for Connolly and the others," he begins by way of some kind of odd apology. "It's for my da. Your da."

"My dad isn't your dad, Corrigan. If he was anything like you, I'd be ashamed to call a bastard like that my father."

I half expect another slap, but his features remain oddly impassive, and I'm faintly surprised because he's beginning to look somewhat tired. He continues as if he hasn't heard me. "Like I said, it's for my da, the way he died. For Bobby Sands and the others. The people who were slain in Gibraltar. Mairead O'Farrell. Remember her?"

"No, I can't say I do. Please Corrigan, don't do this. Do what you want with me, but he's a cripple, an old man. He can't do you any harm. Besides, what will Sandford do when you don't hand him over in exchange for the ransom?"

"Oh, Aidan, don't you think I hadn't thought of that? So Treveleyan ain't much now, but he has powerful folk in high places. Maybe in the British Parliament. The treacherous bastards who've been trying to rule the Irish ever since the dawn of time, just because they don't think that we have a couple of wee brain cells between us. By the time we pick up the ransom we'll be gone."

"So where does that leave me, you bastard?"

The familiarly glacial smile returns in all its glory. "I have plans for my brother."

"I'm telling you for the umpteenth time that I'm not your brother. Dermot McRaney is my father. My mother wouldn't have lowered herself to have had an affair with your father, knowing what he was. And my son? What happens to him?" I attempt to wrest myself free of the manacles, but only succeed in increasing the pain, working up a sweat, giving birth to a headache. "And Dashurie?" I add, when he hasn't so far spoken. "She told me she's expecting your child. What a waste of a young life to give birth to a monster's kid."

The resounding crack he delivers to my jaw sends me reeling against the back of the hard wooden seat, while I feel the blood well up from a split lip.

"That's none of your fuckin' business. That's between me and her."

"Fuck you, Corrigan. Please stop this… this fiasco. You can't commit such an atrocity. It's murder. Won't people hear the shot?"

"Silenced pistols. We'll prop him up. He's drugged. See, I do have some compassion."

"Oh sure you do. You're all fuckin' heart."

His hand is upraised, about to strike me again. "Go on, fuckin' hit me if it makes you feel better," I taunt. But the hand is lowered, as if he thinks better of it.

He says, "You ever see the solitary black cross where our heroes were buried in Kilmainham?"

"Sure I saw it. When I was a kid. But I didn't understand, Corrigan. I didn't fuckin' understand." Tears blur my vision, so I can barely see. "Please don't kill Treveleyan. Take your money and go. Please."

I can't help but recoil when the cold black glove touches my cheek. "Don't lie to yourself, Aidan."

"What the fuck's that supposed to mean?"

"Take a look at yourself in the mirror, see how much we resemble one another. It's who you are. You lie because you understand, no matter how much you deny it. That cross. I bet you were upset. It's such a lonely spot."

I had to admit the memory of visiting Kilmainham, of seeing the black iron cross over the solitary mound, had given me nightmares for a while. It was the fear that those long dead heroes would ultimately rise from the mound and amorphously drift into my room at night.

Instead I tell him that it was a long time ago, that I had been a kid and I scarcely recollect much about it. My words are allowed to trail, when Pug pops his head around the door and implores, "Me and Billy want to get this over with, Mister C." I can't but help the feeling that the fat man wishes for no part in this.

Corrigan says, "To take your mind off what we're about to do, Aidan." He savours his words. "Perhaps you'd like to watch a film."

"A film?" Now what the fuck does he have in mind? "What kind of film?"

Corrigan retrieves the mobile from his jacket and scrolls through it for a while, before he finds what he's looking for. "It's not too long. I'll find something to prop it up so you can see it."

A sense of unease begins to contour my spinal column. I'm certain that any film Corrigan makes would be an unsavoury one. How correct I am in my assumption. He positions the mobile on the table, resting it against a telephone directory.

Powerless, anchored to the chair, I can only stare in pure disbelief. The paedophile Jimmy Brennan immediately appears on the screen, wearing his customary inane grin. Then I see my son. He's naked from the waist down. He's still bound and gagged, helpless to prevent this evil man. Patrick's eyes are filled with terror, almost close to passing out, when Brennan slips a hand toward his nether regions.

Now I really am a wild, crazed animal demanding release from his cage. I scream, "Bastard! Bastard!" at him through my tears.

Brennan mouths, "He's a wee pretty boy ain't he? Just my type, so he is."

"You promised you wouldn't harm my son if I do as you ask. Haven't I done that already, Corrigan?" I say with a last vestige of desperation.

"If you believe that I'm the kind of man to keep promises then you're a bigger fool than I took you for.'"

Chapter
Twenty Eight

The Cellar

The sound of the shot outside the dilapidated building is muffled by the silencers. I'm glad I've been spared witnessing Sir George Treveleyan's murder. For murder it surely is, no matter how Corrigan serves to dress it up, with his 'examples' to be made. Nobody deserves such a horrendous punishment. Sir George had already become a broken man, but I couldn't help but feel that the guy was dying anyway. There was something strangely different in his make-up from the man I had initially met when he had helped me locate my kidnapped brother. Then he was powerful with his knowledge, his use of remote viewing. Lately I had no occasion to witness any of this about Sir George. Now he had been reduced to a drugged, lifeless manikin. The man who had derived his secrets from Tibet was no more.

Sir George and my son. Neither one I can help. I can only suffer their plight, helplessly looking on.

The dawn breaks as the sun struggles to infiltrate the grimy window, the one I've stared at for such a length of time that my eyes have become stiff and sore. The curtain is diaphanous enough to allow a meagre sight of the desolation beyond. It causes me to wonder yet again where we are. Our location has invariably been something to concentrate on while I mentally traverse every part of Kent that I'm familiar with. To no avail.

They must have disposed of Treveleyan's body, because if they return him to Sandford the chances of obtaining their requested €1million will be null and void. I hear the slam, like a car boot being closed. I long to yell at them and attempt to free my already ravaged and bleeding wrists from the manacles. Except now, even moving them slightly, a pain shoots through my arms making me wonder if I've managed to damage a tendon. The event of another maniacally wild attempt to free myself on witnessing what Brennan was doing to my son has left me far too exhausted.

Dashurie enters the room, carrying a bowl containing a greyish white substance that loosely passes for porridge. Corrigan's gloved hand is upraised, and he immediately dashes the bowl from hers when she presents it to me. I yell at him, "What the fuck did you do that for, you bastard?" The bowl shatters against the wall, the sound echoing resonantly on the bare boards.

"It's not fit for pigs," Corrigan retorts, his expression one of arrogance and disdain.

"I would have eaten it," I attempt to placate her.

Dashurie apologises, her words barely audible. When she suggests fetching a cloth Corrigan commands she pick it up with her hands. She says, "I'm sorry," but it's me she addresses. She bends to her task. I can't help but notice that she winces as if she is in pain as she gingerly lowers herself to the uncarpeted floor.

"No man's gonna want you. You'll never please any man," Corrigan spits tersely. "The only woman in a man's life that's of any use is his ma."

"I am sorry," she murmurs, tears falling unchecked from downcast eyes. She collects up the broken pieces, the mess left by the porridge, into trembling hands, unmindful that a broken piece has left a finger bleeding. I draw Corrigan's attention to it.

"She can't do anything fuckin' right. Not even clear away her own mess." His response is typically acerbic.

Dashurie departs, disappearing into the back room. I demand of Corrigan why he chooses to treat her the way he does. I remind him that she was his butterfly, his princess at the Maze Hill house.

"Because she didn't have to do anything but look pretty. Now here, when I need her to cook and do women stuff, she turns out to be fuckin' useless. Besides, I've grown tired of her meekness, her 'I'm so sorry, Danny'." He makes a rather ludicrous attempt to imitate Dashurie's voice, adding, "simpering wee bitch".

"I would have eaten the porridge. I'm fuckin' hungry enough. Look, I know I'm in no position to argue, but lay off her will you? She's still a child. Don't spoil her from meeting a nice boy later." I deliberately soften my tone while he paces the floor. His expression is thoughtful, planting a cigarette between his lips.

"I could use one of those. I haven't had a smoke in ages. That isn't making my temper any better."

"You ain't getting one now. It'll mean untying one of your hands."

"I doubt if I could hold it anyway. I can hardly feel my hands as it is."

"You shouldn't have made such a fuss then, should you?"

"You blame me? Jesus. So, isn't a condemned man deserving of a cigarette."

Corrigan paces. His expression remaining thoughtful, as if he's thinking about it.

Before spinning on his heel, he pauses to confront me squarely now. "What makes you think you're a condemned man?"

"Well, you either have to let us go, me and Patrick, or kill us. You don't have Treveleyan now. No doubt you'll collect your money and get out of the country. You also know that the first opportunity I have that I won't hesitate to kill you. I don't need a weapon to do it. You called me a wild animal. Maybe that's what I've become, what you've made me, Corrigan. A wild animal that's crazy enough to tear you apart."

"I'd like to take you with me."

"What the fuck, Corrigan? There's no way I'd go with you. I'd rather you killed me. Just let Patrick go. Drop him off somewhere.

That's all I ask."

"Your son is insurance."

"If I went with you, what would I become?"

"You would join us. Your strength, your proficiency with weapons. Plus you are of our faith and a countryman."

"Never, you bastard. You might as well blow me away right now. Just let my son go. When you leave here, what about Dashurie? Stop treating her like a fuckin' dishrag. She deserves a life, Corrigan."

"I've grown tired of her anyway." He waves a hand about him indiscriminately. "In fact, she disgusts me with her stupid whining. I don't even want to fuck her now she's got herself in that way."

"You got her in that way."

"Did I?" His tone is filled with such disbelief that I regard him in surprise.

"Well you fucked her, Corrigan. You should have used..."

Again the swirling around on his heels. "Did I? Did I?"

"Why do you keep saying that?" I can't avoid a frown.

"I wasn't the only one who got into her panties."

"You're saying old Elvis and the fat man been screwing her?" I ask, in surprise.

"God, no, I wouldn't let those infidels touch her."

"Who then?"

The familiar glacial smile returns to his face. The smile extends as he regards me pointedly. It's then that the particular penny drops, making my senses reel so predominantly that I'm beginning to feel physically sick.

"Me? You... you can't pin that on me, Corrigan. Sure she tried it on, but I said nothing doing. That's why she scratched my face, remember? Because I rejected her."

"A pity, a pity." He commences pacing the floor again, his boots echoing noisily on the bare boards, the sound conducive to shudder through my very being. I can't help but growl, "What you fuckin' talking about now, you bastard?"

Once again the surreptitious savouring of his words, which I am unfailing to observe, invariably bodes ill. "Sure enough I was getting bored with that wee Albania tart. I realise now that you can't beat a nice wee Irish girl. Do you know any?"

There's an unmistakable sensation of bile rising in my mouth because I sense what is coming. All I can do is respond in the negative.

"Now that's a wee lie for a start, Aidan. Didn't you marry one? What's her name? Caitlan?"

"Don't you dare touch her, Corrigan." I make yet another futile attempt to escape the manacles, only to release a further drizzle of blood seeping down my arms. "I really will kill you, you bastard. You touch my family…" I automatically freeze, my blood running cold, when I think of my wife and baby at home.

"You're in no position to do anything, Aidan. I've seen her. She's very pretty. Small and slight, just the way I like 'em. With her lovely long dark hair. She doesn't wear any paint and powder. Sure she doesn't need it. You're a lucky bastard."

"You sound jealous, Corrigan. If you weren't such a bastard, and fucked about with an event that happened at the beginning of the last century, then you too could find a nice Irish girl, if that's what you want."

"I don't need your fuckin' advice." Another crashing blow is delivered to my cheek, causing my head to spin violently against that hard chair rest again. The blow opens up my already lacerated lip. I spit blood at Corrigan. "Anyway, I reckon you're too far gone for any decent girl to look at you, Corrigan!"

"It's time, Mister C." Billy Symondy is framed in the archway.

It's time. I can't help but wonder uneasily what that might mean.

"Okay, okay, I'll fuckin' be there," Corrigan growls impatiently. "And you," the leather encased finger points in my direction, "you fuckin' know nothing, Mister. If I want your woman I'll fuckin' take her, especially when I tell her about Dashurie."

All I can do is hiss, "Bastard," at his retreating back.

I wait until darkness descends again. The nights come and go.

I've eaten what little Dashurie manages to offer up. When I enquire after my son, I'm duly informed he's been fed. Tonight there is a full moon and Symondy jokes about me turning into a werewolf. He says something about me beginning to resemble some throw-back creature, with my wild hair and blood running down my chin, which has been lacerated by Corrigan's ring. My wrists are now painful and stiff. It's as if, with Treveleyan gone, either Dashurie or I are ostensibly the sport of their hilarity.

Symondy delights in relating how they propped Treveleyan up against a wall and blew him away. He suggests that Sir George resembled a scarecrow, drugged and helpless with his shattered spine. "Course he knew nothing about it, not with the tranquiliser inside him."

The moon shines full into my eyes; it penetrates the thin curtain, preventing me from sleep. I'm freezing cold. With precious little food inside me and barely enough to drink, I wonder if it is Corrigan's intention to allow me to die of either malnutrition or hypothermia.

The silence which has fallen over the place allows me both to doze fitfully, in spite of the full moon, and to take stock of my predicament. There is only Corrigan and Dashurie here now. Occasionally Brennan emerges for food, and to further torment me as to his plans for my son, but I'm far too weak and exhausted to even rise to his onerous taunts.

In spite of a splitting headache, I manage to drift off. The softest touch of a hand on mine practically has me jumping out of my skin. With a finger to her lips, in an endeavour to silence me, Dashurie is at my side. The sapphire coloured robe she pulls about herself is a far cry from the sensuous young woman who had come to me for sex. I recollect how Corrigan had cited me for Dashurie's pregnancy. What would that do to Caitlan?

CHAPTER TWENTY EIGHT

"What are you doing here, Dashurie?" I hiss sotto voce. "Where are the others?"

"Danny is asleep. Pug and Billy still gone for ransom. I have something for you."

Through sleep-bleary eyes, grown sore from lack of proper sleep, I make an attempt to focus on the child/woman standing before me.

All I can do is murmur, "Not now, sweetheart," misinterpreting her meaning.

"Shush, not talk too much." She lowers her voice conspiratorially, so I can barely hear her. Reaching into her robe, she produces a set of keys, dangling them before my startled vision, making my senses reel at the sight of them.

"What are those for?" I dare ask hopefully.

"Keys to place. This one." She selects a solitary key from the set of six. "To cellar. That is where your son is being held. He look like you, doesn't he?"

"Sure he does. But aren't you forgetting something, sweetheart." I attempt to raise a manacled wrist, but can't help wince with pain, wondering if I've ever be able to use my hands again. They've become so painful. Blood had long since congealed behind the iron strappings.

Dashurie produces another key and sets to unlocking the manacles.

"Why are you doing this ? I'm grateful, but you've put your life in danger."

"I know. I no longer care. You kind to me. You need to be with your son. I can't see him the way he is."

"You've seen him? Is he okay?"

"He okay for now, but a very frightened little boy. I cry for you both."

Easing my hands from the iron grips is a painful process, and I wince against the pain when it shudders through me. It's difficult not to scream aloud with the effort, until Dashurie warns we stay quiet. "If Danny find us, he'll kill us both. Patrick too. He will be so angry."

I am free, but my body has become as stiff as my hands, and I'm compelled to lean on Dashurie. I mutter how I feel as if I've aged thirty years.

"You still fit." She makes a transient attempt at humour, only for the briefest of smiles to be replaced by an inherent sadness once more.

"I don't feel it. So where's this cellar?'

"Follow. I will show you. We have to be quiet. Danny a light sleeper."

"Why are you doing this now?"

"Because I want you to help me get away. He say I'm useless. I believe, when baby born, he will kill me and that Mrs Ryan will care for child."

"Jesus, Dashurie, we can't let that happen." I manage to slide an arm about her shoulder momentarily.

"He hate women so much. I not know why. The woman in the cellar…"

I regard her nonplussed. "What woman? There's a woman in the cellar? Jesus, Dashurie."

"Not talk now. We go to cellar."

I wonder what atrocities Corrigan houses in this place. Thoughts of which return me to the night Mitchell and I discovered all those condemning DVDs in Cartright's basement.

In a voice that is barely above a whisper, I enquire where Brennan is.

"He sleeps in cellar. He have a gun. I could not get you a gun."

In the process of restoring the life into my fingers, I explain that even if I had a gun, I doubt I could use it. My hands are far too stiff and sore.

I follow Dashurie through into another room, which turns out to be little more than a kind of lean-to. It further testifies to the fact that the place is merely a shack. The desolation of the landscape puzzles me and I ask her where we are.

Dashurie's eyes flicker upward. She gnaws at her lower lip with consternation. "I not know what they call it. Like you, I blindfolded too. Now, come with me." She places her hand in mine. It's small and delicate, barely felt, except for the fact the hand is strangely cold. There is little heating in this place against the November chill. She escorts me from the wooden framework room.

It seems that she takes charge, for I have no idea where we are going, or what I am to expect. My stomach knots at seeing my son again. Will he blame me for the misfortunes that have overtaken him?

A short flight of wooden stairs descend into the bowels of the old shack. In bare feet I make precious little sound on the bare boards, although each step is a painful one.

The stench of stale air permeates the room, admixed with an unmistakeable acrid smell, not dissimilar to burning flesh. I catch myself shivering involuntarily, that has nothing to do with the cold. Now I'm anxious about what Dashurie is leading me to. Has Corrigan used her to lie to me? Is my son already dead? This is a trap. They are planning to kill me in the aftermath of Corrigan making sure my hands are far too painful to either use a weapon, or to ultimately kill him without one.

The cellar is bare and dank. The only light suffusing the room emanates from a small window and a flickering shadeless bulb.

"Patrick," I breathe his name, my heart racing. Dashurie places a finger to her lips, warning me to silence. Patrick's hands are bound behind him to the rungs of a chair. His mouth is taped. Raising his eyes at my entrance, the darkness vanishes a fraction to be replaced by hope. Brennan lies on a hard wooden bed in a far corner of the room. His incessant snoring fills, and disturbs the otherwise comparative stillness.

The room, roughly measuring ten by ten square, contains another bed. A prone figure is outlined against a thin sheet. I stiffen, half expecting it to be a corpse beneath the sheet, until the figure moves. Easing back the sheet gradually, like a spectre rising from the tomb, I see closely for the first time it is undeniably a woman. This must be the one Dashurie had spoken of. I observe that her head is shaven. While every conceivable inch of her scalp has been plastered flat by brownish coloured feathers. My gasp is involuntary.

The woman gingerly pulls herself up in the bed, hugging the diaphanous material about a body that is naked, apart from a pair of combat trousers, partially glimpsed in the filmy outline. Her breasts, the rest of her, apart from her face, is covered in the selfsame feathers. Her breathing is rapid and belaboured, almost raspy, serving to indicate the hot tar that incorporates the feathers, has doubtlessly affected her lungs. The pain and anguish reflected on her face tells its own terrible story. Her hands are bound behind her, duct tape seals her mouth, which I rush to remove.

Lorna Allardyce murmurs a grateful thanks from sore and bruised lips.

Chapter Twenty Nine

Means Of Escape

Brennan remains asleep, while I maintain a weather eye on him every time he stirs.

Lorna collapses back onto the bed, tears in her eyes. I apologise for hurting her when I'd removed the tape. She merely nods and clutches my arm.

I whisper the obvious question: what have they done to her? I can't help but think of Dennis Mitchell and Jason Lang. The little girl on the DVD in Cartright's cellar. I'm scarcely aware that I have clenched an angry fist against my leg.

LJ mouths, "You'd better see to your son, Aidan." Her voice is cracked and husky. I have been so overwhelmed with both shock and disbelief to see what they have done to this beautiful woman – Leanne's sister – that I remain unmoving momentarily, tears springing to my eyes.

Still maintaining an eye on Brennan, I undo the bonds about Patrick's arms and legs and peel the tape from his mouth. Dashurie whispers, "What you going to do?" in a frightened voice.

"Get the fuck out of here, that's what I'm going to do," I tell her offhandedly.

The instant Patrick is free, he eases his stiff limbs from the chair with my help. I'm still scared that he'll hate me after what he's been through. If he does, that fact will be far more painful than anything that Corrigan can throw at me, but he deigns to fling himself into my arms. "Oh, Daddy, you've come to take me home. I was so frightened." His eyes are dark and imploring when they rise into mine, which allows the terrible guilt to wash over me again. "It's all over now," I placate, even though I'm mentally crossing fingers.

I stiffen when Brennan stirs again throwing back the blanket.

LJ swings her legs over the edge of the bed, pulling the sheet around her. She attempts to cover her unfettered breasts, obviously with embarrassment. Her upper body is completely covered by the same brown speckled feathers. Even in the pallid lighting, I can't help observe the evidence of the treacly black stains from the tar. It's obvious she is in so much pain. I am helpless to know what to do, except to promise to get her, get all of us, out of here.

Lorna shakes her head. "Don't worry about me. Just take Dashurie and Patrick."

"I'm not leaving you here, that's for sure. So, how... how did it happen?" I ask her.

"I followed those two, Symondy and the fat guy, to this place."

"Where are we exactly? I was blindfolded, and so was Dashurie."

"And I missed it." She makes a transient attempt at humour, which falls noticeably short. A hand, one that isn't covered in feathers, rises to her face. I observe the element of pain written there.

"Dungeness, Kent. It's a headland, near Romney Marsh."

"So the old man was right," I murmur.

"The old man?"

"Treveleyan thought that's where we were. I suppose you knew..." But I cannot find the words to express the guilt I feel over Sir George's untimely demise.

LJ nods painfully. "Maybe it was a blessed release, Aidan," she says and closes her eyes momentarily.

"A blessed release? I don't understand. I brought him here because these bastards were holding my son. I've felt guilty ever since." Patrick continues to cling to me. I ruffle his hair and cuddle him close in my relief that he is restored to me. Brennan sleeps on, mumbles something, before turning on his side so that he no longer faces us. We'd all transferred into a kind of frozen silence in the eventuality of him waking up.

I ask LJ what she means by a 'blessed release' in a whisper.

"Sir George was dying of cancer."

The cold that permeates my spinal column has little to do with the temperature. I whisper, "Sir George had cancer?"

"Of the lungs. I know he didn't deserve to die the way he did. I know because Corrigan delighted in telling me. But a bullet was swifter than what would have happened later. He'd refused treatment. But you've spent more than enough time. You need to get out of here, get the authorities. Don't try going up against them yourself. Brennan's going to wake soon. Kill him before he does." Despite the constriction of her throat, LJ's plea is impassioned. "He has a gun under his pillow, but you can't use that. The shot will be heard."

"Please, Dad, can't we go home now? I don't want to stay here any longer." Patrick tugs at my bare arm. I attempt not to wince with the pain. As if noticing them for the first time he wants to know why my hands are bandaged.

"I do that for your father. Danny Corrigan have him manacled to a chair. Now we should go before he wake up," Dashurie urges, her voice rising in panic, her gaze wary when she regards Brennan.

"Dashurie's right," LJ agrees, "but you can't let that bastard live. I'd do it but you're stronger than me."

"Not in front of my son."

"You don't have a choice."

I move toward the sleeping man, aware that when he wakes he'll automatically reach for his gun. There will be a struggle. Exhausted as I am, pitted against the freshness of his sleep, he may succeed in killing me in front of Patrick. Yet I wonder if I can actually wrap my sore hands about his throat.

"No, Daddy." Patrick buries his head against my chest, his hand urgently clutching mine.

I know that LJ is right. Symondy and Pug are absent. Corrigan sleeps in another room. With Brennan dead, Corrigan will be out on his own. I begin the search for the gun.

"Under his pillow," LJ reminds me.

Brennan sleeps with his mouth open, snoring loudly, admixed with interminable pig-like grunts. I'm aware that I have precious little time.

Dashurie more resembles a child than ever, appearing younger than her sixteen years. She explains to Patrick that sometimes people have to do things they really don't want to do. That includes his daddy.

LJ struggles to maintain a sitting position on the bed. She holds her head as if she's having trouble supporting her neck. She obviously requires medical attention. I can't imagine how much pain she is in right now.

Brennan must have heard my approach, because, jerking abruptly awake, with an astonished, "What the fuck?" he attempts to scramble for his pistol. But I'm swift to intercept him. As stiff and sore as my hands are, they manage to locate the soft tissue around Brennan's throat. Thumbs press either side of his larynx. I exert as much pressure as I'm able. He continues his struggling in an attempt to reach his gun.

With my fingers spreadeagled about his throat, I squeeze and squeeze. "This is for what you have done to my son, you bastard," I gasp.

"Mister... Mister Corrigan said I..."

I have neither the inclination or patience to listen to his last pleas to save his worthless life. Despite the inexorable pain throbbing through my hands, I ease the pillow from beneath his head. His mouth has already begun to turn a bluish colour. As the pillow presses down onto his face, it finally sucks out his final breath.

I locate the weapon and pass it to LJ.

"Take it. You might need it."

My gaze is instinctively directed to my son. His face is white, rendered ghostly in the pallid illumination of that solitary bare bulb.

I shake my head. Surveying my surroundings, perhaps for the first time, my eyes alight on that solitary window. Following my gaze, Dashurie wants to know what I am going to do.

"He's getting the hell out of here," LJ tells her. "This place is pretty desolate, but there's a road."

"You're coming with us," I stress, brooking no argument from her.

"I'll take my chance. Besides, I have another weapon." She allows herself a vague smile, the familiar green eyes snapping wide. Reaching to the pocket of her trousers, she extracts a silver plated cigarette lighter.

"I didn't think you smoked," I quip.

"I don't. Now get the fuck out of here, McRaney, and take Dashurie and Patrick with you before that bastard wakes up. I'll try and hold him off." She raises the pistol with a slightly trembling hand.

"You need medical attention, sweetheart," I tell her. "You're coming, even if I have to carry you."

The smile returns, if only briefly. "You know I'd love nothing better, but you get yourselves out first. Look at me. Beneath all this, I have no…"

I shush her to silence. She's obviously upset by the way she looks, all her beautiful hair shaven. I attempt to placate her that once the docs have finished with her, her hair will grow again. Her only response is to avert her gaze, tears filling her eyes.

The window is no more than three or four feet across, and in possession of a cracked sill. I guess neither Dashurie or Patrick will have much trouble easing themselves through the narrow aperture. Nevertheless I am not certain that I will be able to squeeze through. I'm fairly wiry, and muscular, so I suggest it might be simpler to break the pane, perhaps with the gun butt. LJ adds it might be easier to allow the children through. Perhaps they might be able to open the front door. She suggests that the building is quite ramshackle. I smile at this woman's erstwhile resourcefulness affectionately.

Dashurie is swift to retort that she is not a child.

"Of course you're not, sweetheart," LJ says, "but you don't really have time to argue the point."

Before I prepare to leave, I opt to cover Brennan's dead face with the sheet.

Patrick clutches my hand so tightly that his nails practically dig into my palms. He obviously is undesirous of letting me go. I've got my son back. He's got his dad. I cuddle him again, tears in my eyes. LJ regards us both with abject concern and an easily interpreted regret. I think of her own son, Gabriel. I promise that I'll get help, and get her out of there.

"Just get yourselves out, please, Aidan!" Her voice grows ever constricted in her urgency.

I help Patrick to climb through the window. I tense expectantly when the pane squeals noisily. "Dungeness you say?" I remind.

"That's where we are. Now go! Go! You want this?" She holds out the pistol, but once again I tell her that she might have need of it.

"I promise you I'll get help." I press a hand to her shoulder, observing the tears standing in her eyes. She can barely speak when she grasps my hand, indicating that I should get out now.

I haul Patrick onto my shoulder, easing him through the window. Still he clings onto me.

"You won't leave me will you, Daddy?" He swipes a palm at the tears in his eyes.

"No, Patrick. I'll be right behind you. I love you."

"I love you too." His hands clasp my neck, but I am compelled to release him. Soon, it will be day break, and Corrigan will realise that I'm no longer manacled to the chair.

Patrick is finally through and I hear him drop down the other side. Now it is Dashurie's turn. I tell her, when she's through, to wait outside for me. She asks why we couldn't use the outer door instead of such a small aperture. An obvious question. I explain that we'll only disturb Corrigan.

"Not if you kill him."

"My hands are too painful. Now, no more arguments," I say authoritatively.

For her height she is surprisingly light. Dashurie is now the normal sixteen year old, no longer the honey trap temptress that Corrigan intended her to be.

She is halfway through the window when the door bursting open admits Danny Corrigan. There's a Heckler and Koch pistol upraised in his right hand. A terrible look of vengeance and anger is etched on his countenance. "You fuckin' bastards! You'll never escape. Only in a fuckin' pine box. Aidan, I'm surprised that you would betray your own brother."

"I'm not your fuckin' brother, I told you that. You're nothing to me, Corrigan."

I have already broken the glass, even though I've succeeded in opening up my wounds again. I observe that LJ has concealed the gun beneath the sheet.

Corrigan, raising the gun, levers the trigger. The initial shot finds Dashurie half in and out of the window. Her fear of injuring herself on the jagged pane is no longer of importance. The reverberation of the shot travels the room with the cataclysmic force of a small mortar shell. Crimson is swift to fountain up through a punctured vein in the nape of her neck. Another bullet finds her chest, exploding the alabaster white skin. She collapses, a fluttering butterfly, to the ground. Her screams forever silenced, blood pooling around her. Shock and disbelief registers on us.

LJ raises the pistol, slamming the clip, but not before Corrigan triggers another shot. My head buzzes, as if a swarm of bees have penetrated my skull.

The sensation of wetness is hot. An excruciating white heat is spreading down my arm.

I realise in the split second that it takes to draw breath, I have been shot.

Chapter Thirty

No More Bad Guys

Lorna Allardyce fires the automatic at Corrigan's ravaged face as he bounds toward us. The initial shot slams him against the wall. An expression of surprise and disbelief appears on his face, as blood suppurates from the trajectory of the bullet exiting through his brain. When she aims the pistol at the ceiling, the impetus succeeds in bringing half the plaster crashing down on top of him. Blood flowers and spreads up through his tunic. Another slug hammers into his brow, between the eyes, where a crimson sediment slowly trickles.

I rush to help Dashurie, touching a hand to lifeless fingers. Blood continues to pool behind her as if she lies on a crimson pillow.

"She's dead, Aidan," LJ reminds me, breathlessly. She lapses back onto the pillow, the pistol slipping from her grasp, exhausted by her efforts. "Just go, please, your son is waiting," she urges in a scarcely audible voice.

I grip her hand. Her eyes are partially closing as she fights to remain conscious. "LJ, please, please, don't die on me."

"The others will be back soon. You can't help either Dashurie or me now."

Outside the window, Patrick practically screams my name. I tell her, or rather command, that she leave with me.

"I have a weapon, I told you. I don't mean the pistol."

"I hate to leave you."

"I know, but please, just fuckin' go, will you?" she hisses through gritted teeth. I'm guessing the pain is growing steadily unbearable now.

"Just fuckin' go, you stupid Irish bastard. You need to get that bullet out. You're bleeding all over the place."

With my concern for her I have barely noticed the wound I hold with my hand over it.

Hazarding a cursory glance at the woman on the bed, I promise her that I'll get help. Managing to tear up some of the surprisingly rotted bedsheets, I bind it around my arm as a makeshift bandage.

In the process of strapping up my arm, wrapping the sheet tightly about it, I move through the old building. Catching sight of the chair where I was imprisoned, I can't avoid an involuntary shiver. I close my eyes momentarily, gritting my teeth against the white-hot pain that shudders through me. The door stands open, and my son waits there expectantly. I half expect him to rush into my arms. Yet he merely stands there frozen and immobile. His head is lowered, while he sobs disconsolately. I take him into my arm, while holding the other across my chest. He regards me as if I were a stranger. The eyes that return my gaze, so much like my own, are filled with trepidation. I tell him that we should go, call the police and get help for LJ.

Still he fails to respond. I busy myself securing the makeshift bandage.

"You're hurt, Daddy." His words, though sympathetic, contain an element of stoicism too, almost as if it should be an accepted fact.

Blood continues to seep though the sheeting, while a blackness teeters in my vision. I will not to give in to it. I'm aware that we have precious little time. Not only am I certain that LJ will take her own life, but that Symondy and Pug will be showing up soon.

Corrigan is dead, both from a bullet and LJ's strategic shot at the ceiling, bringing half of the plaster down. If he really was my half brother then the fact has hopefully passed into history.

When Patrick appears totally unable to move, I yell at him again that we should get out of here. He regards me as if coming awake, nonplussed and scared. I tell him, even with my injured arm, I'll carry him. "We have to go. Now, Patrick!"

He hurls himself into my arms; I feel his body tremble with long pent-up sobs wracking him. The sob is borne of disconsolation, and is so heart rending that I entertain the sensation of tears pricking my own eyes as I hold this child, my child, trembling and frightened against me. I am so regretful of the suffering and hurt I've caused to those I love since my release from prison. All the bad people that have pursued me so indefatigably. Finally he allows me to take his hand. Now I scan my surroundings properly, and for the first time.

The length of a desolate shingle beach stretches ahead of us. Beyond that, it is difficult to make out the white road, which is drawing closer. I perceive that it is less of a road and more of a deserted wooden rail track. Various sea birds whirl and call above us. Some of the birds swoop quite low, causing Patrick to duck his head as if he is scared the low flying birds will take him off. He directs my attention to the lighthouse in the distance. Its beacon stands out with vivid clarity against the barren desert. As neither of us are in possession of a phone, I refer to us finding the nearest telephone box. Several hut dwellings, similar to the one we have left, huddle together in this barren wilderness as if for comfort. A creamy white building, with a round tower-like shape is embellished and thrown into a marginal relief against the dark rolling desolation. The soulful cries of the birds only add to the lonesome depression of the place. I can see why Corrigan should have chosen such a habitation.

Patrick remains traumatised. I, for my part, linger half in and out of consciousness, with the pain that is becoming practically intolerable now. I entertain the sensation of that overgrown wooden track rushing up to meet me. How it would be so effortless to abandon myself to that incalculable whiteness. My head throbs in accompaniment with my shoulder. When I run the pain shoots through me.

So this is what it feels like to be shot. When you're the guy who's holding the gun, I guess you don't realise, not until you become the victim. Nevertheless I am aware of the impact a bullet has on the body. The danger of infection, resulting in the amputation of the infected limb. Things aren't all they appear in the movies. When the good guy gets shot one week, but is perfectly fine the next. I have no idea the resultant damage that might have been done to the nerves, or the tissue. Splintered bone. Already the arm is beginning to grow numb so that my fingers are unable to grip.

The old Aidan McRaney would have gone in search of Symondy and Pug, but I have my son to consider. My concern also lies with Lorna Allardyce.

Patrick stumbles. I enquire if he's okay. A cursory nod is all I receive. The pain seems to be all around me now. It's only my sheer strength of will that prevents me from lapsing into unconsciousness. Maybe it's the intolerable cold. In haste to escape, I made no attempt to search for either boots or a jacket. Patrick still wears his school clothes. At least he's wearing his shoes. My feet are lacerated and bleeding from the stone and shingle, all culminating in further pain searing through me.

At times I can't avoid such incredible shivering, at others heat overcomes me, as if I'm burning up. All conducive to reminding me that if I don't soon get help, I'm in danger of collapsing and bleeding to death. The sheet is rendered comparatively useless.

When Patrick grabs my uninjured arm, he animatedly directs my attention to the solitary signpost rising up from the shingle, partially buried in the scrub and grass. I attempt to focus my gaze. I can just make out the pointers.

CHAPTER THIRTY

"Lydd and Romney, Dad. Which way do we go?" He regards me with the utmost concern. "You're not going to die, are you, Dad?"

The question surprises me, and I tell him, with a brief incline of my head, that I'm not going to die. At least, I mentally cross my fingers, that the sustained blood loss won't result in that eventuality. I suggest we head for Lydd.

When we finally manage to locate a phone box, outside another shack like building, Patrick helps me inside. I'm half in and out of consciousness, with my son practically screaming at me to hang in there. "Don't go to sleep, Dad. I'm scared you'll die if you do." I attempt a half smile, hopefully to reassure him.

He offers to dial the number, while I try to staunch the blood by tying the sheet tighter, but to no avail. I really do need to get that bullet out, or I'm in danger of losing my arm. The agonising pain coursing through me has become so unbearable. Now it seems that my son has taken charge.

He asks, "Everything will be okay, won't it?"

"Sure it will," I tell him, kissing the top of his head. I tell him how much I love him.

"Love you too," he says through his tears. "It's 999 isn't it? The emergency number? We need an ambulance, don't we?" he enquires expectantly.

"And the police."

Patrick explains as much to the man, whose voice I hear on the other end of the line.

"He wants to know where we are," he says, a hand covering the mouthpiece.

"Dungeness. There's a signpost that says Lydd." Patrick holds the phone while I attempt to speak into it.

Patrick practically shouts into the receiver, "By the way, my Dad's been shot!"

Cracking open the phone box, we step out, my son supporting

me. He's scared I'm about to lose consciousness as I drift in and out. I'm also aware he's anxious of the worst case scenario: I'll die of my wounds. That's not going to happen, I assure both him and myself. Not after all the battles that I have been through.

I take a pause to rest my head against the telephone booth, when Patrick draws my attention to the evidence of billowing smoke on the horizon. "There's a fire, Dad!"

"A fire?" I had already closed my eyes; now I'm coming fully awake when Patrick tugs on my uninjured arm.

The semi darkness is illumined by the tongues of flame lighting up the sky. The crackle of splintering wood and exploding glass shatters the dawn, a pinkish halo in the distance.

"It looks as if the fire is coming from that old place where we were imprisoned." My son sounds far older than his years.

Symondy and Pug must have returned. That's what she was waiting for. Her last vestige of hope, the cigarette lighter.

"LJ," I breathe her name huskily.

Patrick says nothing, merely nodding his understanding.

The smoke drifts towards us across that vast desert of desolation with the rising of the wind.

The wail of approaching police sirens and flashing lights sweep through the darkness, coupled with the fire, illumining our surroundings.

I'm close to drifting into unconsciousness. Even the alarm present in Patrick's voice fails to rouse me. Someone drapes a blanket around my shoulders. An ambulance man attempts to explain to my son that he needs to check me over, because Patrick is scared that if he dares to move from my side I'll drift into unconsciousness and pass away.

A sleek black Mercedes rolls to a halt where Patrick and I occupy a seat offered by the ambulance crew. Patrick also has a blanket draped about him. My shoulder is bandaged and I'm about to be carted off to hospital. I'm anxious that my wife and sister should be informed, only to be told that they will attend to all that at the hospital. The main concern is getting that bullet out.

The Merc parks, and a man and a woman step out. I'm astonished to observe DCI Duncan Sandford. He is accompanied by his daughter Caroline, garbed in jeans, a beige sheepskin jacket thrown over a white polo jumper. A rather burly, old school police officer, Sandford is immaculately clad in a dark suede suit jacket. His moustache is neatly trimmed.

The last time I had seen the Detective Chief Inspector, he had simply been a D.I., and was in the courtroom when I'd been sentenced. It was only later, after I'd done three years, that I learned Sandford had bought one of my paintings.

"Aidan, my boy, how are you?"

Tears prick my eyes, because he sounds so much like Sir George Treveleyan when he greets me that way.

"We heard everything that happened." Caro Sandford places a commiserating hand on my shoulder. My other arm is strapped up against my chest.

"So sorry about Sir George. A sad loss." Sandford shakes his head gravely, his mouth clenched. "Those bastards. At least they had the decency to return his body. He'd been drugged. So he must have known little about it, I suppose." The policeman affords himself an involuntary shudder. "But you did a good job, Aidan. Sir George would have been proud. Sorry it had to involve your son." He deals Patrick a small enfeebled smile.

"And Lorna Allardyce. Corrigan had her tarred and feathered," I remind him. "I believe she died in the flames."

"Oh my God, poor Lorna." Appearing suitably shocked, Caro traces a gloved hand over her jawline.

Sandford shakes his head once more. "There'll be a memorial in her honour of course."

I'm certain her family will be pleased to hear that. The Sandfords appear upset by the news. But LJ, like myself, we were simply expendable. Like me, she too was an ex-con. Would Bridget, Ruairi, Caitlan and Harry be attending my memorial service too?

Nevertheless I fail to vouchsafe my thoughts.

"Poor Lorna." Sandford tuts, shaking his head once more. "She was such an asset to the Agency. Leanne Harlow, your..." The powerfully built police officer brings a palm to his face, behind which he coughs discreetly.

"My girlfriend," I supply wearily.

"I still have your painting, you know."

"She was a good friend too. Lorna I mean," Caro interjects impatiently and flicks a thinly disguised look of exasperation at her father. "She always said that after her sister was killed she had no interest in life anymore. I know she wouldn't have wanted to live like... like that." Her hesitancy is painful, while tears appear in her eyes. "She was a beautiful woman. What about the Albanian girl?"

"They all perished in the flames. She was already dead. Corrigan killed her," I relate.

"Look, you need to get into hospital. When you're feeling better, perhaps you can come down to the station," Sandford mutters indecisively, when an ambulance man says, "We really do need to get this man into hospital, Sir."

"Of course, but I'd like to say..." Sandford has to have the final word of course. "They've closed the lodge and arrested that woman Mrs Ryan. Sir George saw the potential in you. No doubt there'll be a ceremony. Red carpet treatment I shouldn't wonder."

My entire body is wracked with pain. I'm freezing. All I can add to that statement is that I did nothing. After all I was manacled to a chair for most of it. Not that I'd relay that to the Sandfords of course. "Lorna Allardyce laid down her life," I manage to retort. "She should be awarded something posthumously."

"As indeed she will, Aidan. Indeed she will," Sandford replies laconically.

Overcome with tiredness now that it's all over, Patrick has fallen asleep on my shoulder. The ambulance man waits to escort us inside the vehicle.

"Come on, Daddy." Caro takes her father's arm. She wishes me a speedy recovery, and to look after my little boy. "He looks like you, doesn't he?" She smiles. "It's quite uncanny."

I have never been more relieved to escape, to place as much distance between Sandford and his daughter, when Patrick and I are escorted into the ambulance.

Coming awake now, and rubbing at his eyes, he regards me diligently. He asks, "There won't be any more bad guys will there, Dad?"

All I can do is offer him a transient smile, and promise, "No, son, no more bad guys. Not ever."

THE END